Season of Passion

Season of Passion

SADIE MATTHEWS

HODDER

First published in Great Britain in 2014 by Hodder & Stoughton
An Hachette UK company

First published in paperback in 2014

1

A CIP catalogue record for this title is available from the British Library

Paperback ISBN 978 1 444 78116 8
Ebook ISBN 978 1 444 78117 5

Typeset by Hewer Text UK Ltd, Edinburgh
Printed and bound by Clays Ltd, St Ives plc

Hodder & Stoughton policy is to use papers that are natural, renewable
and recyclable products and made from wood grown in sustainable
forests. The logging and manufacturing processes are expected to
conform to the environmental regulations of the country of origin.

Hodder & Stoughton Ltd
338 Euston Road
London NW1 3BH

www.hodder.co.uk

To
C.C.

PROLOGUE

A delicious ripple of harp music floats through the air, and a pair of white doors opens wide to reveal the bride. She stands there quite alone for a moment, an enchanting figure in a beautiful gown of silk and lace, her hair glittering with tiny crystals, then her father steps forward and offers her his arm, so that they can advance into the room together.

I both love and hate weddings: it's impossible not to respond to the sense of romance and hope, and the way that the happy couple are sprinkled with glamorous bridal dust. I adore the almost palpable love and encouragement in the air, like a warm feathery duvet of affection nestling around the bride and groom.

But I hate weddings because I know I won't have one myself. How can I, when the man I love will never, ever love me back?

I'm standing in the third row of little gilt chairs in the elegantly austere town hall of the Marais district in Paris. The harpist conjures liquid notes of angelic music as we all turn to watch the bride come in. She is so beautiful, in a dress of palest grey silk, a long slender sheath enveloped in lace, her bare shoulders rising from the scalloped edging. She's carrying grey roses too, with the faintest hint of lavender in their delicate petals. Her fair hair is styled into a chignon and she's not wearing a veil, just fragile crystal-encrusted stems that shimmer and flash in her hair, although

1

I almost wish she were: her face is so aglow with love and happiness that she's nearly too much to look at as she walks towards her fiancé. He gazes back at her, an expression of intensity on his face, as though all the meaning in his life is bound up in the girl coming slowly towards him. I feel almost dizzy from the sight of such emotion, and I reach out and clutch the chair in front of me as she passes.

The bride reaches her groom and they look into one another's eyes and smile with such absolute trust and intimacy that it reveals everything about the love they share, the kind of love I yearn for but know I will never have. The ceremony begins.

The strange thing is that I have absolutely no idea what I'm doing here.

CHAPTER ONE

The invitation arrived out of the blue only a few days before the wedding itself: a pretty pale blue card engraved in dark blue flowing type, inviting me to the wedding of Beth Villiers and Dominic Stone. I would have assumed it was sent by accident if it weren't for the fact that the name Beth Villiers rang a very faint bell. I just couldn't quite place it.

'Beth . . .' I muttered to myself. 'Do I know a Beth?' I scrunched up my nose trying to remember and quickly unscrunched when I realised what I was doing. I've got to be careful about my face – it's an actress's tool, after all and I don't want to get wrinkles before I'm due them. The problem is I can't help showing everything I feel on my face. I try to keep my expression neutral when I'm not acting but I always forget within minutes, and go back to frowning, widening my eyes, pursing my lips or smiling broadly, and generally being expressive. And even when I think I'm being poker-faced, everyone knows exactly what I'm thinking. They call it wearing my heart on my sleeve, but it's really about showing every emotion in my eyes and mouth. It makes me very bad at lying. My twin sister Summer is much better at keeping things under wraps; besides, with her big blue eyes and fair hair, she's always the picture of innocence anyway. That's why my dad always turned to me when he wanted to know anything and why, much to Summer's annoyance, he always guessed when we'd been up to no good.

'Flora,' she'd say crossly, 'you've got to learn to look as though you're not guilty!'

'I do try,' I'd reply mournfully. 'I can't help it.'

'Some actress you're going to be,' she retorted. 'Why on earth can't you act innocent?'

But it turns out that acting a character is not the same as being a good deceiver.

Now I stared at the invitation, racking my brains. 'Beth . . .?'

I must know her. Why would someone I don't know invite me to her wedding? How would she know my address to send the invitation? And with such short notice! It's really weird.

I walked over to the desk and picked up my phone. In my contacts list I tapped in the name 'Beth Villiers' and there it was – a name and a number, no address. I stared at it, astonished.

So I do know her!

I turned over the invitation and noticed writing on the back. It read:

Dear Flora
   I know time is short, but we'd be so happy if you could come. I think you'd meet some interesting people.
   All the best
   Beth

At that moment, as I read her name, the realisation flooded into my mind and I gasped. *I know who she is!*

Just a few weeks ago, my older sister Freya had got

herself entangled in a very strange adventure. It started when her car flew off the icy road as she was being driven down the dangerous mountain road from our house in the Alps to the airport. Luckily, the bodyguard, Miles Murray, was ex-SAS and highly skilled in winter conditions. Thanks to his skill, they survived the crash and found a place to shelter until they could be rescued. I don't know the full story of what happened in that tiny hut in the storm, but one thing is for sure: my sister and her bodyguard emerged a lot closer friends than when they went in. Naturally she hid her burgeoning relationship from our controlling father, particularly as he suspected that the bodyguard might have had some kind of hand in planning the accident in the first place. Crazy, but that's my dad. It comes from being a very successful and wealthy businessman with three daughters who are tabloid bait, whether we like it or not: it creates a certain paranoia. When he found out about Freya and her blossoming relationship with Miles, there was hell to pay and then things took an even more bizarre turn. My sister simply disappeared. It was then that Beth contacted me, to reassure me that Freya was okay.

'I'm a friend of your sister,' she said in a soft English accent. 'She wants me to let you know that she's fine. She'll be in touch as soon as she can.'

'Thanks,' I replied, a little puzzled because I had no idea that Freya was in any danger. As far as I was aware, she was at a hotel on the other side of Paris, enjoying herself. I had pictured her relaxing in the luxurious spa or dining in her suite after a long bath, a movie playing on the television. I was not expecting to see her until the next day.

Beth said, 'You can call me any time if you're worried. I'll text you my details.'

'Okay,' I said, frowning, quickly clearing my brow when I realised I was doing it. I wasn't sure why I would be worried, or how this girl could help me if I were, but it seemed rude to say anything else. Then a thought occurred to me and I said, 'Will she still be coming here tomorrow? She's supposed to be staying with me.'

The silence on the other end of the line made a quiver of anxiety ripple out over my skin. Then Beth spoke. 'I don't think so, Flora. Unless you hear otherwise, she'll not be able to make it. I'm sorry I can't say more, I really am.'

This sounded serious. I began to absorb what this Beth person was telling me, and my anxiety levels rose a little further. 'Wait, it sounds like she's in trouble – what about her bodyguard? She came to Paris with Thierry, didn't she? Where is he?'

'She's not with Thierry. But she's being well looked after, I promise, and she's not in any danger. As I said, she's perfectly safe now.'

'Now?' I say sharply. 'What do you mean, *now*? What's happened? Is it anything to do with Miles Murray?'

'I really can't say, I'm sorry. She'll be in touch soon, I'm sure,' Beth replied. 'Goodbye, Flora. Don't forget you can ring me if you want. I just wish I had more I could tell you.'

The next moment she was gone, and I was left pressing my disconnected phone to my ear, staring into space as thoughts whirled around my mind. My sister's life had been so complicated lately and I'd been looking forward to sitting down with her and hearing all about it. Could I really believe that strange voice on the other end of the line, no matter how pleasant and trustworthy it sounded? I immediately tried Freya's phone, but it went straight to her voicemail.

I left a message and waited. She didn't call me back, and

I had a drama class to go to, so I decided to hold off on doing anything more until afterwards. When I got out, tired from a gruelling session of physical work, there was a message on my own voicemail. Cursing that I'd managed to miss her, I listened to the recording.

'Hi, darlin'.' Freya sounded happier than I'd heard her for a long time. 'Listen, everything's okay but I'm going to ground for a bit. You know how crazy things have been for me and how much the press are on my tail. So I'm going to vanish. Don't worry about me; I'm totally fine. I'll explain to Dad, and I'll be in touch when I can. Bye!' Then she added, 'Oh, I almost forgot. Listen, this is very important. Don't tell Jane-Elizabeth anything you wouldn't want Dad or Estelle to know. Okay? I'll explain why when I see you. But it's vital you keep things to yourself if you want them to stay private. That includes emails. Lots of love. See you soon!'

That was the last I heard from her for a while. If she hadn't sounded so ecstatically happy, I would have been very concerned, but the tone in her voice put my mind at rest. I had a feeling that she was with Miles, her bodyguard, and at once I felt happier. He'd already saved her life once. If anyone was going to look after Freya, it was Miles.

But her words about Jane-Elizabeth worried me. We all adored Jane-Elizabeth, my father's longstanding and trusted personal assistant. She'd always balanced her loyalty to my father with her love for us girls, and her role as our surrogate mother. If there was anyone who could be considered utterly dependable, it was her. So why was Freya warning me to take care?

'I got the same message,' Summer said when I called her.

She'd been staying in London and was about to head to Venice for a short break with some friends. Wherever we were, we always made sure to keep in touch every day. Now that I was settled in Paris during my term times, I was beginning to realise just how much we all flitted around the world.

'Did you speak to her?' I asked.

'Just for a moment. She was on a plane and had to switch her phone off,' she said. 'But she took special care to tell me not to say anything personal to Jane-Elizabeth.'

I frowned, twisting a lock of my long hair round a finger, a habit of mine when I'm thinking. 'That's so odd, isn't it?'

'Yes . . . but I've played it safe so far. I'm keeping back anything really personal until Freya can tell us exactly what she means.'

'Me too.' I paused, then asked, 'How did she sound to you?'

'In an extremely good mood.' Summer laughed. 'I had a feeling she was heading somewhere with someone rather special.'

'You mean Miles Murray?'

'Who else?'

I whistled lightly. 'Dad will go mad. You know what he threatened her with if she saw him again.'

'He'll go completely crazy.'

We were both silent as we contemplated Freya's act of reckless disobedience. It certainly took courage to go against our father: none of us had ever pushed him to his limits, but I had a feeling it would not be pretty.

'We'll be able to see for ourselves next week,' Summer said. 'Are you coming home for Christmas?'

'Of course. I'm leaving at the end of the week. Do you think Freya will turn up?'

'I'd lay good money that she won't. And I think we both know how Dad will take it.'

We weren't wrong. When I arrived back at the Alpine mountaintop house that we all called home, my father was in the most thunderous mood I'd ever seen. Everyone tiptoed around him, fearful of setting off the anger we could tell was simmering just below the surface and ready to boil over at the slightest provocation. I had the feeling that he didn't know what to do with the emotion that Freya's disobedience was stirring in him. My father didn't become one of the most successful businessmen in the world without expecting people to do precisely as he wanted, and he's always made a point of knowing exactly where his daughters are. Until now, he's been confident that all he had to do was click his fingers and we'd come running. Now he had no idea where Freya was and it was driving him mad. He had threatened to cut her off if she saw Miles again, but she had audaciously cut *him* off, and chosen Miles instead. It wasn't treatment my father was accustomed to, and I couldn't help admiring my sister's spirit: I've always been too in awe of my father to rebel against him. But now, none of us had a clue as to her whereabouts.

'Girls, have you heard from Freya?' Jane-Elizabeth said, coming in to the snug where Summer and I were watching television together. She looked just the same as always – the smooth, plump face that appeared far younger than her years, dark hair with its streak of grey at the front, a bright cashmere scarf over a black tunic top – and yet I wondered if she were now different: no longer the cosy maternal figure we all loved so much, but something a little more dangerous.

If only Freya had told me what she meant! I just can't believe that Jane-Elizabeth has anything but our best interests at heart. And yet . . .

We both shook our heads. Summer looked innocently at Jane-Elizabeth, and I marvelled again at my twin's ability to make those blue eyes of hers look as pure as an angel's. I was afraid that Jane-Elizabeth would read my doubts in my face, and I avoided her gaze.

'Flora?' she said at once. 'Do you know?'

'No, of course not.' I looked up at her worried expression. Her face was as familiar as my own. Our mother died when I was only ten and ever since then, Jane-Elizabeth had been part of our family. I couldn't bear to think that she was somehow mixed up in the trouble going on between Freya and my father. But why on earth would Freya warn us off without good reason?

Jane-Elizabeth sat down on the sofa opposite the one where Summer and I were lounging together, frowning. 'It's all so dreadful. I've never known your father in such a frightful mood, or Freya to be so . . . impetuous. Running off with that man! What is she thinking?' She eyed us carefully. 'At least, that's what I'm assuming. That's she's gone off with this Miles person.' She sighed. 'He seemed perfectly nice when he arrived here. If we'd only known what destruction he was going to cause . . .'

'Well,' I said at once, 'Freya would be dead without him! He saved her life, we all know that.'

'Yes, yes, I suppose so.' Jane-Elizabeth sighed again. 'And we'll always be in his debt for that. But to take her away from us!'

'She's gone with him – and I'd be very surprised if she hadn't made up her own mind in the matter,' I replied a little tartly. An expression of hurt flickered in Jane-Elizabeth's dark brown eyes. She wasn't used to me talking to her in such a tone. The next moment she said:

'So she *has* run off with him?'

'I don't know for sure.' I shrugged. 'But it's the obvious conclusion, isn't it? And if I were in her place, I'd do the same.'

I meant it, too. If I were lucky enough to experience what Freya has, I'd do anything to be with the man I loved. I suddenly saw my sister in a new, heroic light. She was rebelling against everything to follow her heart. I admired and envied her. I wanted to be in the same position, so that I could prove my complete devotion to someone the way she had.

But am I brave enough to challenge Dad, if he disapproved? I laughed inside. *Like anyone is ever going to be good enough for his daughters! He's always going to disapprove. And if he knew who I really love . . .*

'You'd do the same? Oh, Flora, don't say that.' Jane-Elizabeth looked really miserable now. 'You girls shouldn't have to see life as a choice between what you want and what your father wants. But what I can't understand is why Freya hasn't been in touch with me. I know she's angry with her dad, but she's never shut me out like this before. It's awful. I really can't bear it.'

'Perhaps,' Summer said in a deceptively casual tone, 'she thinks your first loyalty is to Dad, and you'd have to tell him if she gave away anything about where she is. And about ten minutes after that, someone would be round to put pressure on her to come back.'

I gave my twin sister a quick glance. She was the picture of innocence as usual. It didn't seem as if there was anything loaded in what she was saying. But here we were at the crux of the matter: was Jane-Elizabeth no more than a spy for my father?

'Perhaps,' Jane-Elizabeth conceded unhappily. 'I'm in very difficult situation, but I hope Freya knows that if she needed me, I'd always protect her.'

Summer and I swapped looks. Once, we'd have thought the same. But what were we supposed to think now?

The house was decorated for Christmas. As usual, a professional decorator had been brought in and the place looked a little like a department store, no corner untouched by extremely tasteful seasonal arrangements. Here, huge glass bowls of giant gold baubles; there, swathes of expensive artificial holly twisted artfully around light fittings and banisters. Glowing stars hung daintily from the ceilings, and Christmas trees twinkled around every corner. Under the gigantic twelve-foot spruce jam-packed with lights and decorations, which stood by the great wall of glass overlooking the mountainside and could be seen from miles away, were piles of perfectly wrapped presents. A glossy magazine could easily have used our house for a shoot showing those manicured, tasteful Christmases, the kind where everything is beautifully arranged but there's not a soul in sight.

I remembered the Christmases we used to have before my mother died; the memories were shadowy, but still there. Our old chalet was certainly large and luxurious but compared to this chilly mountain eyrie, it was cosy and comfortable. We did the decorating ourselves, cramming ornaments on the tree, stringing up paper chains we'd made around the kitchen table, and constructing an unsteady but cheerful gingerbread house. My mother was English, and we always celebrated Christmas the way she had. Once she was gone, we tried to carry on her traditions, but after we moved to my father's grand project, this huge mountaintop house built of glass and steel, many were abandoned. It seemed easier to summon a team of decorators to adorn the house for us than to try to keep alive those old habits from a happier time. Christmas had never felt the same again.

Even so, it was strange to be celebrating the day without Freya. The three of us were used to being apart a lot of the time, but not to have our big sister there when we would usually all be together was horrible.

'Are you finding this as grim as I am?' murmured Summer, coming into the drawing room on Christmas morning where the presence of the enormous, sparkling tree and the mountain of gifts seemed to make the day even more hollow. She looked at my outfit. 'I see you've dressed up for the day.'

I glanced down at my black outfit – a wool dress cinched with a patent belt and long black boots – and said, 'Dad needs to know how we feel about all of this. I'm officially in mourning for the fact that Freya isn't here.'

Summer threw herself down on one of the large white leather armchairs. She was typically elegant in a pale pink cashmere jumper falling off one shoulder, and grey jeans. It's impossible for my sister to look anything other than stylish. She doesn't have my taste for dressing up at all. 'This is the worst Christmas ever! We've barely seen Dad and when we do, he's like an ogre with a headache. Have you dared mention Freya to him?'

I shook my head. 'I've barely seen him. He seems to be locked away in the study with Pierre every waking minute.' I shuddered. My father's head of security always gives me the creeps. 'Have you?'

Summer made a face. 'Uh uh. Let sleeping dogs lie, I say.'

'I wonder what Freya is doing,' I said wistfully. I pictured her waking up somewhere in Miles Murray's arms, radiant with happiness, and I was surprised how much I wished she were here. 'I wonder if she's missing us at all.'

As if in answer, the phone in my dress pocket chirruped and I pulled it out. A text had arrived.

'It's from Freya, look!'

Summer got up and came over to join me gazing at the message. It contained a photograph: Freya, sitting cross-legged on a rug by a blazing fire, wearing jeans and a Fair Isle sweater, grinning happily at the camera, her brown eyes alight with pleasure. Underneath she'd written:

Happy Christmas, girls! I'm missing you very much and will be in touch SOON. I'm safe and well and enjoying myself xxx

'Where is she?' said Summer wonderingly.

'There aren't many clues there. She could be anywhere,' I replied, scrutinising the photograph. I glanced at Summer. 'How long do you think she can keep up this vanishing act?'

Summer was about to reply when a cool voice said: 'You two seem very absorbed. Anything interesting?'

We both looked up to see Estelle, my father's girlfriend, coming into the drawing room. She was in one of her usual clinging dresses, tottering along in high heels, her face made up and her long brown hair tumbling glossily over her shoulders, but she looked a little paler and more strained than usual. She walked rapidly towards us, inquisitive about whatever it was on the screen of my phone, and I quickly made the picture vanish to the home screen.

'Nothing,' I said and then smiled at her. 'Happy Christmas, Estelle.'

She gazed back at me suspiciously and then said, 'Happy Christmas, Flora. And you too, of course, Summer.'

'Happy Christmas.' Summer managed to sound sincere enough but I knew she felt as much warmth towards Estelle as I did. That wasn't much at all. 'Where's Dad?'

'In his study, taking a call. He'll be here soon,' she said tersely, and I got the distinct impression that it wasn't much fun for Estelle being around my father at the moment. *She's got used to being able to wrap him around her little finger. Usually he's obsessed with her and how he can look after her. But now that Freya's disappeared, he can't think of anything else.* I couldn't help laughing internally, feeling a little more cheerful now that we'd had our text from Freya. *It serves her right. Now we'll see how much she really likes being round my father.*

All of us were of the same opinion: Estelle was with my father for one reason only, and it wasn't because he was God's gift to women. Dad was utterly enraptured by her, and we all tried to get on with her for his sake, despite the fact that none of us could like or trust her. It was hard to forget that she'd once been our personal assistant, and now seemed to take a special pleasure in lording it over us.

And I couldn't help suspecting that whatever was keeping my father in his study had something to do with Freya. No doubt he had a team of private investigators on her tail, the expensive kind who worked ceaselessly, even over Christmas. They'd be using every trick in the book to track her down and find her.

Stay hidden as long as you can, Freya. Make them sweat. I know you're safe. Enjoy not being a Hammond sister – savour the freedom while it's still possible.

We chatted in a stilted way to Estelle while the maids brought in the drinks. By the time Dad came to join us, Jane-Elizabeth had appeared, trying to cheer us up by wearing a pair of flashing reindeer's antlers and huge dangling earrings in the shape of Christmas puddings. Like my mother, Jane-Elizabeth is English and has a silly sense of humour. I giggled at the sight of her. I feel more English than anything else, because I was sent to school there, and I get the humour. Freya spent the most time with our mother and she has quite an English outlook but she went to a Swiss boarding school and she sometimes doesn't get the same jokes as I do. Summer is a mixture of English and American owing to her years at a US university. We're a ragbag family, that's for sure.

Dad gave Jane-Elizabeth's antlers a stony look, and she took them off. Then we went through all the remaining family rituals bequeathed to us by my mother: opening presents while drinking mimosas (which my mother used to call 'Buck's Fizz', though of course we were too young to drink it while she was alive), then sitting down to a huge lunch of roast turkey with all the very British trimmings of little sausages, stuffing, roast potatoes and Brussels sprouts with chestnuts. Jane-Elizabeth worked hard to keep our spirits up with a stream of bright chatter, and we tried to reply in the same spirit, but I knew that I didn't want Dad to think that this was normal, or that I was happy about the fact that Freya was missing.

It's his fault, after all, I told myself. *If he hadn't gone mad over her relationship with Miles, she'd still be here.*

I barely spoke or smiled, and Summer was the same. It may have looked sulky, but inside I was intensely sad. We ought to have all been together. It was bad enough that our mother was gone and that we had to endure Estelle, but to lose Freya was awful. Her absence was like a horrible open wound that couldn't be concealed, and that no one was talking about. I wanted to leap to my feet and scream out, 'I can't stand this pretence! Why won't anyone mention her name? Why are we acting as though everything is normal when it's so terrible?'

But I didn't dare, even though my nails were digging into my palms and my jaw hurt with the tension in it.

We opened our presents and muttered our thanks for the expensive trinkets and clothes that Jane-Elizabeth had chosen for us on Dad's behalf. I had a feeling that Estelle had chosen her own gifts – an extraordinary large yellow diamond ring from Graff, and a diamond-encrusted Cartier watch – but she squealed with convincing excitement when she unwrapped them. Meanwhile, a pile of gifts addressed to Freya lay under the tree, but no one mentioned them. In fact, Freya's name wasn't spoken once during the entire day.

I was relieved when I could get away a few days later and escape back to Paris. Summer was joining friends for a skiing holiday.

We left Estelle and Jane-Elizabeth to look after my father, whose mood was even worse, if that was possible. He still refused to talk about the fact that our sister was not there.

* * *

17

I watch as the civil ceremony unfolds. The registrar wears a plain dark suit, with a medal of office hanging from a striped ribbon of red, white and blue, and the vows are taken in French, which both the bride and groom speak in an English accent. My ear has tuned in very well to the French tongue since I've been living here and I'm fluent enough to be mistaken for a native French speaker. I look curiously at the other guests as the bride and groom sign the legal documents handed to them by the registrar, sitting down on red velvet and gold chairs in front of the registrar's polished oak table to do so.

I can tell which side is the bride's. Beth's father has joined his wife, who is tearful but smiling in a turquoise silk suit and a hat that definitely doesn't look as though it was bought in Paris. Two good-looking young men stand with them, one with someone at his side who is unmistakably a girlfriend. She looks ill at ease and a little out of place, as though now she's here in these understatedly elegant sur-roundings, she's regretting the fuchsia feather fascinator that bobs over her head in a kind of outrageous magnificence.

Are the men Beth's brothers?

In the rows behind are more family and friends, all with a distinctive English look about them. I don't know why it's so noticeable but it is. Despite being in their best clothes, they seem more casual than the other guests, more distinct-ive and individual. I can tell that the guests on the other side are from other parts of the world. They are dressed more discreetly but expensively, aiming not to stand out but to demonstrate perfect and costly good taste.

I can't spot anyone who looks like Dominic's parents but a pretty woman who shares the same velvety brown eyes, olive skin and soft dark hair must be his sister. She has an American elegance about her, and I feel drawn to her aura of warmth. There are plenty of polished, attractive women on Dominic's side of the room. He must have been quite a heartbreaker before he met Beth.

I glance over at them as they complete their legal documents. The aura of joy around them is almost palpable. Dominic's heart-breaking days are over, I'm sure of that. He gazes at his new wife with naked delight.

The registrar stands up and pronounces the ceremony at an end, and the room breaks into spontaneous applause as husband and wife kiss happily. Music strikes up from somewhere – a joyous trumpet voluntary – and the happy couple smile delightedly at their friends and family as they walk down the centre aisle together and we turn to follow them out.

It's then that I see Freya.

CHAPTER TWO

'Freya?' I gasp, disbelieving and then I say more loudly, 'Freya!' But my voice is lost in the babble of chatter and music.

I know I saw her. I glimpsed her just for a moment at the back of the room, and then she slipped out and disappeared, just before the newlyweds got there.

But it was her! She's here.

I call after her again, and attempt to make my way down the aisle to where the guests are crowding the way out, stopping to chat and laugh with each other, wallowing in that post-ceremonial sense of good feeling. I push my way through as politely as I can but it's hard to restrain myself from shoving the silk- and wool-covered backs that impede my progress. By the time I make my way out to the wide, marble-floored corridor outside, it's empty, with no sign of anyone having been there, not even the bride and groom.

'What the . . .?' I looked around, confused. 'Where are they?'

I turn to my left and head towards the main entrance, my high-heeled shoes clicking on the stone floor, wondering what to do next. As I pass a large, polished wood door, it suddenly opens and Beth pokes her head out.

'Flora!' she says in a loud whisper.

I stop short and stare. It's a little surreal to see a bride peeking out in such a secretive way. 'Yes?'

She beckons me over, her eyes wide and beseeching, and I go to her. 'Come in here,' she says briefly and disappears into the room behind the door. I step inside after her, and there is Dominic, still radiating a happy glow, and my sister Freya, half-sitting on a table inside. She always looks elegant, and today is no different: she's chic in a beautiful, pale-green tweed suit and shocking-pink silk stilettos, the suit's boxy shape suiting her sharp bob and long legs. But Freya looks different nonetheless: there's a kind of dizzying energy about her and a change in her face.

She's brighter, her eyes are sparkling.

I realise with an odd start that she must be happy.

Have I really never seen her happy before? Maybe it's been years since she was truly at peace. But I can see that she is now. Freya, as the eldest of us, was the closest to our mother. She was with her through the terrible weeks when my mother's illness really took hold. After Mama's death, Freya was never the same again. She became the sharp, angry, prickly older sister I knew so well. Summer and I had each other, so it was easy to bond together against her. For a couple of years we even had a club called The League Against Freya, and enjoyed concocting plans to torment her. She always rose predictably well to our bait, storming around in furious rages, banning us from her room, from her sight, from breathing the same air as she did. We all mellowed as we grew older, and became friends again.

But I've never seen her like this.

'Flora!' She jumps up and comes towards me, her arms open wide. 'It's so good to see you!' In the next moment, I am engulfed in a huge hug, the soft tweed of her suit pressed to my face, a gentle cloud of scent enveloping me. She kisses my cheek.

21

'What are you doing here?' I gasp, pulling back to look at her again. It feels like an age since I last saw her.

'I'm here to see you, of course!' She smiles happily at me.

Beth says in her gentle voice, 'I suppose you wondered why you'd got a wedding invitation from me. As we don't really know each other.'

'Well, I did wonder,' I say, and laugh. 'I suppose I guessed something like this would happen.' I turn back to my sister. 'Freya, where on earth have you been? We've all been so worried about you.'

'Really?' She looks guilty as she leads me over to some chairs to sit down. 'I hoped that my text at Christmas would set your minds at rest.'

'It did for a while, but it's been weeks since then . . .'

Dominic coughs loudly and we look round to see him and Beth standing by the door, holding hands. 'We're going to leave you ladies to talk,' he says, his eyes twinkling. 'We've got a wedding reception to attend and people are going to start wondering where we are.'

'Of course!' Freya laughs and goes over to them to kiss them goodbye. 'Thank you so much for all your help. I owe you both so much.' She takes Beth's hand in hers. 'Especially you, Beth. You look so beautiful. I hope you have a marvellous wedding day.'

'Oh, I already am,' Beth says. She looks radiant. 'Goodbye, Freya, and don't forget to keep in touch. Goodbye, Flora. Will we see you at the reception?'

'I . . . I don't know,' I reply. 'But thank you for asking me today. I appreciate it.'

'Not at all. Let me know if I can ever help you.' She smiles at me, and then exchanges a glance with her new husband. They open the door, letting the noise of the crowd outside float in, and disappear through it to a rapturous welcome.

I turn back to Freya. 'They seem lovely.'

'They are.' Freya looks thoughtful. 'I owe them so much. They helped me when I needed it. They reunited Miles and me.'

'So it's true, then? You and Miles are back together?'

Freya nods, unable to conceal the joyous smile spreading over her face. 'Yes. And I'm happier than I've ever been.' She looks suddenly anxious. 'I must seem horribly selfish to you – leaving you all, disappearing without a word and hardly being in touch since. Do you and Summer hate me?'

'Of course not!' I'm filled with a rush of affection for her, and a kind of envious excitement at what has happened to her. 'You're in love – properly, really! You've got to seize the opportunity while you can. I know I would.'

Freya looks at me gratefully. 'Thanks. I know you would, too. You're such a passionate, romantic person, you'd definitely do the same.'

'I wouldn't think twice,' I say fervently, and a picture floats through my mind: I'm in the arms of the man I love, he's gazing at me tenderly, bending his head to kiss me . . . I shake it away. *That will never happen.*

'And . . . Dad?' Freya asks tentatively. 'Does he hate me too?'

I hesitate and see an expression of pain cross her face, though it's quickly replaced by defiance. 'He'll never hate you. But he's angry. And I think he's working hard behind the scenes to find out where you are.'

Freya shrugs. 'I'm sure he will, eventually. But for now, we're keeping a low profile – there are reasons why.'

'Is it the paparazzi? I mean, you were all over the press

just a few months ago.' There had been a series of exposés on Freya's relationship with Miles Murray, the story of the heiress and the bodyguard proving irresistible to the media.

Freya's face darkens. 'It caused a lot of trouble. More than you can know. When the story behind my break-up with Jacob came out, it started major problems for me. That's part of the reason why I've had to go to ground. Miles knows how to hide us until the storm has blown over. That's why I'm not coming back, not for now, anyway.'

'But where are you two? Where are you living?' I ask.

She looks at me, sorrow in her big brown eyes. 'Honey, I can't say. Please – it's for the best. It's not that I don't trust you, I do. But there are reasons why I can't say more.'

'Is it because of Jane-Elizabeth?' I ask, a wistful tone in my voice. I can't bear the thought that Jane-Elizabeth is not to be trusted. 'Summer and I have been very careful around her ever since we got your message.'

She takes my hand. 'Flora, it's not Jane-Elizabeth – she's a victim, the same way that we are. The person who's working against us all is Estelle. She leaked all the stories about me to the press, putting me into real danger and driving a wedge between Dad and me. I never could work out how the paps got photos of me when practically nobody knew where I was. Or how the private story of my break-up with Jacob got out. But Estelle has her nose in everything. She obviously has access to a lot of Dad's private records and emails.'

I gaze back at her, taking this in. 'Of course,' I breathe. 'It makes perfect sense! But that means she's into Dad's emails, Jane-Elizabeth's emails . . .'

'More than that. She's hacked into the whole of the

Hammond system.' Freya's eyes sparkle with anger. 'She's got some kind of agenda.'

'I think we can guess what it is,' I rejoin. 'She wants to cut us off from Dad, and benefit from the family split.'

'She's succeeding for now,' Freya says. 'But although she may have won the battle, the war will be a long one. I'm not prepared to let our family be splintered that easily.'

'Nor am I,' I put in, my voice spirited. 'But our problem is Dad.'

Freya nods. 'He won't hear a word against her for now, and you can be sure that she's clever enough to hide her tracks. That's why I'm staying away for the time being. It must be driving her mad not knowing where I am or what I'm doing. Besides . . .' She glows again. 'I don't want to leave Miles. It's like a glorious honeymoon, going on and on . . .' Her eyes close and a blissful expression crosses her face. 'Oh Flora. I'm so happy.'

I lean over and hug her. 'I'm glad. I really am. Where is Miles?'

'He's here in Paris. We're going back to—' She stops, catching herself. 'Whoops, I nearly said. We're leaving tonight. But I wanted to see you so much – to tell you not to worry, to give you my love and to warn you about Estelle. I think she's ruthless. I think she'll stop at nothing to get what she wants. So be careful – but don't let her know we're on to her.'

'I understand.' I hug her again and she returns it. We stay like that for a while, and I wonder when I'll see her again and where that will be.

'I have to go,' she says, releasing me. 'Give my love to Summer, won't you?'

I nod, suddenly too choked to speak.

'Go to the reception. I'm sure you'll enjoy it.' She smiles at me. 'And you know what it's like at weddings, with all the romance in the air. Maybe you'll meet someone.'

Now that Freya's in love, she wants everyone to be as happy as she is.

I manage to smile back. 'Maybe. You never know.'

I step outside the town hall and try to make myself incon-spicuous, wrapping my gossamer-fine cashmere scarf so that it conceals the lower half of my face. Freya has slipped away towards some exit at the back of the building and I follow the wedding party out on to the pavement, where the bride and groom are making slow progress through their guests towards a waiting Bentley. The reception will be at a stun-ning townhouse not far away, and the guests will walk there. Feeling apart from the general air of celebration, I cross the street and stand outside a cafe opposite, looking back at the crowd in front of the town hall. They are attracting a lot of attention, the beautiful graceful bride drawing all eyes to her.

'Mademoiselle?'

A waiter is standing beside me, looking questioning. I'm standing among the wicker chairs and tables out on the pavement.

'Oh . . .' I glance about. The tables are mostly empty. A man sits at a nearby one, sunk down in a black overcoat, a demi-tasse of black coffee in front of him. On impulse I sit down on the nearest chair. I don't need to make a decision about going to the reception immediately. 'Cafe au lait, please.'

The waiter nods and goes off to get my coffee. I sit back on my chair and watch the little spectacle across the road. The colourful silks and satins of the women's clothes provide a lovely splash of brightness on this dull January day, and there is a general air of excitement and occasion. The bride is now sheltered from the chill by a long white coat and she is gradually getting closer to the car that will take her and Dominic away to the reception, but every step is delayed by someone wanting to kiss her or speak to her.

She's like a star – a glamorous princess everybody wants to be close to.

The waiter brings my coffee and puts it down in front of me, along with the tab. I fish some money out of my purse, put it down on the saucer and he takes it away. Now there's just me and the man nearby, both of us the only customers hardy enough to sit outside on a cold January day. I steal a glance at him, but there's not much to see. He's wearing a hat pulled down low and a scarf up to his chin, the collar of his black overcoat turned up high. I can only see a large nose, the kind that makes me think he has a craggy face with jutting bones and big features. One of those interesting faces that provide so much to look at. I'm fascinated by faces, perhaps because of my acting. I like to see how much of someone's character is revealed in the way they look as well as by their expressions.

I stare covertly over the top of my cup as I sip the hot, milky coffee.

He seems very interested in the wedding party. In fact, he doesn't seem to be taking his eyes off it. He hasn't taken even a taste of his coffee while I've been here.

His gaze seems fixed on something in particular, and I follow the direction of his stare.

Oh. He's looking at . . . at Beth.

I realise that he's staring at the bride with a furious intensity, as though imprinting the sight of her on his brain. I watch her too: Beth's beautiful smiling face is alight with happiness as she at last reaches the open door of the silver Bentley. The chauffeur holds the door open for her as she bends down and takes her place inside. Dominic walks round the car and gets in at the other side. As he does so, I'm sure I notice the man next to me shrink a little further into his black overcoat.

The chauffeur closes the door and takes his place in the driving seat. A moment later, the car draws away to a chorus of claps and cheers. The guests begin to make their way along the pavement towards the reception, a colourful and glamorous parade that makes even jaded Parisians stop and look for a moment.

'Excuse me, mademoiselle – were you at the wedding?' The man nearby has turned and spoken to me. His voice startles me: it's harsh, deep and scratchy, and he speaks French with an accent I can't identify.

I open my mouth, not sure what to say. The encounter with Freya has made me secretive. Should I be volunteering my presence here to a stranger? It's clear now that I need to be very careful about who I confide in.

'I saw you leave the town hall,' he goes on. 'You are one of the guests, aren't you? I wonder if you'd be so kind as to describe the ceremony to me.'

I gaze at him. It's still hard to make out his face but I can see the glitter of blue eyes from beneath the shadow cast by his hat. *Why does he want to know about the ceremony? It seems rather odd.*

He's watching me as I consider his request and he says, 'I can see you think it's strange of me to ask this. The bride and groom are not unknown to me. I wasn't privileged to be invited though.'

I frown, then a thought occurs to me, and it seems to make perfect sense. Before stopping to think, I blurt out: 'Are you the bride's real father, or something like that? A man walked her down the aisle but perhaps . . . that was her stepfather and you're her estranged father, longing to see his daughter on her wedding day . . .'

He stares at me for a moment with a strange expression in the icy blue eyes, then throws back his head and bursts out laughing. 'Oh, I suppose I deserve that! Her father. No.' He laughs again but with a tinge of bitterness. 'I'm not her father. I . . .' He hesitates, and then says in a low, intense voice, 'I love her.'

'Oh!' I blink with astonishment. *Loves her? This craggy man in his big black coat?* Then my heart melts with sympathy for him. 'You love Beth?'

He drops his head so that for a moment I can only see the top of his hat and when he looks up again, his expression is softer and sadder. 'Beth. Yes. I adore her. But she loves someone else. I offered her my heart and she didn't want it.' That hollow laugh again. 'The wedding is the giveaway.'

'I'm so sorry.' I feel awful for him. What must that feel like? To love hopelessly even when the cause is so utterly lost that the woman has married another man? *No matter how bad things get for me, at least I've never had to experience that. Another woman will never do that to me.* 'The wedding was beautiful. They are obviously so happy to be together.' I give him a sympathetic look. 'I'm sorry. That must be hard to hear.'

'It is,' he replies shortly. 'But it's not exactly a surprise. She's never loved anyone else. I only hoped . . . There were times when I believed I could change her mind, make her love me instead . . .' His voice fades away and his eyes flicker with the intensity of his memories.

I lean towards him, moved by his obvious emotions and suddenly desperate to let him know that he is not alone. 'I know how you feel, I really do. I love someone too – someone who will never love me. I know the agony you're going through.'

He looks at me and seems to see me for the first time. 'You?' His tone is of mild surprise, then he says again with more incredulity, 'You? Really?'

I nod. 'I can't help it. I know how stupid it is to be hopelessly in love with someone who can never love me, but there's nothing I can do about it.'

I can tell that his blue eyes are assessing me, and I feel suddenly self-conscious. When I left the house this morning, I was pleased with my appearance. I'm wearing a navy-blue silk shift dress with elegant pumps and a beautifully cut navy coat over the top, a grey silk cashmere scarf at my neck. My thick chestnut hair is pulled back into a loose chignon, and I've emphasised my slanting grey-green eyes with kohl and mascara. Apart from that, I'm only wearing a little pink gloss on my lips. I know I can't match the radiance of the bride we've just seen depart, but it suddenly matters to me that this stranger thinks I'm at least attractive.

'Who is the fool who doesn't want to love you back?' His voice, with its curious rasp, is almost rude in its curtness, but also strangely compelling.

I feel my cheeks redden. 'It's complicated. I can't explain it.' The truth is, I don't want to explain it. I hate even thinking about the reasons why I can't have the man I love.

'He's married and loves his wife.' The man states it as though it's a fact and I don't want to correct him.

'Something like that.'

There's a pause. He lifts his demitasse to his lips and drinks a little of the black liquid. As he replaces it on the saucer, he says, 'I'm sorry.'

'We're sorry for each other,' I reply softly. 'Because we know how it feels.'

'Orphans in the storm,' he says with that bitter laugh. 'Left outside while the celebrations go on within.'

That's exactly how I feel. As if everyone is enveloped in a warm glow and I'm not allowed to share in it. I'm excluded from the joy everybody else experiences.

I realise that he's staring at me intently, then he says softly, 'You are very young. You have your life in front of you to love again. It's different for me.'

I shake my head. 'It's not as easy as that, though. I don't feel that. It doesn't make my pain any less. Besides, why shouldn't *you* love again?'

He says nothing, then lifts his cup to his lips and drains it. He stands up. 'Believe me, mademoiselle, you have a lifetime of passion in front of you. It's different for me. I can't love again. I don't even know how I will tolerate being alive.' He tosses some coins on to the table. 'Goodbye, mademoiselle, and good luck. The remedy to your misery lies closer to hand than you know, I'm quite sure of it.' He turns to leave.

I'm flooded by a sudden sense that I can't simply let him walk away like this. We've opened our hearts to one another and I feel as though we were brought together for a reason. Besides, I am moved by his plight. He doesn't even want to live. Surely I can help him. 'Wait!'

He turns back. 'Yes?'

'Don't go. I . . . I'm alone today. I'm not going to the

31

wedding reception and I don't want to be by myself. Sometimes strangers are more use to us than friends, aren't they? We can say things that we'd never say to people who know us. Perhaps we could keep each other company – just for today.'

The man hesitates, standing there on the cold pavement, his chin buried in his scarf, watching me with those steely blue eyes. He's taller than I'd realised, well built and imposing.

What am I doing? I know nothing about this man! I have a sudden impulse to withdraw my invitation, but there's also a reckless excitement in it.

At last, he speaks. 'Very well. Why not? I'm not the best company, I warn you. But if you think you can tolerate me, then perhaps it will be a comfort to us both.'

I smile at him. 'Good. You can tell me the whole story.'

CHAPTER THREE

It's only when we are walking together down the long boulevard that I feel the first real sense of trepidation.

What have I done? This man is a complete stranger. All I know is that he's stalking Beth on her wedding day. I must be mad to ask him to keep me company – for all I know, he's a nutter. I can just imagine what Pierre would say if he knew – he'd go crazy.

It's been drummed into me from a very early age how careful I have to be about my safety. It's because my sisters and I are regarded as prime kidnap targets. Our father is a very rich man and we're well known to the world because of his wealth. None of us like the attention or the way that we're considered spoilt princesses whose private lives are public property, but that's the price we pay for the privileges we enjoy because of my father's fortune. I've tried to shake off the media labels and all the attention as much as I can, because I long to make it in the world through my talent, not my family money, but I'm realistic enough to know that it will be difficult. Everyone will always assume I've bought whatever success I enjoy. But my real battle is to have a private life without the constant presence of bodyguards. If Pierre, my father's head of security, had his way, I would never take a step outside the door without one – but maybe in the light of what's happened with Freya and *her* bodyguard, he's revising that policy. Not that I have ever been attracted to any of my guards. My latest stand has been to refuse to have one at all. I want to live in Paris as normally as possible, without drawing attention to myself with body-guards and fancy cars and outlandish living. The compromise has been that a guard lives in a tiny studio on the ground floor of my apartment building and I'm supposed to run all my plans past him and be discreetly tailed wherever I go. But, of course, I don't do that. Alphonse is not the brightest spark and it's been quite easy to give him the slip. I don't want some stupid meathead guy plodding around after me all day long. It's not as though they're all Miles Murray, after all.

What would Alphonse do if he could see me now, wandering off with this man?

I almost laugh at the thought. But the problem is that all the fears for our safety are not unfounded. Years ago, the worst did happen and that has fuelled my father's paranoia ever since.

'Where shall we go?' asks the man beside me in that harsh voice of his.

'It's lunchtime,' I reply, trying to sound jaunty. 'I'm hungry. Shall we go and eat somewhere?'

After all, how dangerous can it be to have lunch with someone? I'm not going back to his lair with him or anything like that.

'Lunch,' he says almost thoughtfully. 'Yes. That's a good idea. Where do you suggest?'

I think. I'd like somewhere private, to reduce the chances of my being recognised. But on the other hand, I also need it to be public enough that I'm not in any danger. My instinct tells me that this man isn't going to harm me – as far as I know, he has no idea who I am and he doesn't look the type to read gossip magazines – but even so, I ought to be cautious ...

But caution has never been a part of my nature. I wouldn't be doing this if it had.

'I know somewhere,' I say decisively. 'It's not far.'

'I trust your judgement,' he says in a tone that's hard to read. 'Lead the way.'

Usually for lunch I would choose somewhere light and airy, buzzy with chatter and people. But that doesn't seem right for today. We need quiet and privacy if I'm going to get this reserved man to open up and speak to me. I'm so curious about him, now, as he walks along beside me. He has a story, I can tell, and I want to know what it is. He says nothing, though, as we approach Marcello's, a restaurant I go to when I particularly want to be shielded from the eyes of the world.

'Mademoiselle,' says Jean-Paul, the maître d', 'what a pleasure to see you. We were not expecting you.'

'I know, I haven't reserved, but Jean-Paul, I wondered if you have the small private room available?'

Jean-Paul's gaze flicks over to my companion, and he frowns, then a strange expression crosses his face and he speaks rapidly. 'Of course, mademoiselle ... monsieur ... whatever you wish. Give us only a moment, I beg ...' He summons a waiter over and instructs him in rapid French to prepare the private room.

I turn to my companion. 'They know me here.'

He glances at me, his eyes amused. 'I can tell. You must be a regular.'

I smile at him. Something in me relaxes – from the way he speaks to me and looks at me, I'm sure he can have no idea who I am and that's refreshing. I'm only too aware that my family has been getting more publicity than usual lately, with Freya's private life hitting the headlines, but in a way that's kept the spotlight off me and I've relished the relative anonymity. Within a very short time, we're being led through the restaurant, already quietly busy with its clientele of businessmen, politicians and society ladies, to the private room. I have the distinct sense that it has only recently been vacated. *But surely they wouldn't move another customer just for me? I'm not that important!*

Before I can ask, my coat is being taken by a waiter and a chair is held out for me at the small table in the centre of the room. I sit down, a napkin is shaken out into my lap and a menu put into my hands. Marcello's serves exquisite Italian food and my mouth is already watering at the thought of their truffle tagliatelle and the rosemary roasted sea bass. I look up to tell my companion that he really must try the ribollita when my words die in my mouth. He is standing there, his coat, hat and scarf now held by the departing waiter, and at last I can see him properly.

The man in front of me has gone from an anonymous figure to something else entirely. He has the most powerful presence I've ever known. He's tall and muscled, with the impression of simmering strength under the well-cut jacket of his suit. He's in his late thirties or early forties, and his hair is dark blond with edges of grey at the temples, but it's his face that is most striking: it's too craggy to be conventionally handsome and yet he's extraordinarily attractive, with strong, emphatic features: a prominent nose, a jutting chin, high cheekbones and a broad mouth with a stubborn-looking lower lip. What draws me most are his eyes, which are a brilliant pale blue, the kind that can have the warmth of a summer sky or the chill of ice at any given moment. The strangest thing of all is how familiar he looks.

But where on earth would I know him from?

He can see me staring, and a smile twitches his lips. 'We haven't even been introduced,' he remarks, and sits down opposite me. The chair seems too flimsy to hold his leonine strength. 'What's your name?'

I try to speak but I stumble over my words, my cheeks reddening still further. I'm embarrassed by the way his presence is affecting me, and so surprised by it that I can hardly concentrate on what I'm supposed to be saying. 'I . . . I . . . My name is Flora,' I manage at last, and drop my gaze to the menu.

'Flora. That's very pretty. Does it mean flower?'

I nod. 'Flora was the Roman goddess of the spring.'

'Was she?' I glance up and see him raising his eyebrows at me, a smile still playing around his lips. 'It suits you. You have the look of a pre-Raphaelite goddess yourself.'

'Oh. Thank you.' I blush even harder at the compliment and look back at the menu, though the words are dancing in front of my gaze. 'What would you like? This is my treat, of course.'

'I don't think so.' He doesn't say it with any rudeness but just with a flat rejection of any idea that I might pay for lunch.

Before I can reply, the waiter returns to take our order.

'Mademoiselle?' he asks, his hands behind his back. The waiters at Marcello's always remember every order perfectly without the need of a pad.

'I would like the sea bass, please,' I say, glad of the distraction.

The waiter nods and turns to my companion. 'And for you, Monsieur Dubrovski?'

'I would like the Roman lamb, rare, with a dish of spinach on the side.' He throws down his menu and adds in his rasping voice, 'And a bottle of Soave, please.'

'Of course, monsieur.' The waiter turns to go, which is just as well, as that means he doesn't notice me gaping at him.

'You're ... you're ...' I can hardly get the words out. This is turning into quite a surprising lunch. 'You're Andrei Dubrovski!'

He looks over at me with an unreadable expression. I can't tell whether he's pleased or not that I know who he is. 'That's right,' he says in a neutral voice. 'How do you know my name?'

Answers fly through my brain. I could tell him that he is, after all, one of the most famous Russian businessmen in the world, known for his acumen, wealth and toughness. I could tell him that my father is a self-made tycoon almost in the same league as he is, and that their paths have crossed in the world of business several times. I could tell him that we've been at the same parties and know the same people, and I could even tell him that I was at a party he threw in Moscow a couple of years ago in support of his charities. There is no reason why he would remember me, though. In fact, we were never introduced. I saw him in the distance, the host of the party in his elegant black dinner suit and bow tie, shaking the hands of his prestigious guests and then standing up to deliver a speech urging us to support the evening's worthy cause. The guests gave millions that night.

But I'm not going to say any of that.

I don't want him to know that there's any connection between us. Much better if we remain as separate as possible. Besides, I don't want any word leaking back to my father.

'I've seen your picture in the paper,' I say at last. 'You're a well-known man.'

He shrugs. 'Perhaps. Not as well known as I once was.'

I stare at him. He's right – I haven't seen much about him in the papers lately. He's kept a very low profile for whatever reason. *Beth? Is she the cause?*

'So, Flora, my new friend, you know who I am. I assume you had no idea when we met at the cafe outside the town hall.'

'No. Of course not. I wouldn't have had the temerity to talk to you if I'd realised who you are.' I laugh. 'You don't need someone like me to tell your troubles to. I'm sure you can afford the best therapists in the world.'

He shrugs. 'I don't want them. I don't want to be doctored.' He leans towards me, his magnetic presence almost vibrating in the air between us. I pull in a sharp breath at the power of his nearness. 'I just want to live, if I can. I want to know how I'm going to live, and if the world holds any future for me.'

I stare at him, my breath coming faster. Just then, the door opens and the waiter returns with our wine and some water. Andrei watches him intently as he moves around the table, filling our glasses. Another waiter arrives with a bowl of dark, syrupy balsamic vinegar, a dish of salt crystals and a basket of focaccia and flat bread. As the waiters leave us, I say in a half-whisper, 'Of course you have something to live for.'

Andrei leans back in his chair, one large hand on the

white tablecloth. I can see his tension in the way his thumb flicks up and down, tapping lightly on the table top. 'I don't mean something to live for,' he retorts, but not unkindly. 'I can think of reasons to go on. I don't know *how* to live, not the way I am at the moment. I'm in constant pain, do you understand that?'

I nod. 'I do.'

He looks up at me. I wish I could interpret the expression in those eyes: there seems to be a kindness there, but also a cold distance, and a faint condescension too. 'How would someone as young and beautiful as you possibly know what I'm talking about?'

'I may be young,' I reply. 'But that doesn't mean I don't know how to love and how to feel. It doesn't mean I can't have my heart broken. And beauty has nothing to do with it.'

His stern face softens just a little. The cragginess mellows instantly. *He looks so much nicer when that happens.* 'Who has broken your heart?' he asks, his rasping voice sounding almost gentle. 'Who would be such a fool?'

'It's not exactly his fault,' I say with a wry smile.

'That sounds intriguing.' He picks up a piece of focaccia and dips it into the vinegar. The bread stains brown as it absorbs the liquid. 'You'd better explain.'

I start to tell him the whole story but as I don't want him to guess my identity, I change a few details. Jimmy was our riding and polo instructor but I make him into a friend instead. And really, that's what Jimmy became. He was always a friend to us, more than he ever was a teacher, and we all loved him. His beauty was something incredible – I've never seen a more perfect man. He had dark hair and liquid brown eyes, tanned skin and the features of a model. He was beautifully built as well, with strong thighs and bulging biceps from his riding. More than that, he was sweetness itself to us. Nothing was too much trouble for Jimmy, and he comforted us when we were low, made us laugh and then feel like a million dollars again. All three of us adored him, but I was the one who really, truly loved him.

Andrei nods as I talk, my voice animated as I explain how wonderful Jimmy is. I'm afraid that he thinks it was just a schoolgirl crush on an older man and I don't know how to explain what it meant to me.

'I longed for him to return how I felt,' I say. 'I dreamed that one day he might take me in his arms and kiss me. I yearned for it. I lived for it. That's why what happened was so devastating.'

Andrei eyes me, one eyebrow faintly raised. 'He preferred one of your sisters? You say there are three of you.'

'No, no, it wasn't that. It was much worse.' I eye him suspiciously. 'You aren't . . . laughing at me, are you?'

He shakes his head, looking perfectly serious. 'Of course not. I would never presume to laugh at your feelings. It's only too clear how you feel about this Jimmy.'

I stare down at the tablecloth. So often my feelings are dismissed. 'It's just Flora,' they say. 'She's so dramatic.' As though my response to life is somehow less meaningful than everyone else's because I make no secret of what I feel and when I feel it. My love for Jimmy has been a source of family amusement and no one has ever taken it seriously. My pain has been treated as a joke and my feelings as a kind of ongoing family soap opera. None of them have ever considered how much I've hurt over Jimmy. It feels odd that this man, almost a stranger, is giving my feelings weight, acting as though they matter. It makes me curdle inside with

41

the pain all over again. My eyes sting and I blink hard. I don't want to embarrass myself with tears.

'So what happened?' he asked gently. 'Did he use you and abandon you?'

I shake my head. When I speak, my voice quavers. 'Jimmy would never do anything like that. He loved me too; I know that. He told me. We were so close. We would meet in the summer evenings, and lie together in the garden, holding hands and whispering everything to each other.' I bite my lip at the bittersweet memory.

'And he told you why you couldn't be together,' he prompts.

'Not then. He told me lots of reasons why he couldn't kiss me, or love me . . . because of his closeness to my father, because I was young . . .'

'But none of those were true?'

I shake my head miserably. 'No. He couldn't bring himself to say it. I suppose the only cruel thing Jimmy ever did was to tell me the truth in front of everyone else. He came to the house one day and told us that he was leaving, moving to Los Angeles. He wanted to try and make it as an actor. But there was another reason too. The man he loved was there.'

Andrei nods his head slowly. 'I see. So Jimmy was never going to love a woman, not the way you wanted him to, at least.'

'That's right.' I recall the moment vividly. He hadn't been able to meet my eyes when he made the announcement. Everyone had stood up, Jane-Elizabeth going forward to embrace him, my sisters thrilled and excited, even though they didn't want him to go. They told me afterwards that it took a few moments before they noticed that I'd fainted clean away, felled by the shock. Jimmy was leaving me, and he would never, could never, be mine.

'Was this a long time ago?' Andrei asks.

'Four years.' I close my eyes, thinking over the time it's been since my heart was broken.

'And you've never loved anyone since?'

I open my eyes and stare over at him. 'No. I will never love anyone else. I can only love him. I can't imagine having what I had with him with any other man.'

Andrei seems to consider this and says, 'Have you seen him again?'

I shake my head. 'The others have gone to visit him. In LA. They say his boyfriend is very lovely. Almost as handsome as Jimmy, and incredibly nice too. But I can't bear to see it.' My eyes fill with tears, despite my determination not to cry. 'I just can't bear it!'

'I understand.'

Just then, the door opens and the waiters appear with our food. I don't feel hungry now, but it smells delicious just the same, the woody rosemary and the delicate lemon scent of the fish. Andrei nods his thanks as the waiters put his meal in front of him, and leave.

I say nothing as I struggle to regain my composure. I've not admitted so much to anybody before, and it's almost a relief to have spoken about it in the way I have, but it has brought it all back to me in a swirl of emotion.

'You've suffered,' Andrei says briefly. 'I can see that.'

'I'm still suffering. It hasn't gone away.' I manage to smile at him. 'I think you understand what I mean.'

'Of course.'

We gaze at one another, reading understanding in each other's eyes.

Andrei says softly, 'Perhaps there are ways we can help each other. Now. Tell me how you discovered this place. As it happens, it's one of my favourites.'

We eat and my appetite returns as we talk companionably. He asks me about what I plan for my life and I explain about my course at drama school. Before I know it, I'm telling him about my experiences there and how I feel when I'm on the stage. I'm glad that the conversation has become a little less intense, but even so, there's a strange excitement rolling inside me.

What does he mean, there are ways we can help each other? And what is the story of him and Beth?

It isn't until we've finished our main course and most of the bottle of Soave that the conversation returns to what has brought us together, when I ask him if he is often in Paris.

'Yes,' he replies, pushing away his plate. 'I'm here frequently on business. I move all the time – Paris, New York, London, Moscow, China . . . wherever my work leads me. But, I confess, I made special arrangements to be here today.'

'To see Beth?' I ask tentatively. I'm eager to know the whole story but I don't know whether he'll be as open with me as I've been with him. He doesn't seem like the confiding type.

'That's right.' He frowns, his thumb tapping on the table again. 'I made it my business to know where and when she was getting married. I had to see her on this day. It was important to me.' He glances up at me. 'I once asked her to marry me, you see.'

My heart aches for him. I know that Beth has made the

right choice for her – Dominic is obviously the man she loves – but that doesn't mean I can't feel sympathy for the man who couldn't win her heart. 'I'm sorry,' I say. 'Really.'

'I appreciate that.' His pale blue eyes rake my face. 'To be honest, you're the first person I've been able to confide in. You know a little of what I'm feeling.'

I gaze at him, that strange feeling burning in my stomach. *What is it?* Then I realise. *It's attraction.* I'm attracted to Andrei Dubrovski. The first man to make me feel that way since Jimmy.

Oh my goodness. I wasn't expecting that.

CHAPTER FOUR

That night, I dream vividly about Jimmy. It's been a while since I've dreamed of him, and this one is peculiarly intense. Seeing him in my dreams is a painful pleasure: it's so wonderful to be back with him, to feel him near me, but even though he's happy to see me too, full of love and kindness, he's never able to give me the passion I want, no matter how much I beg and coax and plead. This dream is no different: we're lying in a hammock together, somewhere hot and beautiful, the sun glinting on his dark hair and gilding his tanned skin. Jimmy looks at me with that sad, wistful expression in his beautiful brown eyes and says in his languid Southern drawl, 'It's just no good, honey. I can't give you what you need. You know that.'

'But Jimmy, you love me, don't you?' I ask him.

'Sure I do, baby.' He strokes my hair. 'But you need a man who can give you what I can't.'

'You have everything I need,' I protest, wanting to believe it even though I know the truth.

'But what I have isn't for you, you know that. You need . . .' He leans forward and touches me, running his hand over my arm and then down the curve of my hip. 'You need . . .' He brushes his hand up under my skirt and smooths it against my panties. At once, I feel a dart of fire rush through me. 'Baby, you need someone who's hungry for you. I want you to have that. I don't want you to wait for me, do you understand?'

I can hardly breathe with the desire for him to touch me again, but he doesn't. Instead, he closes his eyes, yawns and turns away, pulling his hand from me. I know with a plunging sadness that I leave him cold. My skin, my nearness, my body – they don't affect him at all. The fire that burns in me for him will never be quenched.

I wake into the darkness of my bedroom and lie there, blinking away my misery. I have waited for Jimmy. Like some kind of modern-day Vestal Virgin, I've dedicated my body to him even though he will never want or need it. Before now, I've always found a kind of nobility in that, but suddenly it seems ridiculous. I'm young and hungry for life and all it can give me. Isn't it madness to deny myself a taste of what Jimmy can never offer?

I roll on to my back and stare up at the dark ceiling.

After all, I can still love Jimmy. I can keep my heart for him. But perhaps it's time to let my body experience what it's capable of. What it's made for . . .

I remember the powerful masculine presence of Andrei Dubrovski, and the way he made me feel. My skin prickled whenever he came close to me, my pulse sped up and my breath came fast and shallow. Since we parted outside the restaurant, I've felt curiously wired, tingling all over, a pitching excitement inside me.

'So, Miss Flora,' he said as we made our farewells. 'I'm in Paris for a while longer. Perhaps we should meet again.'

'Perhaps,' I replied.

He took my number, thumbing it quickly into his phone. 'I will be in touch.'

I could see he was about to leave. 'Wait – let me take your number too.'

He raised his eyebrows at me, smiling. 'Of course.' He

gave it to me and I tapped it into my phone. 'Goodbye.'
Slipping the phone into his pocket, he bent to kiss my cheek
and then was gone, striding off down the boulevard in the
direction of the Louvre.

I have no idea if he will call me or not, or what will
happen if he does. But as I lie there in the darkness, I can't
help thinking that somehow, Jimmy has given me permission to follow that path wherever it will lead me.

I don't hear anything for two days, and the effect of our
lunch almost wears off. I've begun to think I imagined the
power of his presence and the magnetic attraction I felt for
him. In my mind, the lunch becomes just a curious coinci-
dence, one of those odd happenings that are left by the
wayside as life moves on. Besides, I have plenty to think
about. My classes at drama school take up all my days, and
in the evening I study, learn lines and rehearse on my own
in my apartment. I know I could be out with my fellow
students but I don't feel entirely at ease with them. The ones
who want to be my friend make me suspicious in case it's
only my relative fame and my father's money that interest
them. The others seem to dislike me for the same reasons.
I'm sure a friend or two will emerge in time but until then,
I'm a loner.

But two evenings later, I can't get the thought of him out
of my mind. I keep seeing his craggy, handsome face, the
muscled shoulders beneath the suit jacket, and remember
that rasping voice of his. Each time I think of him, a tiny
shiver goes through me. He hasn't texted me, perhaps he
won't, but I have the strongest feeling I mustn't let him slip
through my fingers. The memory of Jimmy in my dream
mixes together with Dubrovki's passion for Beth to make

me edgy and needy. An idea forms in my mind and as it emerges into my consciousness, I realise that it's been growing in my subconscious ever since I met Andrei. But am I brave enough to do it?

There's only one way to find out. I pick up my phone and type out a text.

Andrei, are you still in Paris? Would you like to meet? Flora

Before I can change my mind, I press send. It vanishes and I stare at my screen with a fearful apprehension. It's gone now. I hope I don't regret sending it.

Then, of course, I hear nothing for an hour. I check the phone every few minutes but it remains resolutely silent, until I'm making a cup of tea and the little chirrup sounds to announce the arrival of a text. I pick up the phone, breathless. It's from him.

Miss Flora, how are you? I've been busy working, forgive me. I'm free this evening, though, and would love to meet you. Your friend Andrei.

I read the odd missive a few times. It's hard to decipher the tone, which is friendly and yet a little formal. Does he really want to meet me, or is he just being polite? Perhaps I should tell him I've changed my mind. But . . . I know I have to do this. I tap out a reply.

Yes, let's meet. Where are you?

A reply arrives almost at once.

Come to the bar at Le Meurice. I will see you there.

I frown. The Hotel Meurice is across town in the middle of Paris, not that close to the Marais area where I live. It's a little arrogant of him to summon me to him like that, isn't it?

But I can't resist. And this was my idea, after all. I push away my supper and go to the bedroom to change.

Half an hour later, wearing a simple black silk dress under my coat, I make my way down to the street, slipping past my bodyguard's apartment without his noticing. I sometimes wonder if he's forgotten entirely that he's supposed to be looking after me, and just enjoys whiling away his hours in the little studio, watching television and eating. But at least it means I can enjoy my freedom. It's dark outside and the evening is cold. I shiver a little as I flag down a taxi and ask the driver to take me to Le Meurice.

Is this crazy? I ask myself as we glide through Paris, following the lights that edge the Seine. *Am I getting myself into a tricky situation? There's still time to turn back.*

But I know I won't.

The bar inside Le Meurice is small but very stylish, panelled in dark wood and furnished with antique chairs around polished ebony tables. The waiters, smart in bottle-green jackets, mix cocktails with expert hands, serving to the people sitting on the high stools around the bar itself, or to the smart customers talking quietly at the tables. As I walk in from the hotel lobby, I see him at once. He's leaning against the bar, one foot crossed over the other, in a languidly casual pose as he reads something on his telephone screen. He's wearing another gorgeous suit, so sharply cut across the shoulders that it must be bespoke. The dark-blond hair is short and spiky as though he's not long out of the shower, and the expression on his face is serious, a furrow between the dark brows as he scrutinises the screen in front of him. I stand in the doorway looking at him for a moment, and as if he can feel my gaze upon him, he looks up and sees me. A smile curves his lips and his harsh face softens.

It's amazing what a smile can do.

I walk towards him and he stands up straight, leaning towards me to drop a kiss on my cheek as I reach him.

'Miss Flora,' he says, and the gravelly sound of his voice sets my skin bumping lightly and a tiny shiver rippling down my spine.

'Good evening, Andrei.'

'What would you like to drink? I recommend the pear martini. They mix the best in Paris here.'

'That sounds delicious, thank you.' I look around. I've visited Le Meurice before but not lately. Since I started my new life at drama school, I've tried to avoid places like this: expensive and exclusive, not the kind of place where aspiring drama students hang out at all. I've headed for the cheaper places around the Left Bank and in Pigalle or Montmartre. I don't want to be just another glossy heiress slapping down her credit card without a second thought, cosseted and kept away from the real world. But still, it is nice to be back.

Andrei orders our drinks and leads me over to a table where we sit down.

'I was wondering if you were still in Paris,' I say, looking around. The bar is quiet but it's early yet. 'You said you were going to be in touch.'

Andrei looks at me thoughtfully and my skin tingles where his gaze lands on me. 'You're right. I was taking my time before I contacted you, that's true. I needed to think about it. Do you want to know why?'

'Perhaps,' I say in an offhand voice. He intrigues me and I'd very much like to know why, but I want to play it cool with him. *Although it's a bit late for that. If I wanted to be cool, I should have waited for him to make the first move.*

He leans in towards me, pressing his fingertips together, his expression serious. 'I have to be careful. I can see what a vulnerable state you are in, Flora. Your broken heart, the tears that rush to your eyes, your longing for the love of a man you can never have – I can tell that you are the kind of girl it would be easy to hurt.'

I stare back, astonished. 'Hurt by *you*?' I ask, incredulous. 'We barely know each other! Besides, I told you. I love Jimmy. That's not about to change, no matter what you might think.'

'No, of course not,' he says almost graciously. 'I didn't mean that you're changeable or inconstant. Love makes anyone vulnerable, you must concede that. Perhaps I sounded arrogant. I apologise. I only meant that when two people find companionship and comfort in the face of suffering, it's easy for emotions to become more heightened than they might otherwise. And if the friendship does not develop as one hoped, it's possible to feel a double rejection. I'm aware that we're both in raw states. A wound can be helped to heal – or easily made worse. Do you see what I mean?'

'I . . . I think so.'

'I myself am vulnerable.'

I run my eyes over his face. It's hard to imagine that this

strong, tough-looking man can be hurt. But I remember the flat, honest way in which he talked about his unrequited love for Beth. I believed completely that he felt those emotions, and perhaps in those blue eyes there's something tender. 'Really?'

'Of course. You know that. You saw me outside the town hall.'

'That's true.'

'I need to be careful as well. I too have a heart to protect.'

I colour a little and say quietly, 'But you love Beth.'

'That's true. But you know what it's like. We orphans in the storm sometimes huddle a little too closely together.' The waiter comes over and puts our drinks in front of us. When he's gone, Andrei says quietly, 'That's why I wanted to be sure of my motives before I texted you.'

'And your motives are?'

He sips his Scotch and says, 'I think we can be a friend to one another.'

A strange disappointment seizes me. 'A friend.'

I realise at once that I've already decided what I want from Dubrovski, and it isn't friendship. *It's experience.*

'That's right.' He smiles again, his broad mouth twitching with amusement. 'I don't have many friends. It will be novel for me. And perhaps you can enlighten me about the hearts and minds of women. They seem to be a mystery to me.'

'I can't speak for all women,' I reply, 'any more than you could speak for all men. I can only speak for myself.'

He gazes at me and then says briskly, 'Very true. That was rather a stupid thing to say. Perhaps I mean that I want an uncomplicated friendship with a woman I like and admire.' He pauses, then asks, 'And you? What do you want?'

I lift my drink to my lips and sip the pale liquid. It's sweet at first but then the sourness of the alcohol burns down my throat. It flies out into my blood, buzzing there and giving me a lift of courage. I remember my dream and the way Jimmy touched me and said, 'You need someone who's hungry for you. I want you to have that.' I remember the fire that darted through me, the need that burned in my belly and between my legs. The memory emboldens me.

'There is something I want,' I say quietly, putting my drink back on the table.

'Yes?'

'First, I need to ask you something. It's a little . . . presumptuous. I hope you'll excuse that.'

He raises his eyebrows at me and nods. 'Yes. Go on.'

I hesitate, then take the plunge. 'Did you ever . . . sleep with Beth?'

The question makes his blue eyes turn steely and his mouth harden. For a moment I'm afraid that I've gone too far. I'm about to apologise and retract my question, when he speaks, his voice low and rasping. 'No,' he says, looking me straight in the eye. 'I never did. And I assume you never slept with Jimmy.'

I laugh wryly. 'It never came close to that. Not surprisingly.' Then I take another drink, a gulp this time. I need the courage. 'So here's what I suggest. We're both in love with other people. I know you think I'm very vulnerable but I'm tougher than you imagine. There's no danger that we can be emotionally hurt by each other. And neither of us can have the comfort of physical closeness with the one we love. So . . .' Despite my bravado, I can feel my cheeks flaming. It's harder to say than I thought. *Oh, just go for it, Flora! Say it! I'm sure he guesses anyway!* 'So . . . I thought ... why don't we find that comfort with each other?'

There. It's out there now.

My hand is shaking a little as I take another hasty drink, almost emptying my pear martini, and then put the glass back on the table. I hardly dare to look at Andrei and see how he has taken my suggestion but when I do steal a glance, I can see that his blue eyes have become hooded, and his expression is unreadable.

He has a very good line in keeping a poker face. It's so hard to know what he's thinking.

I'm mortified for a moment, wishing I could take back my audacious suggestion. How could I ask something like that from a man who is virtually a stranger to me? What must he think? My embarrassment grows until I can scarcely bear it a moment longer, and I'm about to leap up and demand my coat from the bellboy so I can disappear into the cold Paris night. Then Andrei speaks.

'I've never had an invitation quite like that before,' he says softly. He's looking up at me and smiling, properly. His blue eyes are gentle, the colour of a summer sea. 'I'm not quite sure of the correct way to respond.'

'Please,' I manage to stumble out, 'if you'd rather not, I understand ...'

'Rather not? Flora ...' His voice sinks down to a rasping level that means I have to lean in a little to hear him. 'You're a beautiful girl. It's an invitation I'm flattered to receive – more than flattered. I'm honoured. But I see many pitfalls. You may think you're ready for such an arrangement but I would hate for you to regret a step like this.'

My blushes are dying away. I'm regaining my courage. Perhaps this is going to work after all. If there's the faintest chance, then I want to seize it. 'Please don't think about the pitfalls. I've told you, I love someone else. My heart is completely impervious to you, just as yours will be to me. I don't want love or a relationship or anything like that. I only want you to think of what we can offer to each other. I want you to show me a side of life that Jimmy can never give me. And in return, I'll give you some of the . . . the . . . comfort . . . that you can't get from Beth.'

'This is not what I was expecting.' He's staring at me intently. 'And you make it sound so simple.'

'It *is* simple.' I lean closer towards him, suddenly more determined than I've been in a very long time. 'Please, Andrei. I may seem cold-blooded but I know what I want.'

'Oh Flora,' he breathes. 'Cold-blooded is not what you seem. Quite the opposite.' His eyes glitter at me. 'But this is a big decision. I'm honoured, as I say, but still, I can't rush into it no matter how much I would like to. I need to think about it. And so do you. Why don't we both consider what we might want from the arrangement you suggest? And then . . . if we agree . . . perhaps . . . just perhaps . . . we can make it work.'

CHAPTER FIVE

'Move your body, Flora! Make it express how you feel. I want to see *passion*.'

I try to respond to my tutor's commands. I want to lose myself in the moment, convey emotion as purely as I can without the barrier of self-consciousness, letting my movements talk directly to my audience. This part of the drama course concentrates on mime, dance and movement alone, and now that I'm getting used to doing without words and losing my sense of embarrassment, I love it. There's so much that can be said without words and at last I can see a purpose in the way my face expresses so much.

Besides, I'm working hard in my classes. It's helping to keep my mind off the excitement that possesses me whenever I think about Andrei and what is developing between us.

'Very good, very good.' My tutor walks towards me, clapping lightly.

I straighten up, breathless and delighted by his praise.

'You're improving in every class, Flora,' he says approvingly. 'There's a new looseness about you. You're not perfect yet – but you're getting there.' He turns to the other watching students. 'Right, you, Simone. Your turn. I hope you've done your homework as well as Flora has.'

My pleasure in my tutor's approval is soured on my way out of class when Simone bumps into me hard, her sweaty towel pressing into my cheek, and hisses, 'I suppose you paid Monsieur to say that stupid stuff. You're no better than anyone else in the class, so don't let it go to your head.'

Before I can reply, she's walked off with her group of friends, all of them laughing over their shoulders at me.

I stare after them, my face burning, filled with humiliation and fury. *They're just jealous,* I tell myself, but it's hard not to be hurt and to wonder if they're right. Obviously I haven't paid anyone to praise me, but is my tutor being nice to me because of who I am?

Don't be silly, I tell myself sternly. *Why would he? What can he gain from it?*

Nevertheless, my joy in the afternoon has vanished and I walk home lost in depression, keeping my head down and staring at the pavement. It's only when I'm climbing the stairs to my apartment that I look at my phone and see an email has arrived in my inbox. It's from Andrei. I gave him the address of an account I set up especially, one that doesn't identify me.

My stomach whirls over and my fingers tremble a little. I don't want to open the message on my telephone. Instead, I hurry inside, go to my laptop and fire it up. A moment later, I'm able to click on the message and open it.

Miss Flora
I've had time to think over your proposition. You're very persuasive, and you've made me believe that this is truly what you want. I understand it. I also desire closeness and intimacy, but, like you, I can't give my heart.
    Therefore what you suggest makes perfect sense.
    I hope you've had time to think over what you

would like from this arrangement. Enclosed are my
suggestions. Perhaps you should frame your thoughts
before you read mine, so that you can be sure you're
not being influenced by me.

I look forward to hearing from you.
Regards
Andrei

There is an attachment to the email. Andrei has suggested
that I do not read it yet, but I'm not that self-disciplined.
I'm eager to see what he has suggested. I click on it and it
opens on the screen.

The arrangement between Flora X and Andrei Dubrovski

I look at my name. *Flora X. I like that. Me, and yet –*
anonymous. I read on.

It is agreed that for purposes of mutual comfort and sat-
isfaction, Miss X and Mr Dubrovski intend to enjoy each
other physically, at times and places to be agreed. There
will be no payment and no obligation resulting from any
congress. Both parties are required to undertake a health
check prior to any intimacy, but it is the responsibility of
Miss X to ensure there is adequate birth control.

I blink at this. *Birth control?* It makes it all very real.
What am I doing, agreeing to sleep with a stranger like this?
Then I mentally pull myself up. *This was my idea, remember?*
And it isn't going to be hearts and flowers, so if he wants
to talk about birth control, then he's only being sensible.
I turn back to the document.

*Although it is understood that there is to be no payment
with regard to any physical activity, M Dubrovski under-
takes to pay any expenses in regards to travel, meals,
hotel rooms, specific attire and so on in the course of
agreed meetings.*

*Miss X agrees that she is prepared to be broad-minded
and accommodating to the requests of M Dubrovski,
although she is always to be permitted to refuse to partake in any activity that she does not wish to.*

I realise that my mouth is a little dry. I swallow, and a
shiver of trepidation plays out over my skin. I wonder what
kind of activities he has in mind, and how far I might allow
myself to go.

*In return, M Dubrovski is prepared to fulfil any
requests made of him by Miss X, with the same conditions applying.*

*In the case of any unusual request being made, a
verbal agreement as to its restrictions and boundaries
will be made at the time and both parties will honour
this agreement, on pain of compensation to be fixed by
the injured party.*

What is he talking about? I wonder. I'll have to ask
Andrei what that means.

*As expressly set out here, no party will have any obli-
gation to the other of any kind, financial, emotional or
otherwise, as a result of an intimate relationship willingly
entered into. Two copies of this document will be signed,
one to be retained by each party.*

Beneath, there is a space for our signatures.

I realise that my heart is racing. This is real. I've set something in motion and it's suddenly become serious. It might actually happen. If I want it to, it will.

I do want it to. More than that. I need it to.

I think for a moment, only half seeing the words on the screen in front of me. I'm on the brink of something extraordinary, I can sense that.

An adventure. I remember all the things that happened to Freya lately. *Now it's my time. I wonder where I'm going to be led?*

I type out my reply:

Dear M Dubrovski
Thank you for your email and for the document you attached. I agree to its terms and I look forward to the implementation of our agreement. I will arrange to see my doctor for the health check you suggest and will forward the results to you. I trust you will do the same.

My desires chime with yours and I have only these additions to the agreement: first, that the costs of our rendezvous can also be met by me, if I should choose. I also request that you do not attempt to discover my surname; I would prefer to be known to you as Miss X. Finally, I ask that you do not be afraid to broaden my experience as you see fit.

I shall wait to hear from you as regards our first appointment, and I will bring two signed copies of the document with me.

Yours sincerely
Flora X

I read it over and then send it whizzing away. I'm almost aghast at what I've done, and afraid of what I've set in motion.

But how can I be a true actress if I don't know how to live?

I'm sure I've done the right thing.

I wish I could ask Jimmy for his advice, but this isn't something I can discuss with him. And anyway, I told him that I can't be in contact with him, not while I feel about him the way I do. It's just too painful for me. I know he longs for us to be close again, but I can't do it, not while I know that the deepest part of his heart belongs to someone else.

Instead I send an email to my doctor, requesting an appointment for the next day. The birth control aspect is not a problem. I'm already on a contraceptive pill to deal with issues with my erratic and very hormonal menstrual cycle.

Now I can only wait to hear what Andrei has in mind for me.

The next day I cut a class to go to my appointment. It's the first one I've not turned up for, and I hope that my good record means I won't get into too much trouble. The doctor checks me over, takes my blood tests and tells me the results will be available in a few days.

'But you seem in excellent health,' he says, pleased to deliver good news. 'Do you have any reason to suspect you have any sexually transmitted conditions?'

'No reason at all,' I say candidly.

'No – I would be most surprised if you had.' He writes some notes swiftly. 'All seems to be in order. But if you have any queries, please don't hesitate to ask me.'

On the way back from the surgery, I don't hurry back to the Academie as I thought I would. Instead, I wander along the Rue du Faubourg Saint-Honoré, gazing into the windows of the shops as I go. There are famous names along here – expensive designer boutiques with windows full of beautiful clothes – but up until now I've consciously avoided them. They don't fit the life I want to live now, and instead I've been shopping in quirky boutiques and vintage stores off the beaten track. Now I find myself loitering in front of the shops that stock expensive lingerie, gazing at the silk and lace confections worn by the mannequins. A set of peach silk underwear catches my eye and on impulse I dart in.

A shop assistant steps forward. 'May I help you, Mademoiselle?'

'Oh . . . well . . . I noticed in the window – the peach . . .'

'Oh yes, a charming choice, please, allow me . . .'

The next moment, I've been gently propelled into a dressing room and the assistant has expertly assessed my bust and hips, and then she is soon back with me, holding the soft flimsy garments in exactly my size. 'You must try them, Mademoiselle. This colour will look adorable against your skin and with your hair . . .'

She leaves discreetly, so that I can strip off and put on the underwear. It's smooth and silky with a delicately scratchy edge of creamy lace along the edges. I flush as I look at my body. I'm pale, my breasts rising in two small globes from the padded cups of the bra. I'm slim enough, thank goodness, but a million miles away from the smooth, glossy bodies of the women I see in magazines. I can't let a man see me like this. I need treatments, to be softened and prepared and made scented and smooth so that this beautiful underwear is given a proper setting. My hair needs attention; I'm so used to winding up the thick curls and putting them into a makeshift ponytail or loose bun, and not thinking about them again until the end of the day.

'Do you need anything, Mademoiselle?' calls the assistant through the curtain.

'No, I'm fine.'

'Can I bring you something else to try?'

'No, thank you – I'm happy with these. They'll do for now.' I quickly slip out of the underwear and get dressed.

On the way home, I pass a beauty salon, and go in to book myself an appointment for the following afternoon, hoping that Andrei doesn't make a date with me before I have time to prepare myself.

Summer Skypes me that evening. She's yet to find some focus in her life, and flits around with a gang of her friends, partying and amusing herself. Right now she's in New York attending a girlfriend's lavish birthday bash. She spends a lot of time in America after going to university there.

'Hey, how are you?' she asks. Her voice has taken on an American twang, as it often does when she's over there. 'How are things?'

I gaze at my twin sister over the Internet connection. I want to tell her about what I've done, but I'm too cautious to do it like this. Despite our security men putting the best possible firewalls in place, I don't trust this kind of communication. Besides, from what Freya said, our greatest risk might be behind the firewalls all the time.

'I'm fine,' I say, smiling. 'How are you?'

'Good. Any news from the queen bee?'

She's using our agreed nickname for Freya when we're talking about her over the phone or the web.

I shake my head. 'Not a thing since I saw her at the wedding. I'm sure she's doing fine though – I told you how happy she seemed.'

Summer laughs. 'I bet she is.' There's a pause and Summer's gaze slides away from the camera. She looks like me in small, subtle ways. Her colouring is different, but we've got the same nose and full round mouth. 'Flora . . .'

'Yes?'

'I'm going to see Jimmy next week. In LA. Is that okay?'

The news is like a punch to my stomach. I hate that other people can drop in and see Jimmy whenever they like, and I can't. The thought of Summer and Jimmy together makes me want to burst into tears with jealousy and dismay. 'Of course not,' I say lightly, hoping my inner reaction to the news isn't obvious. 'You must give him my love.'

Summer looks at me with sympathy in her blue eyes. 'Of course I will,' she says gently. 'I know he misses you, Flora.'

'That's nice. I miss him too. Tell him that, won't you?'

'Why don't you come over and tell him yourself?'

For a moment, I imagine seeing Jimmy again, gazing into his brown eyes, being held in his strong arms and kissing his dark smooth skin, and a wave of utter longing possesses me. *But I can't do that. It hurts too much in the long run.* Like an addict returning to drugs, I'd just be caught up in the thing that gives me pleasure and yet destroys me at the same time. I shake my head. 'No. Not yet.'

'Maybe some time, then.' Summer understands. She knows how I feel about Jimmy, and I know she's desperately sorry.

Because being in love with a gay man is pretty futile in the end.

I smile at her. 'Yes, maybe some time.' I say it even though I can't imagine a time when I'll be strong enough to face him.

'Okay. Listen, I'll call you tomorrow.' Summer blows a kiss to me. 'Love you.'

'Love you too.' I blow a kiss back. Then my sister's picture vanishes from the screen and I'm alone, and miserable again.

That's when the email pops into my secret account, and flashes up on the screen for me to see.

Miss X
Meet me on Friday night at the Palais Garnier. Be at the evening performance of Carmen. *Your ticket will await you on the desk in my name.*
Andrei

I stare at it.
So. It's beginning.

CHAPTER SIX

It's a busy Friday evening in Paris. The traffic is heavy, the headlights glaring in endless streams down the boulevards and snarled up around the big junctions. It's a cold night and the darkness is damp and penetratingly chilly. People everywhere are hurrying, eager to get home or into the warmth of restaurants and bars, cinemas and theatres, and out of the winter evening.

My taxi crawls through the rush-hour traffic, giving me plenty of time to stare at the people dashing about. I'm wearing my new peach silk underwear under a white crepe dress, and my hair has been blow-dried into smooth chestnut waves. Under my dress, my body is smooth and moisturised, scent sprayed on my skin. I feel more glamorous than I have for a long time, in my high shoes that sparkle a discreet silver in the shadows of the taxi, but at the same time, I feel almost sick with nerves. In my purse there are two folded sheets, each one signed by me in bold handwriting: *Flora X.*

The boldness is deceptive. I feel anything but sure of what I'm doing.

It's not too late, whispers a voice in my head. We're coming up towards the opera house now, a huge and opulent building in the style of the Second Empire that dominates the meeting point of the Boulevard des Capucines with the rue Auber and rue Lafayette. Between its ornate columns sit busts of the great composers – Beethoven and Rossini among others – and the pediment below the green verdigris dome holds two great gilded statues of winged classical figures. It's a stunning building, utterly capturing a particular type of Parisian grandeur, and I know already that the inside is even more over the top and sumptuous.

The opera-goers, elegant couples mostly, beautifully dressed, are making their way inside for the evening's performance, ready to be entertained by the story of doomed passion and death as they sit in their velvet seats beneath painted ceilings.

'You can let me out here,' I say to the driver, passing him a ten-euro note. He draws obediently to a halt, even though we were scarcely moving, and I get out, my heels tapping on the glistening wet pavement, wrap my white coat a little more tightly around me and join the people heading into the Palais Garnier.

I wait for my ticket at the Billetterie, looking about me to see if I can spot Andrei, but he's nowhere to be seen in the crowds.

'A ticket in the name of Monsieur Andrei Dubrovski,' I say when I finally reach the window.

The ticket is swiftly found and passed through to me. At that moment, a black-coated attendant appears beside me.

'Mademoiselle. This way if you please,' he says with a smile and a bow.

'Thank you.' I follow as he leads me through the milling crowds and out to the grand staircase, a breathtaking creation in white marble that leads up to the Grand Foyer. Everywhere there is gilt and statuary, ornate decoration and classical painting, glittering chandeliers and red velvet alcoves. I follow my guide, wondering where I'm being led. We go through the Grand Foyer, which sparkles with gold and crystal, and then through a marble loggia, passing many little doors, before finally I'm led down a small staircase and through a door. I'm standing in a box that seems to be lined entirely in red velvet, that looks out over the spectacular auditorium and the vast stage with its *trompe l'œil* curtain on the safety screen. From the painted ceiling hangs a huge chandelier, and everywhere I look there are surfaces that are carved and gilded or covered in red velvet. The little box holds two velvet and polished wood chairs and in its shady recesses, a bottle of champagne chills beside two slender flutes.

'May I take your coat, Mademoiselle?' asks my attendant. 'Monsieur Dubrovski wishes me to tell you that he will be here soon.'

'Thank you.' I slide the white coat off my shoulders and give it to him, before sitting down on one of the little chairs. The auditorium around me is filling up with people. The attendant takes my coat and hangs it at the back of the box, then returns with a glass of champagne, bows and leaves.

I sip my drink, and watch the people filling up the seats below me. I'm glad of this pause, a chance for me to calm my nerves and gather myself together before Andrei arrives.

Where is he?

I scan the audience but he's not likely to be there. Perhaps even now he's climbing the grand staircase, making his way towards me. I feel a shiver of pleasurable apprehension seize me between the shoulder blades, but I try not to imagine what might happen later. I need to stay calm.

A few minutes later the orchestra begins to tune up in the great pit before the stage. I look at my watch. The performance is about to begin. Where is Andrei? Nearly all the seats are full now. Then the house lights dim, the babble of chatter subsides and the safety curtain rises. The conductor emerges to applause and there's a moment of silence before he raises his baton and the orchestra begins Bizet's exuberant overture.

I'm still alone in this box. My nervousness is beginning to be replaced by annoyance.

Some date this is! Am I supposed to watch the damn opera on my own?

But, I remind myself, it's not a date. This is an arrangement.

That doesn't mean he doesn't have to show me some common courtesy. He should be on time.

I damp down my crossness and try to lose myself in the music. The first scene begins: the soldiers hang around the Seville square, as Michaela comes looking for her lover José, and the girls gather for their work at the cigarette factory. I'm soon lost in the music and forget that I'm on my own until, as Carmen, beautiful and provocative, sings that love cannot be tamed, I sense a presence beside me. Andrei is there, taking his place in the chair beside me, his frame seeming too strong and bulky for the seat's elegant narrowness.

Carmen is swaying about the stage, her ruffled skirt held high on one hip, a red flower tucked behind her ear, warning that if she loves a man, he has to take care. Her rich mezzo-soprano rolls out over the audience, enchanting them with her *Habanera* even as she embodies reckless passion and danger.

'I apologise for my lateness,' Andrei mutters. 'I was unavoidably delayed.'

I say nothing but continue watching Carmen as she taunts Don José, plucking the flower from her ear and flinging it at him. We sit in silence, soaking in the music until we reach the interval, the house lights come up and I turn to look at Andrei. His blue eyes are hooded and unreadable.

The attendant is with us before we can speak, pouring out more champagne and bringing a plate of devilled oysters to us.

'Leave us, please,' Andrei commands, and a moment later we're on our own.

'Where were you?' I ask, sipping my drink.

'I was held up. I regret it. You don't mind?'

'Of course not.' I shrug lightly.

'It is not the best of starts,' he concedes gruffly. 'I hope you'll let me make it up to you.'

When I look over at him, he's smiling, the broad mouth amused, and his eyes are sparkling. I can't help relenting and I smile back. 'Of course,' I say.

The blue eyes darken with strange promise and my skin tingles with the power of his gaze. 'I think we should drink this champagne and enjoy the opera,' he says in a low voice.

'I agree completely,' I reply.

When the lights lower for the next act, his nearness begins to disturb me. As the story grows more powerful and desperate, I feel sure that he's closer to me than before, his arm almost touching mine, but I'm soon lost in the tale unfolding before us. I know what's going to happen but even so, I'm yearning for the tragedy to be averted. I'm utterly caught up in the action and I forget Andrei as I watch the characters act out the final scenes. As the climax approaches, I find it hard to stay in my seat; I long to jump up and shout out a warning and when the end comes, I'm so affected that I turn spontaneously to Andrei and bury my face in his chest. He seems surprised but after a moment, his arm wraps around me and holds me tight. When I lift my face to him, I'm sobbing and my cheeks are wet with tears.

Andrei looks instantly concerned. 'Are you all right? Do you feel unwell?'

'Oh God,' I choke out. 'It's too . . . awful!'

He looks startled. 'What is?'

I point to the stage. 'That!'

'It's just an opera. It's not real.'

I stare up at him, sniffing. 'How can you say that? Didn't you see what happened?'

'I saw some good singers performing well. It was an excellent production.'

I wipe away my tears. 'Didn't it touch you? I'm in pieces!'

He smiles at me, looking a little bewildered. 'I can see that. I don't know what it's like to react the way you do – as if it was real.'

'It was real to me,' I declare. I take a deep breath. 'I think I'm recovering though.'

He slips his arm away from me as though he's suddenly realised he's still embracing me, and we avert our gazes from each other, a little embarrassed.

'Come on,' he says, standing up. 'Shall we go?'

I nod. The attendant comes forward from where he has been lingering in the shadows since the opera ended and gives us our coats. Then we make our way out of the box and through the last of the opera-goers, down the grand staircase and out into the cold Paris night.

'Are you hungry?' Andrei asks. There's a curious awkwardness between us again.

I thought it would be easier than this. I shake my head.

'Nor am I. Then let's go.'

'To Le Meurice?'

'Not this time.' Andrei pulls out his phone and taps a short message. Almost at once a long sleek black car glides up beside us, seemingly oblivious of other traffic or restrictions. Andrei opens the door and looks at me.

For the first time, I feel afraid. Getting in a strange car with a man I barely know seems like a step away from my world and into another, alien one. Gathering my courage, I climb in, sliding across the smooth leather seats.

'Where are we going?' I ask as he takes his place beside me.

'To see a friend of mine.'

'Oh.' My fear is replaced by disappointment. I'd been expecting something more sensual than that.

'I think you will find her interesting.'

He says no more as the car snakes through the busy traffic, the driver finding gaps that no one else seems to see. I watch the city outside go by, wondering where we are going. We cross the river, the chains of lights along the banks sparkling in the inky water, but I soon lose my sense of the direction we are heading in. After about twenty minutes, we draw up in front of a dark gate on a small street flanked by tall grey stone buildings.

'We're here,' says Andrei.

The driver opens the door for me, and I step out on to the pavement. I don't know this area and all I can do is follow Andrei, his back broad and dark in the black overcoat, as he buzzes us in through the gate and across a courtyard to a glossy front door. It's opened before he can knock and the figure behind it makes me gasp.

73

I cannot tell if it's a man or a woman at first, it is simply a human figure clothed entirely in black leather so tight it covers the body like a second skin. There don't appear to be any holes for breathing or seeing until I notice tiny pin-pricks around the nose, mouth and eyes. Then I guess it must be a man, for the chest is flat beneath the shiny leather and there is a bulge at the groin.

The figure says nothing but lifts its arm to direct us across the marble-floored hall and through a pair of tall doors. I follow Andrei, apprehensive again even though he doesn't appear to be surprised by our greeter.

Through the doors is an exquisite drawing room fur-nished in antiques, with lamps glowing softly on polished walnut tables. On the sofa sits a tiny elderly woman, her slate-grey hair pulled back into a tight bun. She's perfectly dressed in a black dress with a white silk collar and cuffs, her small feet in high black heels. She's stroking a soft white cat that's curled up on the seat beside her. Her coffee cup sits on a table in front of her, except that it is no ordinary table. It is a woman, wearing only black leather underwear studded with metal rivets, on her hands and knees before the old woman. The coffee cup is balanced on the bare skin of her back, and she stays perfectly still so that the cup remains steady. I can't help wondering if the heat of it is burning her back.

The lady looks up. 'Andrei!' she says with a smile.

'Olympe.' He goes over and bends low to kiss her soft lined cheek. 'How are you?'

'Very well.' She looks up at us with pale grey eyes, which darken as she frowns. 'Did Eric not take your coats?'

'No. But I really don't mind . . .'

'No, it's not supportable.'

I watch as she rings a small bell on the arm of the sofa and instantly the black figure steps in from the hall. 'Eric,' Olympe says sternly. 'You've neglected your duties. Take my guests' coats at once.'

The figure's head droops in dejection and he approaches first me and then Andrei, holding out shiny leather hands for our coats.

'You will be punished for this oversight,' raps out Olympe, and I think I can see a shiver of fear – or is it delight? – course down the leather-clad back. Eric leaves us, taking our coats away.

'Sit down, please,' Olympe says in a kindly voice, gesturing to the chairs opposite her. We do, and as I settle on the slippery chintz, I steal a glance at the woman who is acting as Olympe's table. She is young, with fair hair tied back in a tight plait. She stares fixedly at the carpet in front of her and appears oblivious to everything else. Then I notice that the heel of Olympe's shoe is on one of her splayed fingers and that from time to time, Olympe is grinding down hard on the finger. The woman never flinches.

What's going on? Am I going to have to do this? A fearful horror fills me. *I don't want to be hurt.* I look over at Andrei, as if hoping to read in his face what he intends to happen to me. I know I asked him to broaden my horizons but this is much further than I was expecting to go. Will I have to be a slave to this old woman, like Eric in his claustrophobic outfit and the woman who even now is having her finger crushed under Olympe's heel?

As I'm thinking this, I realise that the old woman's piercing grey eyes are fixed on me. Then she speaks. 'And who are you, my dear?'

Before I can answer, Andrei says, 'This is Flora.'

'What brings you here, Flora?'

I hesitate, wondering what I'm supposed to say. 'Andrei,' I reply at last. 'And I have no idea why.'

She raises one pencilled eyebrow at me. 'Perhaps you are willing. Submissive. Perhaps you wish to learn docility.'

'I don't think so,' I say hastily. 'I have no desire for pain.'

Olympe looks at me, her expression inscrutable, and she nods slowly. 'I see.'

Andrei speaks again. 'I simply wanted you to meet Flora. For now.'

Olympe smiles. 'And it is a pleasure. You're as fresh and delightful as your name, Flora. Now – I have a favour. Will you please go next door – you see the door there – and find a book for me on the shelves. It is most particular. It is called *The Ceremony* and it has a green cover.'

'Of course.' I stand up.

'Such a pretty white dress,' murmurs Olympe, looking at me. 'I approve.' She gestures to the door as if she has forgotten that I'm not one of her slaves. 'Over there.'

I flick a glance to Andrei, who watches me without a word, then turn and make my way through the doors and into another room, lined with books. Olympe's library. There must be hundreds of volumes, stacked floor to ceiling. *How on earth am I going to find one book among all of these? All I know is that it has a green cover.* Just as I think this, I see that in one block of shelves, every volume is bound in red leather with gilt lettering on the spine. All except one, which is green. I go over and extract the book. On the cover is stamped in black letters THE CEREMONY. There is no author name.

Well, that was easier than I expected.

I'm delighted to have performed my task so quickly and I move back towards the doors. I can hear voices coming from the room beyond and through the crack by the hinge, I can see Olympe, small and elegant, listening to Andrei.

'I'm worried,' he's saying. 'She's very young. Not just in age, but in her character. I took her to the opera just now and she was in floods of tears by the end. She's very sensitive.'

'That is a good thing, rather than not, Andrei. What use is a woman with a hardened heart, with no emotional access to the world? I can see in this girl's eyes that she stands on the brink, ready to embrace everything that lies beyond the mundane and the everyday.'

'As you have, Olympe.'

Olympe smiles again, her bright red lips curving upwards. 'I made a choice many years ago that I would exist on a plane that most people never experience. But I've paid the price, don't forget. I have no children, no husband. And I've never been in love.'

'That may be a blessing, Olympe. You've been spared that particular agony.'

'Yes. I've experienced many other types.' She smiles again. 'And inflicted it too. But the pain of love I've never known. That doesn't prevent me having an opinion, however. This girl you've shown me has great potential, I could see that immediately. But beware how fast you take her, and in what direction. She must journey slowly, and of her own volition. Do you understand?'

Andrei says nothing. I can't see him, so I assume that he nods.

'And your own heart, Andrei?' Olympe asks, burying her gnarled fingers in the soft white fur of her cat. 'Is that safe?'

'It's beyond safe. I think, in fact, it has ceased, and I don't expect it to be resurrected.'

'You can never be certain of that, not while you live and breathe.'

'I have no concerns for myself but I'm worried about the girl's heart. She's passionate. Romantic.'

'Oh, she will certainly love you – for as long as you let her.'

'Then perhaps I should stop all this.'

'It's too late for that,' Olympe replies. 'You're already here. You've already taken your first steps. There will be no turning back. I can see that you need her and you won't be able to resist. I don't think you should, either. The two of you will do much for each other.' She glances up at the crack in the door and seems to stare directly at where I'm peering through. 'You can come back in, my dear. You must be lonely in there.'

My heart pounds and my palms dampen. Without hesitating, I obey her. She has an utterly powerful personality, I can understand that now. As I walk back into the drawing room, the old woman fixes me with that magnetic gaze.

'Did you find the book?'

'Yes, Madame.' I hold it out to her, wondering what is in it.

'Thank you.' She takes it. 'Not everybody finds it, you may be surprised to hear. I'm sure it was obvious to you. But some look for ever and never see what is right before them.' Gazing at the worn green cover, she caresses it lightly with her palm. 'Perhaps you will be ready for the ceremony one day, who knows?'

A curl of apprehension snakes through my belly as I wonder what the ceremony might entail. My eyes go to the woman kneeling wordless and motionless in front of Olympe. The little shoe is off her finger now, but I see that a small line of biting silver clamps has been fixed to one thigh. The skin is bright red around the teeth of the clamps and dead white for a few centimetres beyond. I have the impulse to rush over and pull them off the girl's leg, even though she is as still and quiet as though they were completely painless.

She must want it. She must have agreed to this.

I don't understand it at all.

'Now.' Olympe stands up. She is so small, and yet a great sense of strength and power comes from her little body. 'You must go upstairs and make yourselves comfortable.' She lifts the coffee cup from the back of the woman in front of her and presses the woman's nearest leg with her shoe. 'I am busy now.'

The woman on her hands and knees moves obediently. I wonder what will happen here when we have left.

Perhaps one of Olympe's mysterious ceremonies. Perhaps nothing at all.

I realise suddenly that Andrei has taken my hand and we are moving towards the door.

'Goodbye, Flora. I've no doubt I will see you soon.'

'Goodbye,' I say politely.

'Open your spirit,' Olympe says suddenly. 'Your spirit is what matters, my child. Refine it, purify it. Subdue and then recreate it.'

'Yes,' I say, wondering what she means.

Then Andrei is leading me out of the drawing room and back into the marble hall.

'What is all that about?' I ask him in a whisper.

He glances down at me, his eyes the most intense blue

I've ever seen, but he says nothing. I sense, suddenly and with absolute certainty, that he is aroused, and the realisation is almost a shock.

So many times I lay close to Jimmy, pressed against his beautiful body, his hands entwined in mine, and I never sensed a squeak of desire. The warmth between us was soft, caring, fuzzily romantic, almost childlike in its purity. Now, just in the touch of Andrei's large hand on mine, I feel the sizzle of his desire. He's hungry for my flesh, like a great lion that I've befriended that has now turned on me with dripping jaws and a rosy red tongue licking its lips.

I know all this without even really thinking it. As he leads me up the stairs, I become dazed, overcome with all the emotions racing through me. The knowledge of Andrei's lust has aroused me in a way I haven't experienced before. I sense my body's potential to take me to places beyond the physical moment.

We have reached the top of the staircase. Andrei seems to know this place well. We walk along the carpeted corridor and stop in front of a door. Andrei looks down at me, then opens it. Inside it is complete darkness. He steps in, pulling me in after him, and the door shuts behind us.

What now?

CHAPTER SEVEN

At once, in the velvet darkness, Andrei's lips are on mine, but he doesn't kiss me. Instead he mutters against my mouth. 'Flora. You've enchanted me tonight with your beauty and your spirit. Are you ready and willing to put our agreement into practice?'

My pulse is racing. The nearness of his hard male body is sending tremors out all over me. It isn't handsomeness that's seducing me, but the raw power in his limbs, the breadth of his chest, the hardness of his shoulders. It's pounding the air out of me, making me gasp for breath.

'Yes,' I say, the word coming out on an exhalation. 'Yes.'

His lips press hard on mine, but still, there's no kiss, as though he's retraining himself. My mouth wants to open under his, let him in to possess me, but he's almost locking me shut with the hard pressure on my lips.

He growls against me, as though he can't prevent himself. He's breathing hard too. His hands touch my hips, full of restrained power. 'Are you sure?'

'Yes,' I say. I'm certain now. I'm on this ride and I don't want to get off. My body is alive to his, my whole being prickling with the fire of longing. I know he wants me: I can feel the tremor in his body as he touches me. *But it's not really me he wants. It's Beth.* I don't care. I know it's my body that's spurring the need in him. It's I who will experience what happens next.

The darkness is lifting a little as I become accustomed to it. I can make out his shadowy shape, the glimmer of his eyes, as he moves his hands round to the back of my dress and finds the zip. He pulls it slowly but firmly so that the dress peels away along my spine and over the curve of my bottom. He pushes it downwards and I wiggle my hips so that I can slough off the dress. It falls to my feet and I step out. I'm wearing only the peach silk underwear now, and my silver high heels. He cannot see me but his hands begin to move over my skin and as he touches the soft silk, cupping my breast gently, he groans a little.

The deep rasping sound sends a burst of powerful excitement through me. It burns through my belly and makes me swell and moisten between my legs. Every nerve in me begins to respond to him and the power of his body. His fingers go to my hair, twisting up locks of it as he drops his mouth on mine again. Still he doesn't kiss me, just presses his lips to mine, moving them across my mouth in a tantalising brush.

Kiss me, Andrei, I beg him silently. It's as though all the pent-up desire I ever felt for Jimmy is boiling to the surface now. I'm more desperate than I've ever been, mad for the desire growing in me to be slaked at last. I've dealt with frustration for so long now . . . for years I've worshipped a man, longed for his touch, yearned for his desire. Now I have what I've wanted: a man, huge and hungry for me. I can barely wait another minute. But Andrei is firmly in control here. I have to move at his pace. I want to touch him and reach out my arms to embrace him. My fingers want to slip under his jacket, unbutton his shirt, feel the warm skin beneath. But as soon as I stretch out to touch him, he stops me. He grabs my wrists and holds them together, keeping me away from him.

'Not yet,' he says in a low voice. With one hand, he holds my wrists firmly. With the other, he works nimbly at his collar and the next moment he is pulling his tie free. Before I know what is happening, he has taken my hands behind my back and is securing my wrists together with the tie.

'What are you doing?' I ask breathlessly.

'I'm not going to hurt you, don't worry.' His tone is soft but his hands are firm as he binds me. 'This is just for a little while. So we can get accustomed to one another.'

I don't know what he means but there's no time to think about it because as soon as I'm bound, he lifts me up and carries me across the room, then lowers me on to a bed. I can see nothing but I can feel the smooth surface of a silken cover against my skin. Andrei places me on my stomach, my hands tied in the small of my back, my cheek against the bed. My eyes are wide open in the darkness but I can see virtually nothing. I can hear Andrei's breathing and sense his body close to mine as he stands over me. His hand comes down on the back of my neck, then his fingers trail over my skin, tracing down over my spine. Everywhere he touches tingles with electric excitement as his fingertip travels down my back, over the silk clasp of my bra, down into the valley and up again over the curve of my backside. Now his finger is stroking down the silk of my knickers, finding the cleft between my buttocks and heading downwards to the place where my thighs join. I'm already swollen there, and I can feel the dampness in the silk panties, testament to what the touch of Andrei's finger is doing to me.

'Do you like this?' he says in his hoarse voice. 'Do you like me touching you?'

'Yes,' I answer.

'Do you want more?'

'Yes.'

'You are delectable. I want to touch you. I want to lose myself in your softness. May I do that?'

'Yes.' It comes out almost as a whimper. I'm parting my thighs while hardly aware I'm doing it. I want to give him access to the soft wet heart of me. I want that probing finger to find me and push inside.

Please.

The voice is only in my head.

He lies down on the bed, on the side that my head is turned away from, so that it feels as though he is behind me. I can feel the crisp white cotton of his shirt on my skin. He's taken off his jacket but otherwise he's completely dressed and it's oddly exciting to be almost naked next to him. It adds to my sensation that I'm his creature tonight – not a slave, like the woman on her hands and knees, but a delicious temptation to be relished and enjoyed and given pleasure to.

I want to know what he can do for me. I want to feel everything I've been denied. And, I realise, I want to pretend that it's Jimmy doing these things. *This is my way of making love with Jimmy the only way that's possible. In my mind.*

I'm still lying on my stomach, my legs parted, my hands bound. Andrei's finger is stroking the silk knickers, pressing down harder every time he smooths his way down between my buttocks to where my sex is longing for him. I'm very wet now, I can tell. His fingertip plays at the slippery entrance under the silk, tantalising me before pulling back, and then returning.

I can't help myself moaning lightly. The darkness is focusing everything to what I can feel around the curve of my buttocks and in the soft wetness below them. I rub myself against the bedcover, feeling my nipples hard against the fabric of my bra. My wrists strain a little against the tie bound round them. The sensation of being restrained is more exciting than I'd envisaged, allowing me to concentrate even more on the sensations gathering between my legs.

Andrei doesn't seem able to take his finger away from me this time. He's pressing it at the entrance, playing with me, tormenting me, and then, suddenly, pushing his finger inside me, making me sigh with pleasure as I feel it press in. There's a growl in Andrei's throat as he dips into me, pushing his finger in and out of my depths. He adds another, two fingers now, hard and insistent, plunging in and out of me. My clitoris, swollen with desire, rubs against my knickers and the bed, filling me with delicious sensations. Andrei carries on fucking me with his fingers, adding a third, stretching me out around them as he presses them in as deep as he can. He pulls them out, and drags their wetness down my back, then returns to push them inside me again, in and out.

'Ahhh,' I sigh, unable to stop myself pressing down on his fingers, pushing out my buttocks so that they touch the wool of his trousers. While his fingers thrust deliciously into me, his lips touch the back of my neck, and he kisses the skin there, then grazes it with his teeth, nipping gently at me, licking me with tiny touches of his tongue. It's tormentingly delicious. The pleasure is growing in me, and I realise I'm moving my hips rhythmically, letting my bud rub hard against the bed while his hard fingers fill me up.

I could come like this. Oh God, I could come soon . . .

It's been so long. I've lived like a nun, abjuring my bodily needs, ignoring the yearnings that come from my core and resolutely turning away from thoughts that could lead me towards desire. And now . . . my body is waking under Andrei's ministrations. It's revelling in his throaty enjoyment of fucking me with his hand, feeling me stretch, hot and wet, around his fingers. I love that he loves this. I want all he can give and more, but I don't know how long my normally neglected body can stand what he's doing to me.

I'm trembling all over. As he bites my neck and rubs his lips across my skin, he moves his fingers to my clit. It's stiff now, and wet with my juices. His fingertips press hard on it, toying with the hard nub inside, rubbing it deliciously.

'Oh, Andrei,' I say, with something like panic in my voice, 'I can't stand it.'

'Don't fight it,' he mutters, and kisses my shoulder, nipping me.

I don't know where I want his fingers, playing on my bud or deep inside me. I wish he would release his cock and push it in so that I can have both at once, but that's not his plan. He's close to me now, though, and every now and then he pushes himself against my hands and I feel the stiffness under the wool of his suit. It's huge and steel-hard, and every time I touch it, a burst of hot excitement flowers in my stomach. The way it remains concealed behind those expensive, proper clothes of his is even more exciting.

He plunges his fingers back into me and fucks hard in and out and then returns to my clit and now it's more than I can bear. I'm gasping and wriggling under the sensations he's inspiring in me, pressing my bottom out so that I can get a touch of that hard cock on my buttocks. He picks up pace, rubbing me harder and faster as the delicious feelings build in my core and then fill my belly, and then

I can take no more, and the orgasm explodes over me. It's the strongest I've ever experienced, a storm of pleasure breaking over me in a great roll of thunder, shaking me with its fierce power. I'm crying out, shaking under the waves of delight crashing over me, stiff as the orgasm grips me and then gradually relaxing into complete, breathless languor as it leaves me.

'Ohhh,' I sigh, dazed.

'You needed that,' he says in an amused voice. He undoes the tie round my wrists so that my hands are free.

'Oh my goodness, I did.'

'But . . .' His voice is like a purr. 'This is only the beginning. Turn around. Stand up.'

I can already feel the stirrings of fresh desire mixed with a different excitement altogether. *At last. Will it happen?*

In the darkness, I slide to the end of the bed and stand there. Andrei moves so that he is sitting on the edge with his thighs apart. 'Come to me,' he orders.

I step forward so that I'm between his thighs. I can feel the heat radiating out from his core, where that hard prick is straining to be free.

'Undo your bra.'

I unclip the straps of the peachy silk and my breasts, smallish and pert, are bare to him.

'Bring yourself to my mouth.'

I press my chest forward until I feel the soft rasp of his cheek against my nipples. They are hard and sensitive, the brush of his stubble sending hot tingles down to my groin. I'm wet with coming, but even more with the rush of fresh desire I feel there. His mouth is open. I cup my right breast and push it towards him, running my nipple along his lips. His tongue flicks out and touches it, and I sigh so that he knows how much I like that. He licks it again and I press it into his mouth, desperate for him to suck me. He plays with it for a long time, his tongue flicking over its tip, making me pant with desire. Then at last, he closes his lips around it and sucks hard, pulling at it, grazing it with his teeth, cupping the other with his hand and rubbing his thumb over that nipple. I throw back my head, groaning with pleasure. After he has sucked my right nipple to a hard point, he turns to my left and plays with it too, taking his time before he takes it fully into his mouth and bathes it with his tongue.

I'm aflame with lust when he's finished.

'Release me,' he whispers.

I reach down and feel the rock-hard stiffness of his cock pressing up inside his trousers. It's filling the available space and making it hard to unbutton his fly, but I manage, slipping my fingers into the slot and touching the rod that is both hard and velvet smooth at the same time.

'Pull it out.'

It twitches under my hand as I wrap my fingers around it and pull it upwards. It's hot and smooth and much bigger than I'd realised, the girth magnificent. From the pulsing thickness, I can tell he is ready. My climax must have excited him. I stroke it gently as it rears up.

'Do you want it?' he asks.

'Yes,' I breathe longingly. 'I want it.'

'Where?'

'Inside me. I want you in me.'

'Then put yourself on me.'

Andrei leans back on his hands and his cock stands tall and proud, waiting for me to do whatever I want. Breathing hard, my sex hot and wet, I slide off my knickers, then climb up on the bed so that I'm straddling him and poise myself over him, my lips directly above the head of his upright prick.

'You're so big,' I say softly. 'I don't know if I can.'

'Try.'

I put my fingers down to my entrance, feeling how incredibly wet I am. One thing is for sure, I have all the lubrication I need. Putting a hand on his shoulder for balance, I begin to lower myself until my slit is just above the hot smooth head of his cock. I rub myself over it, letting the tip play about in my delicate folds. Andrei moans lightly.

I tease him for a while, letting the eager cock think it is about to slide into me and then pulling away, leaving it wet and hopeful. Sometimes I let it play on my clit, which is swollen again and keen for more stimulation. The action makes Andrei groan as he feels the tip of his cock rubbing me. Then at last I take it in hand and guide it to the entrance of the velvet tunnel where it longs to be. I hold myself there, then take my hand from the huge shaft and let myself sink downwards, engulfing him slowly inside me. I moan as he fills me up, and then, when he's only a third inside, it stops. He can penetrate no further. He thrusts his hips to gain more access but with no success.

I raise myself a little, take a deep breath and with an effort, I force myself down on his prick. The resistance inside me bursts with a spasm of pain and then he goes on up, inside me, deeper than I ever imagined anything could reach. My sex stretches to take him in and as the pain subsides, the feeling of bliss, of completion takes its place.

Andrei growls somewhere in his throat as he feels himself deep in me. I begin to move up and down, riding his hard shaft, loving the deep ramming home he gives me. His hands come forward and clutch my bottom and he helps me move, sliding me along his cock and down again. We're both groaning with the pleasure of it, and for a long while we do nothing but this, every push making us hungry for the next. Then, at last, as we pick up pace, he lifts me and turns me over so that he can climb between my thighs without taking out his cock. He puts his mouth on mine and for the first time he kisses me properly, sending rapturous delight racing through me. Our mouths feel so right together, as though they were made for each other. He thrusts in his eager tongue so that we can kiss madly as he fucks hard. Now his pubic bone is grinding on my hungry clitoris, sending almost unbearable sensations all over my body. I lose myself in the pleasure of his kiss while his prick drives me on ever harder towards a feeling of utter, wanton delight. It is all I hoped it would be and more. I feel the sensation rising in me and I know that he is close too, and the sense of our mutual climax throws us both over the edge in a frenzy of violent joy. My body shudders with it again, this second one more intense and more prolonged than the first, and I feel his prick inside me swell and throb as he shoots out his orgasm. I'm gasping with the intensity of it, almost entirely lost in the fierce sensation. Andrei falls forward on my breast, panting.

After a while, we're back to ourselves. Andrei has rolled off me and we recover side by side.

'That was wonderful, thank you,' he says.

I sigh with repletion. 'Thank you. I loved it.'

'Flora . . .' He hesitates. 'I noticed that . . . there was a barrier to me at first. Was that . . .'

I say as casually as I can, 'Oh, you were my first real lover.'

'What?' I can hear the astonishment in his voice. 'You're a virgin?'

'Was.' I smile into the darkness. 'I'm not now.'

'There's a silence and he says, 'I am very honoured. But you should have said.'

'It's not such a big deal. I'm not entirely inexperienced. I just hadn't ever gone the full way. I wanted it to be a special experience and it was. I don't mean all lovey-dovey, just something memorable and enjoyable. And it was certainly that. So thank you.'

'You're very welcome. I think you must be a natural,' he says admiringly.

'I hope that's a compliment.'

'Oh, it is, believe me.' He drops a small kiss on my forehead. 'I'm still very honoured though. And I like a woman who is prepared to do whatever she needs to get what she wants.'

'I'm glad.' I'm still smiling into the darkness. Andrei Dubrovski is everything I hoped for in a lover. His magnificent cock is more than I could have imagined it would be.

I just hope I get to enjoy it much, much more.

CHAPTER EIGHT

Outwardly I suppose I seem just the same but I feel utterly transformed, as if someone has switched on a light inside me. It is as though I haven't just joined the ranks of ordinary adulthood, where people have sex all the time as part of their daily existence, a vital aspect of being alive. I've leaped beyond that in one bound and into a secret society of the initiated.

Last night was my first real experience of sex and the fact that it took place in the sumptuous townhouse of an aged dominatrix indicates that I'm on the path to something unexpected, unusual. I'm excited by the idea, and I feel as if I'm floating through the world, the air around me vibrating and shimmering with the energy that's been awakened in me. I loved what Andrei did to me and the intensity of my orgasms and I can't wait to repeat the experience. I can hardly concentrate on anything, so I'm glad that it's Saturday and I have the day off my classes. I get up early, my body alive with excitement and energy, and walk round the corner to a cafe where I can sit and watch the world go by and remember everything that happened last night. I sip at my coffee and wonder where Andrei is and what he's thinking. Even though I seem to be watching the men unloading the little van opposite, hauling crates of vegetables into the restaurant over the way, I'm really lost inside my imagination. There I can see Andrei in front of me, his broad chest naked, his shoulders heavy with muscle and his face dark with desire as his impressive cock stands up eager for the fray. The picture makes my stomach swoop with excitement.

At lunchtime there's a message in my inbox.

Miss X
You were much more than I could have dreamed of
last night. I need you again as soon as possible. But are
you prepared to follow where I lead?
Andrei

I send a message back.

Andrei
I want all you can teach me and more. I will obey your
commands and be yours whenever you want me.
Miss X

The reply arrives almost immediately.

That is indeed a promise. I made a similar one myself
once, and I did not regret it. I will send you instruc-
tions later.
A

I wonder what promise he made. Who would Andrei promise to obey? I can't imagine him submitting to anyone. His aura speaks of power and domination. Then an image flashes in front of my mind: a tiny elderly woman stroking a cat and crushing the fingers of her slave under her heel. *Olympe.*

She is the only person I can imagine could tame Andrei. There is more force in that small frame than I have ever seen contained in one person.

Were they lovers?

The idea is a strange one; usually I would find the picture unsettling, the old woman and the younger man, but it is curiously fitting somehow. I don't know how I'll ever dare ask Andrei if I'm right.

A shiver runs over me as I think of Andrei paying obeisance to Olympe. *What would she do to him? Will he want to do the same to me?* I've never imagined such things. *Would I have the courage?*

That is what I'm going to find out.

The next message comes later that day. Andrei asks me to meet at an address that I recognise as being in the same area as Olympe's house.

Come dressed for a dinner party. Wear nothing under your dress.
A

At home, I take a long, leisurely bath, dreaming of what might happen to me in the evening. I look down at my breasts rising from the bubbles of my bath, the pink nipples already tight at the thought of what I'll experience in a few hours, and my hand drifts over my belly and to my mound. I feel the tightening and throb of desire and my finger strokes lightly over my bud, which tingles in response. I've barely looked at myself for years and resolutely ignored my sex, as though punishing myself for not being desirable to Jimmy.

I realise that Andrei's desire for me is answering a need

that I've repressed for far too long. I am desperate to feel that desire: it's awakening me, nourishing me, giving me something back I had no idea I had lost.

I pull my hand away from my body. I don't want to do anything that will take the edge off the hunger I feel for Andrei.

After all, I don't know how long this arrangement will go on for. I don't want to waste a second of it.

The thought that this awakening could soon be over makes me feel bleak, so I push it away and think only of what is to come tonight.

The address is indeed Olympe's house. I recognise the dark gate as soon as I arrive there. I press the buzzer and a tiny blue light flicks on, lighting my face. I'm being watched through a camera. The gate whirs and I push it. It opens under my palm and I step into the courtyard. It's lit by discreet lanterns, showing the beauty of the nineteenth-century townhouse and the pots of shrubs and flowers arranged about the old flagstones. Ahead of me, the glossy front door stands open. As I approach, the leather figure – Eric? Or it could be anyone – steps out from the hall. Wordlessly he takes my coat and then hands me an eye mask covered in sparkling green sequins.

'I'm to wear this?' I ask.

The figure nods.

I slip the mask over my eyes. It's light and comfortable but it's still strange to be gazing out on the world from the eyeholes. Once it's on, I'm directed into the drawing room from where the noise of chatter is already emanating.

Shyly, I walk into the room. It's just as it was yesterday,

except that the woman who was Olympe's table is no longer there. There are around a dozen people inside, the men in dinner jackets and the women in smart dresses, and all are wearing masks. The men wear purple masks. Four of the women – including a small figure with slate-grey hair who can only be Olympe – wear silver masks, the others wear red. I'm the only one wearing green. I recognise Andrei immediately despite the mask. There is no disguising that powerful figure and the dark-blond hair. Behind his purple mask, the blue eyes glitter as he sees me enter, and he comes straight to me.

'You're late,' he murmurs, kissing my cheek.

'Am I?' I look down with surprise at my watch. It's barely two minutes past the appointed time.

'Everybody else was here on time, my dear. Olympe won't like it.' He takes my arm. 'Let me get you a drink.'

He leads me over to a drinks table where a bottle of champagne chills in a bucket and pours some of the sparkling liquid into a coupe glass.

'Two minutes isn't late,' I say quietly. I'm unsettled at the thought that Olympe won't like it. *What will she do?*

Andrei hands me the glass. 'You'll soon learn that obedience is all where Olympe is concerned. She lives to a grand standard of precision and expects everyone around her to do the same. She's most upset by the tiniest infraction. But you're new. Perhaps she'll overlook it.'

I glance over at the small figure surrounded by her guests. She is staring directly back at me, her grey eyes almost the same colour as the silver mask she is wearing. A shiver of apprehension ripples over my skin.

'What do the different colours mean? Who are the women in the silver masks?' I sip the champagne.

'I don't know who they are. That's the whole point of the masks. The women in silver are Olympe's most trusted friends and confidantes. They are all part of her little tribe, as she calls it. The high priestesses in her cult. But I do not know their identities. They are probably well known in their fields, perhaps even famous. One, I suspect, used to live at the Élysée Palace.'

I draw in my breath, looking eagerly at the women. 'How extraordinary.'

'Don't try and find out anything,' Andrei says, a note of warning in his voice. 'That is strictly forbidden. What happens here is entirely removed from our existence outside this place. Do you understand?'

I nod. A thrill of freedom passes over me. I can see why for Andrei, famous himself, this is the kind of liberation he wants – to be able to exist without fear of prying eyes and ever-present phone cameras. And for me, too, it's a wonderful feeling. No one here knows who I am, or cares. This sophisticated crowd would never dream of selling stories about me or passing pictures to the press. I'm free to do as I please. They have no idea who I am either.

'What do the red masks mean?'

'Women who have been initiated into Olympe's wider circle. Your green mask means that you are a novice.'

'How does one become initiated?' I ask, almost afraid of the answer.

'I'm forbidden to tell you,' Andrei replies. 'You may one day be allowed to witness a ceremony. That's not for me to decide. Come. We must join the others.'

The drinks last only another quarter of an hour or so. No one takes much notice of me – perhaps my green mask means I'm not to be spoken to. Andrei is welcomed and he converses easily with the women in silver masks. The men, I notice, do not speak to each other but only to the women. I watch with interest. Everyone is polished, civilised, and the fact that identities are obscured is soon forgotten. At precisely half past the hour, a gong sounds and Olympe leads the way through a pair of double doors opposite the library ones I went through yesterday, into a lavish dining room dominated by a large table set with snowy linen, silver cutlery, crystal, bowls of flowers and candles in silver candelabra. It's a perfect scene, indistinguishable from dozens of other Saturday night dinner parties going on in wealthy households across the city, except that around the room stand figures in shiny leather body suits, our attendants for the evening, and at the head of the table, a black-handled whip with tongues of shiny knotted leather lies next to the place setting.

Andrei leads me to my seat and we wait for Olympe to enter last and take her place at the head of the table. As she walks past me, she stops and smiles up at me.

'Good evening, my dear,' she says in her clear voice.

'Good evening,' I reply.

She beckons me towards her and I bend down to hear what she wishes to say. As soon as my head is at her level, she twists her fingers hard and sharp into my hair, picking up a lock close to my skull and tugging on it with a vicious strength. At the same moment, her fingernails, filed to talon points, dig into the skin of my arm.

I gasp at the sudden wash of pain.

'Do not be late again,' she murmurs, releasing me as quickly as she took hold.

Tears of agony leap to my eyes and I can't help moaning softly. Olympe moves on. No one takes the slightest notice.

I bite my lip to control myself, determined not to show how much she has hurt me. I've been punished. It's humiliating. But all I can do is move on.

And learn from my mistake.

When Olympe has taken her place, we all sit, and the meal is served. The leather-clad figures silently minister to us, placing the food before us, filling our glasses, removing empty plates. When one attendant clinks a plate against a glass, he carefully puts the plate down and goes unbidden to Olympe's side. She picks up her whip and administers a hard blow across the offered back, the leather cracking across the shiny bodysuit. The figure accepts the stroke and returns to work, and nobody says a word or even appears to notice. Each time there is a tiny infraction, this happens and every time, the blow delivered by Olympe gets harder and stronger. She has amazing strength in those delicate-looking arms.

The conversation is of theatre, books and films. Everyone appears educated, cultured and of a good position in society. Andrei turns occasionally to me, but mostly he talks to the woman on his left. The man on my right does not speak to me at all, but I'm happy to observe. The glittering masks sparkle in the candlelight, the eyes behind them shining.

Who are they all? I wonder. *What has brought all these people together in this way?*

When the dessert has been placed in front of us, the silent figures leave. Olympe claps her hands and there is instant silence.

'There are gentlemen here who have been given a task,' declares Olympe. 'The little tribe wishes to taste sweetness now.'

Three of the gentlemen pull out their chairs, and disappear under the table. I wait for them to emerge but nothing happens. Everybody else starts eating their dessert and the conversation resumes.

'What's going on?' I whisper to Andrei.

He leans down to murmur his reply. 'The little tribe is being taken care of. Look at the women in the silver masks.'

I glance at the women. They all appear older than the others, but each is perfectly soignée and glamorous. As they eat their parfait with tiny silver spoons, I can't see anything unusual about them.

'Under the table, the gentlemen are also having their dessert.'

I understand and a bright flush stains my cheeks. 'Oh!'

Andrei seems amused, then says, 'You too could enjoy this if you wish.'

'One of the men?' I say, astonished.

'No. Me.' Andrei stares at me from behind his mask. 'I'm at your command during this meal. If you want me to, I'll pay homage to you right now.'

I blush even harder. My sex throbs with the idea but I'm not an exhibitionist. I steal another glance at the silver-masked women. *But they are hardly exhibitionists either. I would never guess what's happening to them.* Still, no matter how appealing the idea, I don't like the thought of experiencing it in this way.

'Not here,' I say quietly.

Andrei nods. 'As you wish.'

'But . . .' I slide my gaze over to him from behind my own mask. 'You may touch me. If you want to.'

'Your wish is my command,' he says in a low voice. The next moment I feel his huge hand on my thigh. I pick up a sliver of parfait on my spoon and put it in my mouth. The iced sweetness melts on my tongue as Andrei's fingers gently draw up the chiffon of my dress until he is able to touch the skin of my leg.

'Tell me what you thought of the opera, Andrei,' I say. All around us, the remaining couples talk quietly to each other. The little tribe speaks to one another with perfect composure. Only the occasional flicker of a tongue over lips, or a minute gasp, gives away what is happening out of sight.

'I thought it was a magnificent performance,' Andrei says, his low tone making his voice sound hoarser than ever. 'The singer who played Carmen was a mistress of the role.' His fingers trail over my skin and up to the junction of my thighs. An answering moistness springs up there. I take another piece of parfait in my mouth. The chill in my mouth from the iced dessert seems to heighten what I'm feeling under the table as Andrei's large fingers begin to stroke across my mound, finding the bud that's already stiff there, waiting for his touch.

So this is why he told me not to wear underwear . . .

As I eat the delicious dessert, Andrei's fingers toy with my slit, stroking and poking just inside, stroking the oiled juices from there up to the swollen bud at the top and massaging it softly. I let my legs fall apart so that he can get as much access to me as possible, and concentrate on showing nothing on my face despite the pleasure radiating out through me. Apart from a faint movement of his right arm, Andrei appears only to be enjoying his own dessert, albeit a touch clumsily with his left hand.

The delicious feelings building up in me are almost too much to bear, but Andrei is skilful. He's not going to make me come here, just stimulate deliciously until I can think of nothing else but the tickling that plays on my clit.

I look discreetly at the faces of the women in the silver masks and wonder what they are feeling and if any of them has enjoyed a silent orgasm, but they seem utterly normal.

Oh . . . I don't know how long I can stand this.

As if she read my mind, Olympe stands up. Andrei's hand vanishes from my skin. Everyone at once is silent, spoons returning to the plates, eyes turned to her.

'The meal is over,' Olympe says. 'The initiated shall retire downstairs.' She glances at me. 'The novice may choose what she does now, but she is not permitted to join us.' She sees me open my mouth to speak and holds up her hand to prevent me. 'Say nothing. Wait until we have left.'

There is a long pause, then Olympe leaves the table, walking past us all. The silver-masked women stand and follow her, then the women in red masks. Finally all the men stand and leave the room after the women. Three of them emerge from under the table. They appear perfectly composed and just as they looked earlier. Perhaps Olympe's pause was to enable the men to make the ladies and themselves decent again. They walk out after the others without even looking at us.

Andrei and I are left alone in the dining room. He gazes down at me, his blue eyes glittering behind the mask, then he lifts his fingers to my lips. I can scent my own odour on them. Gently he parts my lips and pushes his two fingers inside and, startled, I close my mouth around them and suck at them. A sweet saltiness tastes on my tongue and I massage the fingers with the inside of my mouth, running my tongue around them. Andrei makes a throaty noise and then says, 'Push your chair back from the table.'

Now we are on our own, it seems that Andrei is not simply here to obey my orders. I move my chair back. The chiffon of my skirt is rumpled up high, revealing the naked flesh of my thighs and the shiny red slit between them, gleaming with juice, my bud standing out at the top.

'Open your legs further,' he says and I spread my thighs wider, and my lips move further open, revealing the heart of me. I look at his face and the expression in his eyes as he stares down at me with evident enjoyment. He lifts a silver spoon from the table and scoops up some of the remaining parfait, then he brings it close to my slit. After a second, he pressed the cold bowl of the spoon against me, the chill titillating my clit and making me twitch with the sensation, then he turns the spoon over and tips the parfait over my open lips. It trickles down me, a pale white stream running down to the seat, tickling me as it goes. The next moment, Andrei leaves his seat and kneels in front of me on the floor.

'Lean back, put your hands on the table and don't move them,' he orders.

I obey. He puts his own broad palms on my thighs and strokes his hands up and down my legs, then pushes my knees apart and brings his face close to my mound. I open my legs as wide as I can to allow him as much as access as he wants.

I can hardly breathe. My heart is pounding, and hot desire is twisting through my body, the blood rushing to my sex and making it swell and burn. I long for the touch of his tongue. His face is tantalisingly close to me now. He's letting me burn for it, revving me up with need as he brings his mouth ever closer to my clit. Then with one long movement, he puts his tongue on the ridge of flesh below my

103

entrance and laps upwards, licking up the stream of sweet liquid, making me shiver with pleasure as his hot tongue takes up the chill of the parfait. When he reaches my nub, I sigh with the delightful sensation. He sets to work, licking and lapping at my depths, now pressing his tongue inside me as far it will go and now taking it up to tickle my clit. After a while, he concentrates on it alone, tickling and playing with the button, lifting me to a panting level of lascivious excitement. I can't prevent it, I throw back my head, clutching the table as I shudder with the building strength of my orgasm. His tormenting tongue goes on licking and licking my clit as I stiffen and cry out with the force of my release, letting down a rush of honeyed liquid as I come hard on Andrei's face, the sequins of his mask cutting into my flesh. When he looks up at me, his mouth glistens with the wetness of my climax. I stare down at him, still gasping for breath.

I reach down and run my hands through his hair, ruffling it between my fingers. 'Oh . . . thank you, Andrei,' I manage to say.

'My pleasure – and yours.'

'But what about your pleasure too?' I say. I'm not finished. My desire has only been damped down, it's ready to flare up again in a moment. Surely he must want his own needs satisfied and I long to do for him what he has done for me. His hands are suddenly on my waist and the next thing I know I've been pulled under the table and we are both together under the table. I lie down beside him. He's undoing his trousers and the next moment his great prick is out in his hand, stiff and ready for me. I'm eager for it, and I open my legs so that he can get access to my slit, and he climbs between my thighs. I'm beautifully oiled by my coming, and the large head is pressing at my entrance in a moment, Andrei's body hard between my thighs and heavy on my chest. He grunts and then shoves forward, making me exclaim as the huge thing slides into me, the balls at the base hitting my buttocks.

'So delicious,' he groans as he presses it home, ramming it into me as far as it will go.

I gasp as he thrusts in and out, fucking me as hard as he can. My arms are around him, holding him in, one hand clawing at his buttocks and helping him move his hips so that he can run that huge thing as deep in me as possible.

The situation is deliciously exciting, being on the floor, hidden and yet at risk of exposure if anyone should come in and hear us at it. I know Andrei is already excited by the effect of licking me to a climax just a little earlier and it isn't long before I feel him swelling inside me in the way that tells me his prick is ready to come. I slip my hand down between us and grasp his balls, holding them and then tickling them lightly as he rushes into me. I can feel the place where his thick stem is engulfed by my tight lips, and the friction of our fucking, and it excites me greatly. The touch of my hand on his balls sets Andrei off and he rushes into his climax, roaring as it gushes from him inside me. He jerks hard as it comes, and then subsides to a gentle rocking. I'm still hungry though. I wriggle under him and he understands. His prick is still big and swollen inside me, and he moves it a little harder, pressing down on my needy clitoris, giving it the sensation it craves, sending out the delicious feelings from my centre to the end of every nerve. Rub, rub, rub, with my sex still stretched around him. I can hardly bear it but I also can't bear it to stop. As he watches me, his eyes dark and glassy, I begin to moan and then finally shout as the shuddering pleasure engulfs me, intense and electric as it was the first time he drew the orgasm out of my body. I come hard and long underneath him and when I finally open my eyes, he kisses me deeply.

'How gorgeous you are when you come,' he murmurs. 'I would never get tired of it. You excite me madly every time.'

I sigh happily. 'That's lucky. You do the same for me.'

We smile at each other, acknowledging the chemistry that makes us able to give and receive such pleasure.

'Now,' he says, 'perhaps we should return to the table. I imagine someone will be here soon – though to be honest, what we are doing will be tame compared to what's happening downstairs.'

'What is happening?' I ask curiously as we straighten our clothes and emerge from underneath the table.

'Whatever Olympe wants,' he says evasively. 'Perhaps you'll know one day. Come on, let's get some coffee in the drawing room. I need to recover from that.'

'So do I.' I smile happily, thinking that whatever is happening downstairs, it can't be even half as nice as what we've had up here.

CHAPTER NINE

Is it really only little more than a week since I met Andrei?

I feel a strange fear at the idea that I might not have crossed the road to the cafe after Beth's wedding and might never have seen him. The experience I've shared with him so far has been so overwhelming, so transformative, that I feel a horror for the girl who might have gone on without that in her life.

But it's all right. It did happen.

I can't help wondering what Andrei is making of our arrangement and what he thinks will come of it. Is it just for the short term? He seems to be introducing me to Olympe's world, and from what I understand the members belong for life. He seemed to hint that perhaps one day I might know more about what goes on in her more secret gatherings, though I have an idea. She is a dominatrix. I image that whips and chains and leather gear are her stock-in-trade.

Perhaps I'm only being granted a privileged glimpse, and then the door will shut again. And perhaps that is all that I want. I can't imagine ever wanting Olympe to do such things to me.

I don't know what went on in the downstairs room and the idea of what it might be fills me with fear as much as curiosity. There are people braver than me, people willing to take themselves beyond what I've experienced and beyond the accepted norms of what is pleasurable.

But, I tell myself, *I've only just begun. I'm still learning to taste the delights of sex. I don't need to go beyond that.*

A voice in my head replies:

Not yet.

My life outside my arrangement with Andrei has lost all interest for me. I know I ought to be worrying about Freya, and keeping on my guard against Estelle, but I'm utterly absorbed in this adventure I've embarked upon. My studies at drama school have been all I lived for lately, and now I think of the hours I spend at the Academie as just time I must fill in before I'm able to be with Andrei. Only Summer would have the power to draw me out of this seductive world I've found myself in, but she is very quiet. Usually we speak every day, or as often as we can, but she hasn't called. I know why. It's because she's with Jimmy and she doesn't want to upset me.

The week has begun again. It's a cold Monday and I'm walking between classes, checking my phone as I do obsessively now, hoping that an email would have arrived there, when a strange thought strikes me. I stop where I am, crossing the bleak wintery garden at the back of the Academie, going from the studios to the main building. The bitter wind buffets my face and flicks my hair across my cheeks but I hardly notice.

Summer is with Jimmy. And I've barely given it a thought.

I'm horrified at myself. Little more than a week ago, I was adamant that my heart was totally and utterly his. Just a few days ago, I would have gone pale and shaky, and felt sick with jealousy, at the knowledge that Summer could be with Jimmy when I could not. I would have tortured myself with mental images of them laughing and enjoying themselves together. I would have longed for that for myself.

And now?

I conjure them up before my mind's eye, Summer and Jimmy sipping iced lattes under a brightly coloured umbrella outside a coffee house in LA. Jimmy is as exquisite as ever, his skin tanned a dark coffee colour, his velvety brown eyes dancing with laughter as they share a joke, his perfect mouth smiling and showing those gorgeous teeth. He's as handsome as a matinee idol, as though he's stepped out of a glossy magazine photograph.

I feel what I've always felt for Jimmy. Love. But it's not the same as it was. I'm horrified at myself.

Am I really that fickle? Is that all it took to make me forget him, after all this time? A couple of good fucks?

I feel despairing at myself. How can I trust my emotions if they're so changeable? What about my vows of eternal love for Jimmy, my protestations that my heart was untouchable? What about them?

I remember Olympe's words as I stood in her library listening to her and Andrei talk. She said, 'She will certainly love you – for as long as you let her.' I barely took it in at the time, dismissing it as simply wrong.

I think it over carefully as I go into the dry warmth of the main building. I feel breathless in the overheated atmosphere after the chilly fresh gusts outside. *Do I love Andrei? Have I simply swapped one fruitless passion for another?*

I'm sure that I do not. I love what he does to me. I adore the sensations that he provokes in me, and the whirling pleasure of the orgasms he gives me. Most of all, I love the way he desires my female body and the power it gives me over him. That is what I could never have with Jimmy: in the end, I left him cold, and without desire there is no power play between lovers.

I feel happier. *There. I don't love Andrei. That's good. Maybe this is an important stage in my learning to live without Jimmy. It's a natural process of pulling away. After all, can I really spend the rest of my life loving a man who doesn't love me?*

It had seemed so noble only recently. Now the idea is foolish, and rather unrealistic, the romantic notion of a schoolgirl, not a woman with adult passions and needs.

It occurs to me to wonder what Andrei thinks of me. I am his protégée, perhaps, a plaything to help keep his mind off his own hopeless cause.

I'm sure that's all I am. That was the agreement after all. I must remember to hold myself back a little, perhaps not be too available. I don't want him to take me for granted.

Just then an email bounces up on my phone. I give a tiny gasp of excitement and open it. It's from Andrei.

Come now. I want you. Be at the Luxembourg Gardens in half an hour.

I don't hesitate, but simply walk through the Academie and out of the front door, heading straight out in the direction of the river.

It takes half an hour to reach the gardens and I enjoy the brisk walk, the wind whipping colour into my cheeks. It's freezing and the gardens are virtually empty. A few nannies push babies around in pushchairs but they are well wrapped up. The playgrounds are deserted – the children are in school, and anyway it's too cold for playing outside.

110

I follow the directions that Andrei sent a few minutes ago, and find him sitting on a green bench outside a small boarded-up pavilion that in the summer sells ice creams but now is closed. He's wearing his black overcoat, his hat pulled down low so that only his nose, large and jutting, can be seen as he reads his newspaper. I remember how that nose was buried in my delicate folds, his strong tongue lapping me to ecstasy, and a hot rush of excitement burns through me. The sight of his big, strong hands makes me gasp lightly. Even the sight of his muscled calves outlined against the wool of his trousers makes a ripple of desire surge through me.

I'm not in love, but I am in lust.

I go over and sit next to him. He ignores me for a moment, then slides a blue gaze towards me. 'Good afternoon.' He folds up the newspaper. 'I'm glad you came.'

I smile at him. 'I can't think where you want to have sex here. Do you have a key to the ice-cream parlour or something?'

He laughs a little ruefully. 'No. I'm afraid not. I couldn't concentrate on my business and I needed air, so I came out for a walk and found myself thinking about you.' He fixes me with an intense gaze. 'I wanted to check in with you about how things are going.'

'They're going well,' I say brightly. Then, in a more concerned voice, 'Don't you think?'

'They are going quite delightfully for me.' Andrei smiles at me, his big mouth twisting up at one side. I wish he would smile more often, as it transforms his face from a harsh, almost ugly cragginess to an unexpected handsomeness. 'But Olympe has spoken to me. She wants to know if you wish to be initiated. It is against the rules to be a novice for more than a few weeks.'

I stare at him, trying to read him and finding, as usual, that it's next to impossible. I want to please him, but it's so hard when I can't work out what he wants. 'What do you think?'

Andrei juts out his lip and shrugs. 'It's hard to say. You've not seen what goes on, so how can you judge? And besides, you're young.'

'I'm sure Olympe has initiated younger women than me,' I reply.

Andrei thinks for a moment. 'Yes, you're right. She has. Age really has nothing to do with it, as you can tell from Olympe herself.'

'So . . . ?'

'I'm not sure. You need to feel the desire for what she does. It's not an easy path to take. You must always begin by submitting before you are allowed to graduate to where, for example, her tribe are. They are mistresses themselves now, each with a coterie of willing slaves.'

'Then there's only one thing to do,' I say with a spirit in my voice that surprises even me.

'What?'

'I must see what it is I'd be getting into.'

Andrei looks doubtful. 'I don't know . . .'

'Why did you take me to Olympe's if you didn't expect this?'

He frowns. 'I don't know. Perhaps I shouldn't have introduced you to Olympe. I imagined at first that our arrangement would remain strictly private. And I thought that our liaisons would be altogether more manageable.' His blue eyes land on mine, steely and strong. 'But it hasn't been like that, has it? Since the first moment I tasted you and the deliciousness of your body, I've been possessed by

112

an overwhelming need to have you in the most profound of ways.'

My stomach tightens with hot excitement as he says it. 'I feel the same,' I reply in a low voice.

'I've thought about you every day,' Andrei says. 'And right now, sitting beside you, I'm hard with burning desire for you.'

I glance down and see the outline of his stiff rod pressing out in his trousers. The sight makes my mouth dry with desire and I feel myself grow wet at once. I hunger for his cock immediately.

'Is there somewhere we can go?' I ask in a weak voice.

Andrei looks about. 'There's always somewhere.'

I glance around. There's no one near enough to see us. I reach over and touch the hot stiffness that presses against his trousers. It moves under my fingers and I lick my lips.

Andrei seizes my hand and moves it away from his cock. He stands up. 'Come with me,' he says. I get up and we walk swiftly together to the edge of the park. There I can see the big black car that took us from the opera, the driver sitting in the front seat smoking nonchalantly out of the window. As he sees Andrei striding towards him, he looks panicked and jumps out of the car, tossing away the cigarette and standing at attention. As we get nearer, he pulls open the door to the back seat. Andrei climbs in and I follow. When the driver is back in his seat, Andrei says, 'Turn off communications and all vision. Darken the windows. Then drive.'

At once the glass screen between the driver's seat and the back seat turns black. The windows tint until it's hard to see out of them and I'm certain we cannot be seen from the road. The car begins to move and we are out in the traffic.

Andrei unzips his trousers and pulls out his cock. It's magnificent, stretching up at full length, thick and hard. I want to kiss and suck it at once, but Andrei grips it hard in his fist, moving his hand up and down it.

'Let me have you,' he says.

I immediately unbutton my jeans and push them downwards. I have to stop to unzip my long leather boots and remove them, then I'm able to kick off the jeans and my knickers, leaving my lower half completely naked.

Andrei slowly rubs his cock as he looks at me. 'Put the boots back on,' he orders.

I obey, zipping them up.

'Turn around on the seat. Show me your arse.'

I turn so that I'm kneeling on the wide black leather seat, my arms over the back of it, holding myself up. I have to spread my legs wide to keep steady as the car moves. I wonder if the driver can actually see any of this, but I don't care right now. All I want is that cock in my depths.

'I love to see you in those boots, your beautiful body naked to me,' Andrei says. He gets behind me, clasps me round the waist and a moment later, I feel the tip of his cock pressing on me. I'm already slippery with arousal and he doesn't wait before he thrusts in hard, burying himself in my depths. It is not easy, both of us kneeling on the seat, but the frantic urgency of it makes it all the more exciting. His body is heavy against my back, his prick deep and hard inside me.

'I've got to fuck you now. You drive me wild,' he mutters into my ear, panting as he thrusts home.

I groan. It's so good to have him hot and hard inside me. I press my bottom out so that he can get deeper into me. The car turns a corner and it throws him even more heavily against me and deeper inside. He has me tight around the waist so he can thrust hard and deep. His balls slap against me and then he's so deep, we just jerk hard against each other. His hand slips round to the front and he begins to rub the hard button of my clit. It's delicious, a rapturous feeling filling me as his swollen cock stretches me out and the fingers conjure cries and sighs out of me as they play with me.

'Please fuck me harder, Andrei,' I beg.

He steps up his thrusting and with a sudden movement, he slaps his palm down on the side of my bottom. The smacking sound startles me but the feeling itself is not unpleasant, like a hot sting that comes and goes in an instant. He does it again, my buttock juddering lightly under the blow. It heightens my excitement.

He works his cock deeper inside me and I know it won't be long before he comes, we're both so hungry for it. A moment later, he buries his face in my neck, biting lightly at the skin and then thrusts hard and slow several times and I feel the warm gush of his orgasm fill me up. Immediately I'm sent over the edge and my own climax breaks over me with a fierce electricity. I stiffen and then convulse over his cock, my body gripping him and shaking with pleasure as I come.

Andrei pulls his prick out of me, and a gush of liquid falls from me, making a shiny puddle on the black leather seat. Andrei sits back, his cock already losing its length. He pushes it back inside his trousers and smiles at me.

'Thank you,' he murmurs. 'That was exquisite.'

I turn round and sit back too, returning his smile. 'I thought so too.' I reach for my jeans. 'But how you're going to explain this state of this seat, I don't know.'

* * *

Andrei has the driver take us back to a restaurant in the Latin Quarter and we go inside for something to eat. We talk easily as we have some food, our appetites stimulated by our recent activities.

'I should go home and shower,' I say as the waiter removes our plates. 'I'm beginning to feel like I need it.'

'Where do you live?' Andrei asks, and drains his wine glass of the last remaining Bordeaux.

'In the Marais,' I reply without thinking.

He raises an eyebrow at me. 'A very nice district of Paris.'

I flush a little, even though there's no reason why I shouldn't live there. 'Yes.'

'Do you live alone?'

I say nothing, not sure what I can reveal about myself. I don't want to lie to him but I'm wary of telling him more about myself. It could lead us into all sorts of difficulties. If he ever began to guess our connection, no matter how slight it is, he might decide to call off our arrangement, and the thought of that fills me with horror.

'You don't have to say anything at all,' he says softly, seeing my discomfort. 'Let's keep it as it is. You will remain Miss X.' He lets the name roll over his tongue and repeats it again slowly, 'Miss X', so that it sounds like Miss Sex.

'I think what we have agreed gives us freedom,' I say earnestly. 'We can be ourselves without fear. Don't you agree?'

Andrei nods. 'Yes. And you're right. But I can't help being curious about you. You, at least, know who I am.'

'Yes – but not much more. You keep yourself very removed.' I look at him from under my lashes, fascinated by the way his craggy face changes almost from moment to moment, always showing itself in a different light, becoming harsh and then handsome in a matter of seconds.

'It's safer that way,' he replies. 'At least, that is what I've always found.' He looks away from me, his eyes harder suddenly. 'I've always had to do things my own way, and get what I want. That means that I've had to be ruthless in my life. I can't have people standing in my way, preventing me from achieving my objective. Necessarily I must be cold and seem heartless at times, when it's the only way to get the result I want.'

'But you can't always be cold and heartless,' I say. His strength of will intrigues me. He's like a tragic hero in a play, whose flaw is his refusal to be human. 'What about your family? They must see another side of you.'

A strange look flickers across his face. *Is it pain?* He says gruffly, 'I have no family. I'm an orphan. I lived in institutions until I was old enough to run away and make a life for myself. I was determined that I would become a success, and make the world recognise and respect me.'

I stare at him. 'You've certainly achieved that,' I say with admiration. *But to be alone your whole life ...* I hide my pity, certain that a proud man like Andrei does not want it.

'Hmm.' His mouth tightens. 'It has not always gone the way I wanted.'

'Really?' Then I remember the whole reason we're here, and why we're doing this. 'Beth,' I say softly.

He winces, his eyes closing. Then he looks at me, his eyes broodingly dark and hooded. 'Yes. Beth. I couldn't have her, even though I offered her everything I could think of. And she and Dominic attempted to bring me down and destroy me, after everything I'd done for them.

The past year has been very difficult for me. I almost lost everything I'd built up.'

I look away, examining the faint damask patterns on the tablecloth. I don't know Beth and Dominic well, but they don't look like vengeful, ruthless people. If anything, Andrei has that air about him. I suspect that there is a complicated story behind Andrei's succinct explanation. But I say slowly, 'You loved her, and you couldn't get her.'

He nods. 'She refused to obey.'

I absorb this, wondering if he can see the contradictions in what he says. At last I say in a gentle tone, 'But Andrei, you can't order love. You can't force it. It has to grow.'

'I loved her and needed her,' he said brusquely. 'And she refused me.' He lifts his hand to the waiter and signals for the bill. 'Now, shall we go?'

It seems to me that a large part of Andrei's obsession for Beth is based around the fact that he couldn't win her. He's never described her in terms of who she is and what made him love her. I wonder if he's ever considered her feelings. *Perhaps he really has learned how not to be human. Maybe that was the only way he could survive.*

Andrei is looking at me with one of his unreadable expressions. 'Do you want to go somewhere?'

I look up at him. The attraction between us still crackles but I am distracted by my thoughts, and all that he's revealed to me in the last few minutes. 'I ought to go home now,' I say. 'I'm tired.'

There's a brief pause and Andrei's eyes seem to become icy. Then he sighs. 'Of course. I've taken too much of your day already.' He hands a credit card to the waiter and as he settles the bill he says, 'My driver will take you home. I'm going to walk for a while.'

'When will I see you again?' I ask, anxious suddenly that he might interpret my desire to go home tonight as a cooled enthusiasm for our arrangement.

'Soon, I've no doubt,' he says, his tone clipped. He puts away his credit card and picks up his phone. 'The car will be waiting for you outside. Direct him wherever you want to go.'

I stand up. 'Thank you. Goodnight, Andrei.'

'Goodnight,' he says, but he doesn't look up from his phone.

CHAPTER TEN

That night I'm tormented by the idea that perhaps I've spoiled things between Andrei and me. Did I pry too much? Did I cross the delicate line we'd established between our real lives and our fantasy?

I can't sleep, images of Andrei flashing in front of my mind. I see his glorious cock and wish that I'd gone with him wherever he asked so that I could experience the bliss of feeling it buried inside me to the root. I'm hungry with desire again, a feeling of insatiable need, where getting what I want only increases the appetite for it instead of sating it.

I had no idea this world was there, I think. I've always been a hopeless romantic, in love with somebody – my favourite actor, a hero in a book, the boy who tended the garden – but once Jimmy came into our lives, he was all I dreamed about as I grew into womanhood and became aware of my developing body. There had been times when other boys had tried to kiss me and touch me, and sometimes I'd even let them, just to find out a little of what it was like or even in the vain hope that I might be able to make Jimmy jealous. But when it came down to it, I'd never loved them and so I'd never allowed them to go very far with their marauding fingers and panting mouths. I'd kept myself for Jimmy.

What a waste!

The thought comes unbidden into my mind as I lie

wakeful in bed. I'm almost shocked at my own heresy. A waste to have worshipped Jimmy? He was my moon and stars for years.

But he could never, ever give you what you needed. You were wasting your time.

The voice is frank, brutally honest. I know that it speaks the truth.

But Andrei can.

I decide that I will contact him the next day. After all, our arrangement stipulates that I also can call the shots if I so wish.

I'm not going to let this end. Not yet. I'm not ready for that.

After our encounter in the car, I feel sure that my boots stimulated Andrei when I wore them while naked from the waist down. But they were just ordinary, flat boots that I wear to tramp around Paris in winter. I'm sure I can find something a little more exciting than that.

I skip classes at the Academie, calling in to say that I'm sick, and go shopping in the more louche areas of the city instead. Now that my eyes are open to the possibilities, I see plenty of places that cater to desire. I pass shops with fetish footwear in the windows, others that provide all manner of toys and aids and costumes. I'm not sure how far I want to explore these places, and I'm nervous of going into this new world by myself, but I gather my courage and go in. At first, I'm open-mouthed at everything on offer and the lavish, baroque tastes that are catered for, in leather, rubber, satin and silk, studded with metal and hung with chains. But I'm fascinated by it too, and by the end of the morning, I have a pair of high-heeled black leather boots that lace up to just under my knee, tight and shiny. Compared to many of the things I've seen, they're plain and rather low key, but they're exciting to me. I have a feeling that Andrei is going to like them too.

As I walk back, it occurs to me that my peach silk underwear won't look at all right with these boots. Its soft satiny texture isn't appropriate at all. I need something else. Then I see a small boutique, its dark purple frontage with a window display that is a collection of torsos clad in corsets.

Of course. That's what I need.

Without hesitating, I walk across the street and go inside. A pretty assistant sits behind a counter polishing some of the goods from the display in the glass case front of her. She barely looks up, so that I can examine what's on offer in peace. From rails hang many confections of lingerie and underwear, making me think of courtesans of the nineteenth century, and rows of corsets that bring to mind the cancan dancers at Marcel's or the Moulin Rouge. They are tiny at the waist, and fastened with hooks or else long laces or both. In glass cabinets around the room are all manner of erotic extras; in one, leather cuffs, collars and other accoutrements, along with whips, paddles and rulers. In another, ticklers, and in another dildos of glass, ceramic, silver or latex, some huge, some slender and others small with fat heads that I suspect may be anal plugs. Another cabinet holds eye masks and another a collection of beads, balls and nipple clamps. I hardly know where to look but I can't help remembering Andrei's injunction that I must be broadminded and prepared to acquiesce to his demands.

Is he likely to demand such things from me?

After all, I've only just discovered the heady pleasures of

straight sex. Will he be keen to introduce me to variants so soon?

The truth is that the sight of all the equipment designed to enhance pleasure titillates and arouses me. Why shouldn't I experience all there is in life? Why wait? After all, I'm somewhat of a late starter compared to most of my friends, who've been having sex since they were fifteen or so.

But then, they weren't in love with someone resolutely gay who was never going to introduce them to sex no matter how much it was on offer.

I return to the corsets and look at a mint green one edged with black lace, and a scarlet one with rows of boning that look as though it constricts the waist horribly.

'That is one of our bestsellers,' says the assistant from her place by the counter.

I look up and she's smiling at me, polishing a long glass dildo with evident relish, her slim hand moving up and down it with a cloth.

'Is it?'

'Yes. That boning is very popular.' She looks back at her work.

I flick through others, in all shades and styles. There are leather ones and shiny PVC, ones that cover the breasts and others that sit beneath and cup them. There are corsets that constrict only the waist, leaving the chest completely bare, and others with hoops and chains attached, though for what I don't know.

I go to another that's caught my eye, in classic black, with heavy boning, hooks and eyes and laces too. It sits below the breasts but framing them so that they are shown off to their best advantage.

'Would you like to try it?' asks the assistant.

I nod, and she points me to a changing room with a red velvet curtain concealing the interior. I go in, pulling the curtain shut behind me, and undress quickly. When I'm wearing just my knickers, I try to put the corset on but it's very hard on my own.

The soft voice of the assistant comes through the curtain. 'Would you like some help?'

'Yes – please,' I say, seeing in the mirror that I'm already rather red-faced from trying to strain behind me for the fastenings. She steps inside, taking care not to look at my naked chest in the mirror.

'Here,' she says in a friendly tone. 'Let me help.' With nimble fingers she does up the hooks and eyes, each one pulling the corset in tighter. Then she tugs on the laces until they are nice and tight too, and ties them into a bow at the base of my spine. 'There.' Now she looks at my reflection. 'Lovely.'

I look at myself. I look like someone from the Edwardian age, with my thick hair falling over my bare shoulders, my breasts lifted lightly by the cup of the corset. They seem to nestle in the lace around them, the rosy pink of the nipples bright and winsome against the black. My waist has assumed minute proportions, and is taut with the boning that holds it in. I like the constricted feeling and the way my back feels so very straight inside it.

'Those rather spoil the effect, don't they?' The assistant gestures at my white knickers. 'Take them off.'

I flush. 'Really?'

'Of course. They're ruining it. You won't wear them anyway, will you?' She points to the suspender straps hanging from the corset. 'You need stockings.' She disappears behind the curtain and returns a moment later with a pair of fishnet stockings. She drapes them over a chair and then pulls my knickers down to my ankles so I can step out of them. I'm scarlet with embarrassment but she doesn't seem to notice. Then she helps me step into the stockings and slides them up my legs to fasten them to the little dangling ribbons.

'That's better,' she says. 'Much better.' She gazes at me appreciatively. 'Now you're irresistible.'

I look at my reflection, more like a woman from the past than ever now that I have the stockings on. I know Andrei will like this very much.

'I'll take them,' I say. 'Thank you.'

'Good.' The assistant smiles. 'You've definitely made the right decision. Shall I help you take them off?'

'I won't take them off,' I say, suddenly deciding. 'I'll wear them now.'

She raises her eyebrows just a touch and smiles. 'How charming. Perhaps you have a rendezvous. If so, I wish you pleasure.'

'Thank you,' I say, looking again at my reflection.

As soon as I'm out of the boutique, I stop on the pavement. I've changed back into my jeans but now I'm wearing the high boots too, and I'm aware of the stockings rubbing against my skin as I move. My jumper hides the corset but I know it is there, and my bare nipples poke at the soft cashmere.

I take out my phone and send a message to Andrei.

Miss X would like to see you right now, somewhere very private.

I start walking again but my phone beeps almost immediately with an incoming text.

Olympe is out of town. We can use her house. Meet me there in half an hour.

Walking around in my new underwear is so arousing that I'm afraid that half an hour will ruin me for the rest of the day, so I hail a taxi and then spend twenty minutes in a cafe nearby calming my nerves with a small glass of wine. I'm excited and I don't want more than that in case it numbs my senses. All the time, as I look at the other customers, I wonder what they would think if they knew what I'm wearing and what I'm about to do.

But maybe the world is full of people who've just had sex, are about to have sex, are thinking about sex. Perhaps all of us, under our placid exteriors, are raging for it all the time. Maybe we're all obsessed!

All I know is that my rage for Andrei is like nothing I've known before. My passion for Jimmy seems ethereal and unbodied compared to the all-encompassing physical need I have for Andrei. Just the thought of him hard and dark-eyed with lust makes my pulse speed up, my body respond with a thrill of excitement, and my mouth dry a little.

When half an hour has passed, I go to Olympe's house as directed and this time I'm let in by a demure maid rather than the leather-clad Eric. The place feels different without its mistress present; it's still exquisite and stylish, but there's a sense of energy lacking, as though the house has sunk into a slumber in her absence. Perhaps that's because, when she is here, the air is thick with the contained excitement of her slaves, her tribe and anyone else who is brought into her company. I wonder for a moment what made Olympe devote her life to physical experience and how she has managed to make such a success of it. I'm sure that her story must be fascinating and I hope that Andrei will tell me.

As the maid leads me across the hall towards the drawing room, Andrei appears at the top of a small staircase I hadn't noticed before.

'Flora, hello.' He smiles at the maid. 'Thank you. I'll take Miss Flora downstairs.'

I'm delighted to see him, not just because he looks delicious, but because the thrill of my secret rushes through me.

'Andrei.' I go over to him, more aware than ever of the roughness of my fishnet stockings against my skin, and the tightness of the laces on my boots and at my waist. As I move, I can feel the slipperiness of arousal is already there. When I reach him, I kiss his lips lightly, inhaling the dark musky scent of his aftershave.

His hand brushes over my arm as he kisses me back and the place where he's touched me throbs and tingles. I'm already alive to every sensation he can give me.

I'm looking forward to this.

'Follow me.' He leads me down the narrow staircase to the basement.

'What's down here?' I ask, looking curiously down the dark hallway and the four doorways on either side.

'Olympe's work rooms,' he says drily.

'Does she charge for what she does?'

'Oh no.' Andrei sounds shocked. 'She would never do such a thing. She would never be in the employ of her submissives.'

'Then how does she maintain all of this?'

He shrugs. 'She has money. I don't know how.'

'What's her story?'

'I don't know much. She doesn't talk about herself very often. I'll tell you what I know one of these days.' He smiles down at me, his eyes glimmering in the dim light. 'But I'd much rather concentrate on you at the moment.'

I return his look, thinking again of my secret with an inner thrill. 'That's good. That's my plan too.'

He leads the way to the first door on the right and opens it. I'm not sure what I'm expecting to see, but I'm quite relieved at the normality of the room inside. It's small and panelled, with lamps providing a low light, just enough to show that the walls are hung with antique prints. I squint at them quickly and see that they are rowdily explicit eight-eenth-century pornography. The room is dominated by a large square divan, not quite a sofa and not quite a bed, covered with cushions at one end, and upholstered in a kind of rough tapestry. There are cabinets on either side of it and it faces a bare wall, where there are no lamps or prints, just a floor-to-ceiling velvet curtain that is almost as wide as the entire wall.

'This is the withdrawing room,' Andrei says, raising his eyebrow. 'At least, that is Olympe's nickname for it. I don't suppose there is much withdrawing being done in here.'

I shiver with the involuntary image of Andrei ramming himself home inside me, and swallow hard. 'What is that curtain for? There can't be a window down here?'

'Ah. I'll show you.' He goes over to it, pulls a cord and makes the curtain glide back easily on its track. There is a huge black screen there.

'A television?' I ask.

'In a way. More of a cinema screen. Olympe shows films here occasionally. And when there is live action required . . .' He flicks a hidden switch and the screen turns from black to transparent, showing the room beyond. I gasp. It looks like a fully equipped dungeon, full of strange-looking instruments. There are bars like the kind in our school gymnasium along one wall, opposite hang rows of whips, paddles and riding crops. In the middle of the room is what looks like a medieval rack, with manacles at several positions along its frame, and some kind of riding horse or stool that looks very much like the place for some kind of punishment. There's also a gilt stool with a cushioned kneeling place and raised front that looks like it has hoops attached to it, looking to me like a strange *prie-dieu* that might be seen in a cathedral – except perhaps for the hoops. I wonder what she does to people who kneel there. Everything is finished in expensive materials – fine wood, rich leather and gleaming metal – and I can see shelves full of beautifully made handcuffs, chains and other implements. It reminds me a little of the boutique I was in today, except that in the shop there was an atmosphere of playful pleasure. Here, in Olympe's dungeon, I sense that more solemn and committed rites are performed. This is a place of agony, long drawn out and intense, where the lines between pleasure and pain are deeply blurred. I can imagine Olympe, small and powerful, moving about this place and inflicting the torments her submissives beg for with implacable dedication.

'Have you been in there?' I ask suddenly.

Andrei doesn't answer for a moment and then says, 'Yes. I have.'

'What was it like?'

He regards me with a grave expression. 'It was an

experience that's hard to describe. Imagine being utterly in your body and yet outside it at the same time. It was a little like that. I'm glad I knew it. I only did it once.'

I want to know more but I sense that he will not tell me what it was like to be acted on in that next-door room. I have the flash of an image: it is Andrei stretched over the horse next door, his broad muscled back bare for Olympe to inflict blows on from her stinging whip. I shake it away.

Perhaps I don't want to know about that after all.

'Close the curtain,' I say, and Andrei pulls the cord that sends the curtains swishing silently back into place. Now the little room we're in is private again. He walks over to me and puts his arms around me, gazing down into my face with those piercing blue eyes.

'Perhaps I shouldn't have brought you here. This is more than you need to know.'

'But I don't want to be protected from reality,' I whisper. 'I want it all.'

His mouth lands on mine and he begins to kiss me, a few soft lip-kisses to start with, and then the tip of his tongue probes at my lips and I open to him at once. I can't imagine being anything other than hungry for his kiss, and the sensation of his mouth over mine, his tongue as eager to taste me as I am to taste him, is intoxicating. We seem to fit together so perfectly, and he kisses with a delicious skill that sends my senses soaring. His hands begin to caress me as we kiss, rubbing over my bottom, which he doesn't notice is bare beneath my jeans, and then up my back, while his other hand strokes my breasts.

He pulls away suddenly and eyes me curiously. 'What's this?' he says. 'You're wearing something . . .' He's no doubt felt the boning and laces under my jumper. 'But nothing here ...' His thumb rubs over my nipple, braless and exposed beneath the cashmere. A smile plays on his lips and his eyes glitter. 'What is it?'

'Perhaps you should undress me,' I whisper.

He needs no further instruction. He lifts the soft layer of my jumper and pulls it upwards. I raise my arms so he can take it off over my head. As he sees what lies beneath, he makes a small murmur of appreciation. 'This is beautiful. Very beautiful.'

The jumper is discarded and Andrei gazes at my soft, pale breasts in their nest of lace, the nipples hard and dark, my naked arms and the corset that emphasises the curve of my body, and nips me in so tightly at the waist. I feel seductive and utterly feminine, and I love the knowledge that the sight of my body is driving Andrei wild with desire. When his gaze meets mine again, his eyes are hard with lust.

'You know what to do to me,' he mutters, his breathing coming faster. 'I love to see your body like this.' He dips his head to suck on my nipple, taking it into his mouth and nipping it with his teeth. I push him away, making him release it. He groans as it slips from his mouth. 'I want it ...'

'But you haven't finished,' I say sweetly. 'Have you?'

He gives me a questioning look and then unbuttons my jeans. When he sees that below them I'm wearing no underwear, he makes an appreciative guttural sound in his throat. The little black ribbons stimulate his curiosity and he pushes the jeans downwards, moaning at the sight of my stocking tops.

'Wait,' I say. 'They won't come off that way. I'll have to do it myself.'

'I don't think so,' Andrei says almost roughly. He goes

to the cabinet at the side of the divan and returns in a moment with a pair of scissors. I watch curiously as he makes a cut in the hem of one of the legs of my jeans and then puts down the scissors so that he can grasp the denim and tear it apart. It rips right to the waist, and he repeats the same thing with the other leg. Now my jeans are more like a pair of chaps, hanging open to reveal my legs in their fishnet stockings, the tight black leather boots laced up to the knee. Above them, I'm bare and exposed, and then there is the delightful corset.

Andrei's face is flushed with pleasure as he looks at me. 'Perfect.' With a couple of quick movements, he slices through the waist of my jeans and they fall to the floor.

'Now I'm ready for your pleasure,' I say, and stand with my legs apart so that he can see the beauty of the boots and the way they hug my calves, the intricate laces and the high heels.

Andrei kisses me again, letting his hands roam over me, getting evident delight from the contrast of my skin with the hard corset and its silk and lace, and the heightened curves it produces in my body. Further down, he fondles me where the rim of the stockings meets the satin ribbons, running his finger down under my cleft and sliding it into the hot juices there. I lift one leg, wrapping it round his thigh so he can feel the leather boots, and he runs a hand appreciatively down my leg, along the stockings and then on to the shiny leather.

'Gorgeous,' he says between kisses. 'You're gorgeous.'

He pulls his finger from my cleft and uses the wetness on his finger to anoint my nipples and then returns for more. When two of his fingers are wet to the knuckles, he slides them up my neck to my mouth. I open my lips so that he can press them inside and I suck them hard, taking down the sweet-salt juices that speak of my desire for him.

I want him to show his body to me and I reach out to undress him. He moves my hands away lightly and says, 'In time.'

He wants me to stand in front of him first, so that he can feast his eyes on my body, play in the soft folds of my sex and suck long and hard at my breasts, then kiss the soft globes, my collarbone, my shoulder and my neck. His lips, tongue and teeth are driving me wild as his fingers roam about below, stimulating wild thoughts and desires in me. I want him, of course, but I also don't want this divine playing to stop, as my legs tremble and my breathing quickens.

Suddenly, without a word, he lifts me up and carries me to the divan, putting me face down on it. I spread my legs so that he will have a glorious view of my boots and stockings topped with the soft flesh of my thighs, and the round buttocks above, just below the rim of the corset and the criss-cross of laces that climbs my back. I know he adores this sight from the sound of his breathing, and I can almost feel the strength of his gaze burning into me. He comes forward and begins to massage my buttocks, rubbing and stroking them with increasing pressure, running his hands ever closer to the cleft between them and the entrance to my sex below, which I'm sure must be shiny with moisture, and hot with need. As he rubs my bottom, he grows fiercer with his hands and suddenly he slaps my bottom hard, three times.

I groan, but not with pain. The blows sting but not much. I love the way I can feel them reverberate through the flesh of my buttocks and the way they express his love of my body and what it does to him. He rubs me again, running his fingers hard down to my sex and pressing them into the entrance just enough to dip the tips in. It's unbearably tantalising. I shift my legs further apart, hoping he will be compelled to thrust in several fingers at once to feed my inner hunger, but he doesn't do as I wish. Instead, he slaps my bottom again, harder, another three brisk sharp blows that resound satisfyingly through the room, then bends down to kiss and lick my buttocks. With his mouth busy on my bottom, at last he sends his fingers plunging into me, and I moan as he pushes his long fingers right into me, three of them stretching me out with a delicious irregularity. He begins to pump his hand, pushing in and out as his teeth dig into my buttocks. He sucks up a mouthful of flesh and then releases it, nibbles and grazes at somewhere else, and licks me in long strokes to the small of my back.

I feel as if I'm going to come just from the action of his mouth on my backside and the fingers forcing in and out of me with such enthralling action. But Andrei's not ready for that.

He pulls his dripping fingers out of me, and turns me over so that I can see him. I know my eyes are intense with lust, and my lips are wet where I've been licking them in the pleasure of stimulation. He seems to relish the sight of me in front of him, my breasts and sex bare, the beautiful corset constricting my middle, and the leather boots that are wide apart now, offering my delicate centre to him.

He unbuttons his shirt and takes it off. I take in the sight of him, the bulging muscles and the dark hair curling over his chest, where dark pink nipples are almost hidden. He has well-formed abs and a narrow waist, and I watch hungrily as he undoes his belt, and then his trousers.

I can feel myself throb with need as I catch my first glimpse of that glorious cock of his. It's rock hard, thrusting upwards with a soft domed tip that I long to take in my mouth. As he takes off the trousers, I wriggle forward and slide off the divan so that I'm on my knees in front of him. Without waiting for permission, I take the hot shaft in my hand, and cup his balls with the other, then I begin to lick it, letting my tongue play over the girth of it, relishing its heat and the stiffness. I know he can see this tableau beneath him: the breasts rising from the corset top, the head at his cock, the pink tongue paying homage to the magnificence of his hard prick, one hand shifting the skin while the other tickles his balls, rubbing at the spot behind them.

Andrei is panting. It feels good to give him a little taste of his own medicine as I tantalise him, my tongue moving slowly along the shaft toward the promise of the tip where I'm sure most of his sensation is based. His hand lands on the back of my head and I wonder if he's going to make me take him into my mouth, but he doesn't do more than enjoy the feel of my hair and the movements of my head as I lick and lap him.

I have never done this before but I love it and the action of licking him is giving me a stimulation of my own. I'm acting only on instinct, taking my lead from the way he gasps and closes his eyes when something particularly pleases him. I've always wondered what it might be like to pleasure a man with my mouth and assumed it would be unpleasant, but it's not. It's all I want and yearn for at the moment just as much as Andrei seems to, and I don't think I can wait any longer myself. At last I pull his cock forward – it's so stiff it's not easy – and take the head of it entirely into the warm wetness of my mouth, sucking hard and letting my tongue play over the tip and around the smooth dome. I swirl myself around him, loving the enormous thing with my mouth, sucking and licking as I move my hand up and down the shaft.

'Oh my God,' whispers Andrei, his voice even hoarser with the sensations I'm stimulating in him. His cock seems to be swelling to even greater proportions, filling my mouth. I want to take him right down my throat. 'Be careful. You're going to make me come.'

I want him to come. I want him to spill into my mouth and let me taste what it is he shoots out inside me. I suck and pump him harder. Then he pulls my head away, making me relinquish him with regret.

'That was beautiful. But, Miss X, you acted without my permission. I prefer to know when I'm going to be sucked.' He bends down to his trousers and a moment later he has the belt in his hand. He folds it into a strap. 'Turn round. Bend over the bed.'

I flush, and do as he orders. A moment later, I feel the sting of the belt thwack over my buttocks. I know he's being gentle as it doesn't hurt very much but makes a delicious sound of slapping. He gives me six sharp blows and says, 'What do you want?'

'I want you to fuck me, please.'

'Should I fuck a girl who sucks my cock when I don't give her permission?'

'Yes.' I push my face against the bed. I can feel my bottom wriggling with desire. 'Please. I need it.'

He steps forward and pushes his cock against my backside, prodding me on the buttocks and into the cleft there, making me moan with longing. 'I know you want this. I shouldn't give it to you. But . . .'

'Please,' I moan. 'I beg you . . .'

'Hmm.' He makes me wait and then says, 'Turn over. Put yourself back on the bed and spread your legs.'

I do as he orders, desperate now to have him inside me, full of wild longing that must be satisfied. He kneels up on the bed between my legs, his cock rearing up so that I can see it above me.

I sigh with delight. At last he's going to give it to me. Then he lifts my right leg and crosses it over the left and inspects the view. 'Very pleasing,' he murmurs. Now he can see my boots better, the round curve of my backside and the hole that's waiting from him squeezed between my thighs. 'This is what I want.'

He holds his cock in his fist, the head emerging hot and ready for me, and presses it to the entrance of my sex. I stare up at his face, watching his burning eyes as he observes his cock toying at the juicy entrance and then begins to penetrate me.

The sensation is exquisite, my hole seems much tighter in this position and the way it stretches to engulf him as he pushes forward makes me moan with delight. He has one hand on my upper thigh, pushing it down so that I feel his strength on me, and thrusts his cock forward hard so that he's deep inside.

'Ohhh!' I can't help it, the feeling of him rushing up into me is so incredible. It's almost painful but utter pleasure at the same time. Now he's in, he doesn't intend to stop and he begins to fuck hard, thrusting in and out, his hips jerking against me, his balls banging on the underside of my buttocks.

'Do you want this?' he demands.

'Yes! I want it!' I pant back. My hands pluck

involuntarily at the covering on the divan. 'Keep fucking me, please.'

He goes at me harder, pumping into me, pressing down on my thigh, looking at the leather boots and then at my bottom beneath the laced corset.

I pick up a cushion and bring it to my face, biting into it and using it to stifle the noise I'm making, which is growing close to a shriek. It's glorious pleasure with an edge of something else as he plunges roughly in and out of me. He slaps my hot buttocks again, and they tingle where they've been strapped.

I groan and talk, though I hardly know what I'm saying, only that I'm telling him how much I want it, how I can't stand it, how he mustn't stop.

His prick is bigger and harder than ever inside me. He slaps my bottom again and then, suddenly, roughly, he moves my leg back so that I'm spread open to him, and he's between my thighs. His weight hits my mound, he rubs against my clit as he pounds on me, driving me on to the wanton pleasure I crave. He's full against me now, sucking a nipple, then kissing my mouth with huge, wet, open kisses, fucking hard. I wrap my legs around him, digging the heels of my boots into his thighs and this makes him moan and shudder. He's close now and so am I. I dig my nails into his back, driving him deeper into me, and then the unbearable pleasure whirrs up inside me to a peak and the next moment, I'm caught up in the glorious wave, spinning inside it and conscious only of the bliss I'm experiencing, as Andrei catches the same wave, and comes hard and long inside me, shooting out his climax with a shout that is close to agony.

* * *

'I don't exactly know how I'm going to get home,' I say lazily. We are lying exhausted on the divan in post-coital languor.

'Why would that be a problem? My driver will take you,' Andrei says.

'That's very kind but since you cut my jeans up, I've got nothing to wear on my lower half. Not even a pair of knickers.' I giggle. 'What on earth am I going to do?'

Andrei stares at me for a moment and then laughs heartily. 'François is a good man but I think it's a little unfair to have him drive you home half naked. I'm sure Olympe will have something here. I'll send the maid to have a look.' He checks his watch suddenly. 'And then, sweet Flora, I'm afraid that I must leave you. I have business to attend to this evening.'

'Of course.' A mild depression sinks on me, stifling some of the afterglow of pleasure I've been enjoying. This is just an arrangement, after all. We have done what is in the terms of our agreement. That is an end to it.

But at least I have this. I have Jimmy in my heart and Andrei in my bed.

That thought is supposed to comfort me and I'm surprised to find that it doesn't. In fact, it doesn't sound right at all. I banish it from my mind.

Andrei gets up and stretches. I admire the beauty of his form and how well made he is, from the hard thighs and firm buttocks to the broad shoulders and muscled arms. His cock hangs at the junction of his thighs, no longer stiff, but still impressive. I'm seized by a longing to go to him and take him in my mouth, suck him up to stiffness again and demand that he run another course with me.

But that's not possible. He has to go, and besides, I'll always be hungry for more.

I'm half surprised at myself. I never knew my nature was so lubricious.

Andrei gets dressed and goes to find the maid so that she can find me some clothes. I lie on the divan in the curious room next to the basement in Olympe's house, wondering about the strange adventure I have embarked upon, and where it will lead me.

CHAPTER ELEVEN

I make it home wearing a skirt borrowed from a closet in Olympe's house. It's plain black but has the label of a famous fashion house sewn inside. Somehow that's what I'd expect from anything owned by Olympe. No matter how plain something is, it's bound to be of the highest quality.

I throw away my torn jeans and carefully fold away the corset. I can't wait to wear it again. The effect it had on Andrei was very pleasing indeed. Just the thought of the lust growing in his eyes makes my stomach burn with excitement. I'm glad that my foray into dressing up pleased him so much, and that I reaped the rewards of it.

I wonder how many encounters like this we'll be able to enjoy . . . I hope it is plenty.

I run a bath and lie in it listening to music and thinking about everything that's happened. The image of Beth floats before my mind and I wonder idly if she was ever tempted by Andrei. It must have been a lure, surely, to have a man like Andrei offer his heart. His magnetism and physical appeal are undeniable; Beth would have had to have a will of iron to resist him, wouldn't she? I know I wouldn't be strong enough to say no.

But then, I know what he can do to me. And . . . I run my hand through the soft bubbles on the surface of the water. *The man I love doesn't love me in that way, and never can. Perhaps if I were in love with someone like Dominic, a man who desires a woman, I would be able to resist Andrei.* I try to picture it, and yet I still can't imagine being able to deny myself the delicious pleasures of sex with Andrei. I shiver as I remember what we were doing to each other just a few hours ago in that little room beside the dungeon.

The warm water swirls around my shoulders and breasts. My body feels pleasantly well used, my nipples aching from Andrei's attentions and my sex just a little swollen and sore from the pounding he gave it. The indentations left by the corset have faded but I can still feel the results of the constriction.

Is the dungeon where Olympe performs her ceremonies? I wonder what she does exactly . . .

My curiosity is partly because I'm intrigued by a world where pain and pleasure are so intertwined, and partly because I'm fascinated by Andrei and what led him to be part of that world.

Or more specifically, in thrall to Olympe.

I decide that I will ask him next time we meet and see if perhaps I may be allowed to know a little more about that secret world.

I think I'm brave enough to see what they do. The image of the rack in the basement dungeon floats into my mind and for a moment I imagine myself cuffed to it, my body stretched out, vulnerable and exposed.

No. Not that. I only want to know. Anything more is not for me.

Beth stays in my mind for the next day or so although I don't really know why I'm thinking about her. As I go about my daily life, I wonder what Beth would be doing in my place. How does she like her coffee? What does she eat for breakfast? I wonder what soap she uses, or which face cream. Occasionally I catch myself up and laugh at myself. What does it matter? What difference does it make?

It's almost as if I think that if I use the same cream, I would become more like her, and why would I want to do that?

I push the thoughts away as much as I can, and try to concentrate instead on my work at the Academie, and devoting my energies to that. Despite my attempts to focus, I find my mind wandering. I still check my phone for messages from Andrei every few minutes, wondering where he is and what he's doing. I know I am at liberty to contact him if I want to, but I made the last overture and somehow it seems more fitting that he should arrange the next. I want to be the pursued as much as the pursuer, and I'm sure that a man of Andrei's psychology would think that too. But eventually I can't stop myself from contacting him, though I frame it as something other than a request to see him.

Dear Andrei
I've been thinking about Olympe. I wonder if she would permit me to witness one of her ceremonies. I'd be very interested to see what they involve.
F

There is a long wait for an answer and I wonder if I've done the wrong thing by opening a line of communication that is outside what we agreed. It isn't until the late afternoon that I hear from him.

Hello
I'm sure Olympe would be happy to allow your
request. I will speak to her about it. I'm out of the
country for a day or two. I'll be in touch when I'm
back. Keep your boots well polished for me, won't
you?
A

I smile at this, relieved that he doesn't seem to think I've gone beyond what we agreed by asking to witness Olympe at work. I also feel strangely bereft that Andrei is out of the country and there is no chance of a sudden summons to a rendezvous with him. On the other hand, it means that I'm able to stop checking my messages obsessively and I can, at last, think a little more of the demands of my drama course. I miss him though, and at night I dress up in the corset and boots and look at myself, before making myself climax, imagining Andrei inside me, fucking to the pleasure I experienced in the basement room. It's something but nothing like what I have when I'm with him.

I had no idea what it was like to need someone like this. It's as though I'm incomplete without him, incapable of real satisfaction.

I don't know how I will wait until he comes back.

It's early evening and I'm home from drama school, exhausted by the dance class I had at the end of the day. There's been no word from Andrei and I can only assume he's still away on business.

I'm settling in for a quiet night when I'm startled by a knock on the door of my apartment. No one ever knocks on the door unless I've already buzzed them up beforehand. Perhaps it's someone from inside the building. Perhaps it's even Alphonse, my lazy bodyguard, who does little more than check in with me every morning to make sure I'm still okay.

I pad over to the door and gaze through the peephole. There's a woman outside and I glimpse tendrils of blonde hair escaping from beneath a floppy hat, and a pair of large dark sunglasses that aren't strictly necessary on a cold January day like today. But I have a funny feeling that I know who it is.

I open the door and Summer pulls off her sunglasses, crying out, 'Surprise!'

I gasp with delight and the next moment, we're hugging happily.

'You didn't tell me you were coming!' I say, laughing. 'I could have been out.'

'Where would you be?' Summer says teasingly. 'I understand you never go out any more – you're far too dedicated to your art these days.'

I say nothing, feeling a little fraudulent as I think over how little I've been devoting myself to my classes these days. Instead I pull her into the apartment, saying, 'So when did you arrive? How was LA?'

Summer resists me a little, and says almost apologetically, 'Actually, this is not the only surprise.'

'It isn't?'

She shakes her head. 'Uh uh. I brought someone else to see you.'

A figure steps into my line of vision, someone who's been standing out of sight while I've been engrossed in Summer's arrival. He's tall and tanned with dark hair and exquisite brown eyes. He's smiling at me, his teeth whiter than ever against the mocha colour of his skin.

I gasp, feeling as though all the air has just been punched out of me. 'Jimmy!'

'Hello, Flora,' he said in that familiar American drawl, his voice honeyed and smooth. Once, every fibre in me thrilled to that sound and even now it fills me with pleasure. Jimmy holds out his arms to embrace me. 'It's so good to see you.' Then he wraps me in a strong hug. 'Do you mind me coming over with Summer? It was a crazy impulse, but I've missed you so much.'

'Of course I don't mind.' I kiss his smooth cheek and inhale the lemony scent of his cologne. Being this close to Jimmy would once have set me alight with longing, and I would have trembled all over to feel his body against mine.

And now?

I am both startled and almost amused to discover that I feel nothing beyond the normal pleasure of seeing an old friend. Jimmy is still gorgeous, of course, but now I appreciate his looks with a detached enjoyment that one feels towards a beautiful thing. He does nothing for me.

He leaves me cold.

The thought bursts into my mind with absolute clarity. My friend Jimmy is now just that. My passion for him is dead, snuffed out as quickly and effectively as a candle flame pinched between the fingers.

'Come in,' I say, trying to stay focused despite the revelation chiming through me. 'This calls for a celebration. Let's open some champagne!'

Summer is observing me carefully to see how I'm responding to her surprise. She nods, looking relieved. 'That sounds like a great idea! We can tell you all about what we got up to in LA. Jimmy has the most fabulous gossip, you just won't believe it!'

We spend a happy evening together, talking and laughing. I can't believe the way I'm really enjoying being with Summer again and intrigued by the way my whole relationship with Jimmy has changed tack so easily. Being with him as a friend feels utterly natural and for the first time I can enjoy his company in the same way that Summer can: with gossip and chatter, jokes and laughter. I can experience all the good things about a relationship with him, without that pent-up emotion, the thwarted desire, the sense of hopelessness and rejection that has tainted every moment I've spent with him for years.

Later in the evening, Summer leaves us alone and Jimmy fixes me with those velvet brown eyes of his.

'It's really good to see you, Flora. You seem happy. Really happy.' He smiles over at me, and I see all the affection he has for me in his face. He does love me, in the way he can, I know that. The knowledge fills me with warmth.

'I am,' I say sincerely. 'In my own way. Nothing's perfect of course.'

'Are you seeing someone?' he says, and then adds, 'I hope I'm not being too nosy.'

'Of course not.' I feel my cheeks grow a little hotter. 'As it happens – yes, I am.'

A look of pleasure crosses Jimmy's face. 'I'm very happy to hear that. You deserve it.' He leans forward, suddenly earnest. 'All I've wanted is for you to be happy, Flora, you do know that, don't you?'

I nod. 'Yes. I'm sorry that . . . emotions . . . got in the way of our friendship.'

'You're a passionate girl. I was the only man in your life.

147

I always knew you would not be able to stop your nature.' He smiles ruefully. 'I was flattered but also very worried about you, when you didn't seem able to outgrow your feelings. I thought that as soon as you met other boys, you'd soon forget me. But it never happened.'

'That passionate nature of mine,' I say drily, 'can be a curse sometimes. I couldn't bear to let go of what I felt for you.'

'You found as much romance in your situation as a lovelorn maiden, I think.' Jimmy laughs. 'You're an actress. It's a role you wanted to play.'

I laugh too. 'Maybe that's it. Maybe I was just waiting for another role to come along that I preferred to play instead.'

He looks suddenly serious. 'I hope you've found it.'

I gaze back at him, thinking of the role I've been playing lately. *From lovelorn maiden to Miss X.* 'You know what? I think I have.'

CHAPTER TWELVE

Summer and Jimmy have booked into a hotel and it's late in the evening when they decide it's time to go back there and get some sleep.

While Jimmy is in the bathroom, Summer kisses me goodnight and whispers, 'Is it all okay?'

'It's all great. Thank you for bringing Jimmy.'

'I had to,' she says simply. 'He and I had a big heart-to-heart in LA and we both felt that we couldn't let the situation go on. And . . .' She fixes me with a penetrating look from her big blue eyes. 'I've got the feeling that something important is happening in your life. Is that true?'

I hesitate. I've never lied to my sister and I'm not about to start now. 'Yes – it is. There is something happening. But I can't tell you about it right now. I promise I will when the time is right.'

Summer searches my face for clues and then says, 'All right. I trust you to tell me when you're ready. Just one thing: are you happy?'

My mind is flooded with images of everything I've experienced in the last few weeks. 'Oh yes. I'm happy.'

'Good. You seem different somehow. But I can't quite work out how.'

I smile at her. 'I've done a lot of growing up.'

'Don't do too much,' Summer says with a laugh. 'I don't want you to leave me behind!'

I'm seized by a longing to tell her everything, to confide all of my adventures and ask her what she thinks. *I need to tell her about Andrei!*

But the time isn't right. Not yet.

We spend two happy days together, and my spirits lift higher with each hour. This is more fun than I could possibly have anticipated. Suddenly I understand entirely the relationship that my sisters have always enjoyed with Jimmy, the carefree joking and happiness that I've been so jealous of. Jimmy is far sweeter to me as a friend than he ever was as a putative lover.

We wander around Paris, amusing ourselves, shopping, going to galleries, eating at the coolest cafes and drinking in the best bars. Despite the fact that Jimmy doesn't even live in Paris, he knows far more about the most fashionable places than I do. He makes sure we go to the newest burger and cocktail joint, where only last week some big stars were seen enjoying the very Parisian take on an American classic. He gets a table at the chicest restaurant, where all the customers are young, gorgeous and stylish. I feel young myself for the first time in ages and almost forget to worry about not going to the Academie. I even neglect my secret email account, which I usually check every hour at least.

We're dining at a restaurant that serves eighteen tiny, perfectly manufactured courses full of culinary surprises, a wine to accompany each served in miniature glasses. I'm eating a fricassee of frog legs served on edible leaves made to look like lily pads when my phone flickers to life on the table beside me to alert me to an incoming email.

'Excuse me,' I say, and pick up my phone.

Summer and Jimmy chatter on while I open the message.

Miss X
Where are you? It's been too long. I'm back and I
want to see you. Come to me tonight.
A

I stare at it for a few seconds, then look up at my sister and Jimmy convulsing with laughter over a joke as they pick tentatively at the latest course, waiting to discover what the surprise will be this time.

This is very strange. I have to decide between Andrei and Jimmy. And I want to stay here with my sister and my friend.

For the first time, I see my relationship with Andrei as something strange and unusual. Up until now, it's felt right and natural. But how would I explain it to the others if I got up now and left?

Excuse me, I have to go and see my secret lover who doesn't know my name and likes to have extreme sex with me and take me to his secret sadomasochistic society.

Put that way, it sounds distinctly odd.

I pull myself up. *But it's not like that. Nothing happens that I don't consent to. I'm not a member of that society. And I know all I need to about him.*

'Who's your message from?' Summer says playfully, looking over at me. 'Your mysterious boyfriend?'

I flush a little as I laugh lightly. 'Yes it is, actually.'

'Does he want to join us?' she jokes. 'Go on, Flora, ask him to meet us. We want to see him!'

I glance down at my phone, not sure what to say to this.

'Does he want to see you?' Jimmy asks, not laughing in the way Summer is. He seems to understand that this is something important for me.

I nod. 'One of those last-minute things.'

'You should go,' he says, his dark brown eyes on me as if he can read what's going through my mind.

'No, no ... I haven't seen you in years. Summer and I hardly ever manage to make proper time for each other. I can't just go off and leave you.'

Jimmy looks at me hard and then says, 'Flora, you should go and see this man. We've had the whole day together and all of yesterday too. We've got tomorrow if we want it. But you shouldn't neglect him for our sakes. After all, we can't give you what he can.'

I stare back at him, knowing he understands. He guesses what an enormous journey I've been on, leaving behind the girl I was and learning to be an adult.

'Go on,' Jimmy says quietly. 'I really think you should.'

He's giving me permission, just as he did in my dream.

I smile at him, beaming happily. 'All right then. I will.'

'Oh,' Summer says with pretend grumpiness, 'just go off and leave us then! I guess I'll have to put up with Jimmy on my own.'

'You'll survive,' Jimmy retorts. 'Let Flora go. She needs to.'

'Have fun then,' Summer says with a shrug but I can see from her expression that she's not angry. Maybe she's even a little envious.

'I will.' I get up. 'I'll see you two tomorrow.'

As I leave the restaurant, I send a reply to Andrei.

Where are you? I'm on my way.

Andrei replies almost at once with the name of a grand hotel near the Place de la Concorde. I know it but not well. It won't take long to get there and I hail a taxi on the street corner.

On the way, I realise that I'm free now – totally free of Jimmy. My love has turned into what it was always supposed to be – the love between dear friends. But that leaves my heart empty and unoccupied. I have no one to love.

I hear Olympe's voice in my head again. 'She will certainly love you – for as long as you will let her.'

She was wrong about that. I've managed very well to keep myself free of falling love with Andrei.

I bring his face to mind. That mobile, harsh face with its big nose and jutting chin, the obstinate lower lip and the icy blue eyes. It's a face I find endlessly fascinating. But love? No, I don't think so.

Andrei is waiting for me in the lobby of the hotel, sitting in a chair that faces the door and watching the entrance like a hawk. As soon as I walk in, his eyes are on me and he's on his feet striding towards me.

'Where have you been?' he asked. 'You were going to contact me. There's been nothing.'

'I've been with Jimmy,' I begin, wanting to tell him all about what's happened to me and what I now know about my feelings. But then something occurs to me and I stop. If I no longer love Jimmy, does that nullify our agreement? The whole arrangement is predicated on the idea that our hearts are impervious to one another because we both love other people. If I no longer feel that way, does that mean that Andrei will bring it to a halt?

The thought is awful. As he stands close to me, the power

of his presence washing over me, making me simultaneously weak and full of longing, I realise I can't bear the thought of him not being in my life.

'Jimmy?' His eyes flash and his lip curls with something like scorn. 'So that's why you've not wanted to see me. Has he had some kind of conversion and come back to claim you?'

'No.' I'm startled by the anger I can see in his face. Why should he be cross about me seeing Jimmy? He knows it can never lead to anything, even if he cared – which I'm sure he doesn't. 'It's not like that. He came to clear the air between us. So that we can be friends.'

Andrei is still staring furiously at me. 'Friends?' He almost spits out the word. 'We both know that's not possible.'

I'm silent. I feel caught in a trap. If I say it is, then our arrangement is void. If I say it isn't, then I'll only be fuelling this strange anger of his.

'It wasn't part of our agreement that we should see the people who've caused our misery,' Andrei says in a low, intense voice.

I'm startled. 'What do you mean? That it's forbidden? There was no mention of that.'

'I would have thought that was obvious,' Andrei says harshly. 'I haven't seen Beth. How would you feel if I did?'

I imagine it. I see them together, Beth distant and lovely, Andrei yearning and pained in his rejection. It feels horrible. A surge of jealousy rushes through me at the mental picture I've drawn. *But it shouldn't matter!* 'We said there would be no emotional involvement,' I say almost to myself.

'Common courtesy is something else,' retorts Andrei. 'At the very least, you should have told me you were seeing Jimmy. You've threatened the whole thing.'

He turns as if to stride off, and I grab him by the arm. 'Wait – what are you saying? That it's over?'

'I have to think about it.' His face is colder than I've ever seen. I can't understand how this has happened and I'm filled with panic.

'Don't go,' I implore. 'Why can't we stay the same? Seeing Jimmy doesn't change a thing, I promise.'

He stops, staring at the floor. I wonder if people are watching us, wondering what's happening between us.

'Please.' My voice is low and intense. 'I've been foolish. Stupid. I'm sorry. Forgive me. Don't leave me like this.'

Something in my voice stops him. He looks down at me, his eyes inscrutable. I seize the chance I sense is there.

'I've broken the rules. I deserve to be punished,' I say quietly.

His eyes flicker and he becomes very still.

'You should administer my chastisement.'

His mouth twitches. 'Only if you repent,' he says in a growl.

'I repent. I need absolution.'

Our eyes meet and everything we need to say to one another is there. A dark excitement curls in my belly.

'The penthouse suite. In five minutes.' He turns on his heel and strides out over the lobby towards the lifts.

I release a long breath. For a moment, I looked into a future without Andrei and it was terrible. I know now, for sure, that I do not want this to end.

Ever.

CHAPTER THIRTEEN

I ride up in the lift to the penthouse floor, catching a glimpse of my face in the mirror. I look pale and anxious.

Not exactly as though I'm on the way to an assignation with my lover.

I wonder what Summer and Jimmy would make of this if they could see me now. I almost laugh at the thought. They probably think I'm at some smart restaurant or in a cosy apartment about to have a romantic meal with my boyfriend. Perhaps they're imagining flowers, wine, soft kisses and murmurings of love.

Hah!

The truth is that I'm desperately trying to keep my lover from deserting me by offering my body up to him for whatever he wishes to do to it.

He looked so angry. I've never seen him like that. Is there a side to Andrei I don't know? A place he'll go to that I'm not ready for? After all, he's been in Olympe's dungeon. He knows more than I ever will.

The lift reaches the floor and stops with a little ping. The doors open and I step out into the carpeted hall. No one is about. I can see the door of the penthouse suite, flanked by tables holding vases of flowers.

I go to the door and knock. There's a long pause and then it opens. Andrei is standing there, his face stern and his eyes cold.

'Come in.'

His voice is even chillier than his eyes. I see that he has changed and is now wearing a dark blue robe over silk pyjama trousers.

When I've stepped into the hall he orders me to stop, and the next moment he has slipped a sleep mask over my eyes so that I can't see a thing. I hear the door close behind me. His voice sounds from behind me too.

'Strip off your clothes.'

I obey quickly, undressing fast. I sense that this is not a punishment I need to fear but another game. I understand suddenly what is happening.

It's a way back into our arrangement for Andrei. He nearly threw it away and he doesn't want that. He wants this too – and this is how we'll manage to continue.

At once I feel aroused as I stand there naked, knowing his eyes are on me but not being able to see him. I feel sure that whatever he's planned for me will end up in the most delicious way possible.

Andrei speaks again, now at my side. 'You are going to be punished for breaking the terms of our agreement, do you understand? You shouldn't have seen the man you love without telling me. You undermined everything we've enjoyed so far and I won't tolerate that. But if you take your punishment, then perhaps you will be forgiven.'

'I understand.' I hope I sound meek enough to satisfy him when he is in this severe mood. I feel instinctively that we are playing a game, the kind I've imagined ever since I saw the dungeon in Olympe's house, and knew that Andrei had been there himself. Where there is a dungeon, there must be a punisher and a punished, mustn't there? A master and a slave? I can easily guess that tonight, I will

157

be the one to submit in order to win back the approval I need so much.

'Good. You're lucky that I am able to improvise without the proper equipment. Otherwise you would not be able to be chastised. I'm sure that would disappoint you very much.'

'Very much,' I say obediently. I can sense that complete compliance is the right way to behave.

'You want this punishment, don't you?'

'Yes, I do.'

'Good.' A hand grasps my wrist. 'Follow me.'

I'm led out of the hallway and into a room I cannot see. We walk through that and I sense that I'm being led into another. When we reach a bed, Andrei speaks again.

'Lie down,' he says. 'On your back.'

I do as I'm told. I can feel my nipples raise pertly in the air, stiff with the anticipation of what is going to happen to me. With the sleep mask on, I can see nothing, which makes me alert to the sounds going on around me, and I hear Andrei moving around the room, the opening and closing of doors, the clink of glasses and the movement of equipment of some kind.

I lie quietly until he returns to me. When he speaks, his voice is still stern.

'You must stay completely still, do you understand me?'

'Yes.' I stiffen, trying to remain motionless. Then I gasp as something very cold lands on my belly. It burns there, sticking to my skin. *What is it?* Then I realise. *An ice cube.*

It tickles and freezes me simultaneously, and begins to melt. As soon as the surface becomes liquid, it starts to move on my skin and I expect it to slide off. But an unseen finger holds it on, and then moves it around my belly, trailing icy water all over me. It's all I can do to stay still and restrain myself from brushing away the cube. It is brought up to my nipples and run over the surfaces of them, then up my neck and over my lips and eyelids. It's brought back down, circling my nipples again and then over my stomach and downwards towards my sex. It's rubbed over my bud and down along my slit and then, to my astonishment, it's pressed inside me, lodged into my depths. The sensation is very strange, as the ice melts fast into water. I tingle to it as it fills me with that odd burning coldness and then feel it disappear and a wetness trickle down my thighs.

'Very good,' says the stern voice. 'You barely moved. But . . .' Another ice cube lands on me and the same routine begins again. I struggle to stay motionless under the cube's movement. 'The truth is that you are moving. Which you are forbidden to do. Wait there.'

The second ice cube is rubbed over me in the same way and left to melt inside me. I sense Andrei leave the room and I lie there absolutely still, feeling the damp patch below me grow.

What will he do to me?

He returns with something that he puts at the side of the bed. Then he sits.

It's a chair.

He pulls me up into a sitting position and then moves me off the bed so that I'm standing in front of him. He turns me round, inspecting me, and when I'm facing him again, he tweaks my nipples.

'Pretty,' he says, 'but disobedient. What a shame. Don't

you know that only obedient girls are permitted to enjoy me? Do you want to enjoy me?'

'Yes,' I say, and the yearning is there in my voice. My sex is already alive with need for him. The ice cubes have wakened it well.

'Of course you do. You must earn back the right to have me fuck you, do you understand?'

'Yes.'

'Good. Put yourself over my knee.'

I edge forward blindly, putting out my hands to find his lap. He does nothing to help me but lets me feel where he is and then move myself round so that I can lie on my stomach across his thighs.

'Hold the legs of the chair.'

I put my arms forward and grasp the legs in my hands, holding on tight. My head is low down and my bottom is thrust in the air, my toes only just touching the ground.

'Good,' he says softly. 'Well done. I like the way you're being so compliant. I like to see your bottom there, offered to me. It's so tender. It seems a shame to hurt it but I fear it's the only way you'll understand. So, remember. Take your punishment well and you'll receive your reward.'

I stay very still, waiting. He begins to rub my buttocks, murmuring appreciatively as he does so. Just as they begin to feel caressed and cared for, he draws back his palm and gives me a solid smack on the bottom. I gasp and jerk under it.

'Still!' he orders, and draws back his hand for another stinging slap right over my bottom. I can feel the heat of the blow, the blood rushing to the skin, the pain radiating outwards. I've never been smacked before, and it's a shock.

Smack. He hits my bottom firmly with an open palm.

This isn't like the slaps he likes to give me when he's fucking me, which don't hurt at all. This is a proper smack designed to cause proper pain. Smack again.

'Oh!' I cry out, as it stings harder on the already tender skin.

He smacks harder. 'Ten smacks for you,' he says. There are six more to come and by the time he's finished, my behind is stinging and there are tears in my eyes.

'You took your punishment well,' he concedes. 'But still, there is a little more work to do before you reach your real repentance.'

I'm breathing hard, biting my lip and blinking to hold back the tears of pain. Despite the soreness I'm hot with desire for him. As he smacked me, I could feel the stiffness of his cock against my side, under the robe he is wearing.

'What must I do?'

'You must kiss the rod, of course.'

With that, he moves me into position, letting me down from his lap so that I can slide to the floor and kneel between his knees. I can't see where he is but I put my hands out and at once I can feel the great shaft under my palm. I wrap my hand round it and bring my mouth forward to take the head between my lips.

I begin to kiss and lick it, sucking it into my mouth. My blindness gives me a heightened sense of devotion to the hot, smooth cock in my hands and mouth, and I lick all the way down it to the balls, darting my tongue out to touch them too, tickling them with the tip. This makes Andrei sigh and groan and I know he likes it. I spend a long time tending to the shaft, working my way back up to the top where I take the domed head into my mouth as far back as it will go. I lock my finger and thumb together at the base of his cock so that they form a firm ring, and then grasp the length in my hand, moving it up and down so that the skin rides under my hand, while I use my tongue to stimulate the top. Andrei moans as I suck and manipulate him like this for a long while, feeling him swell under my hands. When I think he can stand it no longer and is about to come in my mouth, he draws his cock out, pushing my head gently away.

'The rod is well kissed,' he says. 'Now. You must let it do its work. Lie down on the floor.'

I lie down beside the chair, not knowing how much room there is for me, but there appears to be a rug underneath me.

Andrei kneels between my legs, pushing them apart with his knees. He moves himself so that his cock is at my slit and pushes forward, making me gasp as his huge girth opens me up. He works it in and begins to fuck away hard. I try to put my arms around him but he won't let me, making me keep them on the floor at my side, holding my right arm firmly as he thrusts in and out.

'How is your punishment?' he asks. 'Have you learned your lesson?'

'Yes,' I moan, pushing my hips up to meet him. The sensation is delicious but I pretend that the insertion of his huge cock is almost painful. 'You're too big for me.'

He fucks harder at this, and dips his head to bite at my nipples and neck. Then he kisses me hard and murmurs into my mouth, 'I loved to see your lovely bottom turn red under my hands.'

'I deserved it,' I whisper. 'I'll never disobey you again.'

We're both excited by the game we're playing, the

pretence that I've truly been punished and that his cock is my punishment. The reality is that my stinging bottom is adding to the hot pleasure I'm getting from his hard, strong movements in and out of me. My ministrations to his cock have excited me unbearably and my bud wants to cling to him and have him bring it to a voluptuous delight. My passions are fired even more strongly when he brings his hand down to rub at my clitoris, even when he treats it roughly and slaps it lightly.

'Hold my cock like you did before,' he orders, and I put my finger and thumb round the base as he fucks on. The pleasure it gives him excites me, making the storm of passion between us rage even more fiercely. His mouth falls on mine and he kisses me deeply, his weight heavy on me now. His cock swells and thickens even more as his climax approaches, and the movement of his body on my bud begins to take over. I thrust my hips up to meet him, and then burst into my climax, shaking and shuddering under him, clawing at his back and almost sobbing with the intoxicating feelings he's giving me. Andrei stiffens too, holds himself still and then I feel him thrust hard three times, each time spilling out his climax inside me. Then he sobs out a word. It sends a wave of misery over me when I hear it. I know what he has sobbed in his moment of ecstasy. It was the name 'Beth'.

When my mask is off, I find myself in a very luxurious hotel suite. Andrei runs me a bath in the huge marble tub and I wallow in the water for a long time, wondering if he knows what he said as he came. It is ironic that this whole session was based around my supposed dealings with Jimmy, when the truth is that I know for sure now that my love for him was illusory – while Andrei's love for Beth seems to be very much alive.

I can't be jealous, this is the deal. No emotional involvement.

I swirl the cooling water around me.

But Andrei seemed emotionally involved when he got so angry at the idea of my seeing Jimmy. It seemed more than he would let on.

I shake my head miserably.

Well, it wasn't the case. He loves Beth. And why shouldn't he? He's a free agent.

When I come out of the bathroom, trying to be cheerful, the atmosphere between us is friendly again. Andrei is his normal self. We order food and eat in the suite, looking out over the golden lights and traffic of the Place de La Concorde. Beyond it, the Eiffel Tower is illuminated against the night sky. This is Paris at its most storybook.

We chat easily enough and later, when I'm dressed, Andrei offers his driver to take me home.

'Does he ever tell you where he takes me to?' I ask, curious.

'Never. And I never ask.' He grins at me. 'Now, take care, Flora and I'll see you soon.' He drops a kiss on my cheek and says conspiratorially, 'And thank you for saving this evening so we could enjoy each other. I was being an idiot. You should ignore me. And I wanted to say – of course you can see Jimmy if you want. That's entirely your prerogative. You do understand that, don't you?'

'Of course,' I say, smiling back and wondering why I feel so intensely miserable about that. I want to make a bargain with him, that I won't see Jimmy if he stops thinking of Beth when we make love.

But what's the point of that? He never will. And besides, I don't want him to. That's not what this is about.

'Goodnight, Andrei.' I kiss his stubbled cheek. 'Sleep well.'

Then I turn to go.

CHAPTER FOURTEEN

The next day is painful for me, in more senses than one. My heart aches with a strange sadness when I remember Andrei sobbing out Beth's name at his climax. I remember how it killed my own pleasure stone dead, leaving me with a horrible hollow feeling.

But there's another hurt I cannot ignore. In my bedroom, I inspect my buttocks in the full-length mirror, and see with a kind of fascinated horror the marks Andrei has left there. They are tender to touch and my whole backside feels bruised and in pain.

I wonder how long the marks will remain, then I realise that simply looking at them is making me aroused, dampness spreading between my legs with a tingle of excitement. I stroke my hand over my breasts and down my belly, letting my fingers touch lightly on my mound. My reflected eyes grow darker and my tongue flicks out over my lips. I'm hungry for more.

When will it ever end, this need I'm possessed by?

I'm touching the soft tip of my nub, letting the sweet feelings wash out from my centre and imagining that in a minute I will be forced to work on it in earnest, to conjure up the pleasure I'm now addicted to, when a small chirrup from my phone alerts me to an incoming message.

Summer and Jimmy? They're bound to ask me about last night. What on earth will I say to them? Will they notice that I'm having trouble sitting down? Or is it Andrei, wanting to inspect the results of his punishment?

I shiver with a delicious anticipation. I can't help remembering the exquisite satisfaction that came from pleasure felt after pain.

I go over and pick up the phone. It is a summons. But not one I was expecting. I have no choice but to obey.

Olympe sits across from me, straight-backed and elegant on her sofa just as she was the first time I saw her. This time she wears a chic navy silk dress with a shirt collar. Her hair is pulled back tightly as before, her lips and nails painted the same blood red. The grey eyes regard me thoughtfully and I feel again the immense power that emanates from her small form.

'I expect you're wondering why I wanted to see you,' she says.

'Yes, Madame,' I reply.

'Andrei tells me that you'd like see one of my ceremonies. Is that right?'

I feel impudent somehow and drop my gaze. 'Yes, Madame. That's correct.'

She stares at me for a moment and then says, 'That can be arranged. In fact, I think the time is most definitely right. You will hear from me in due course.'

'Very well, Madame.' I'm relieved. *That wasn't so hard. Is the interview over?*

Olympe seems to read my mind and holds up her hand. 'There's something else I wish to discuss with you. It is quite simple. I want to ask you about Andrei. I want to know how your relationship with him is developing and what you expect to happen.'

I gaze at her, feeling helpless. I have no idea how to answer those questions, but I know that only absolute honesty will be tolerated. 'I'm afraid that I don't really know, Madame.'

Her pencilled eyebrows lift. 'Is that so? You must know something.'

I hesitate, trying to order my thoughts. I know that for Olympe, precision and clarity are all. 'I thought I knew, Madame. Andrei and I had an agreement, that we would enjoy each other without fear of becoming emotionally involved, but now . . . I'm not sure what is happening. Last night, when I told him that I'd seen the man I once loved, he became enraged and threatened to end our liaison. It was only by asking him to punish me for my transgression that I was able to save it. It seemed that . . .' I trail off, remembering the intensity of it.

'It was more emotional than anything you have ever shared,' supplies Olympe.

I nod. 'We seem to have moved to a different place in our relationship, but I do not know what it is.'

Olympe looks at me wisely and nods. 'Your powers over each other are shifting. It is always the case where love is involved.'

'Love?' I stare back at her, astonished. 'Oh no, Madame. There is no love. He even called out the name of the woman he truly loves while he was making love to me.'

'My dear, that is the agony of releasing the old and accepting the new. Surely you know something of that yourself.'

I stare down at the floor where the patterns of a red and blue Persian carpet swirl richly at my feet. *Do I know that agony?*

Of course I do.

I look up as Olympe goes on. 'The love between you is still nascent. There is time to escape it if you wish. You could turn Andrei's emotions from budding love to hate, or to scorn if you want to. If you need to escape.' She watches me carefully as she says this.

I bite my lips, staring again at the carpet, following the intertwining patterns with my eyes. I can't quite believe what Olympe is saying. *Andrei loves me? He might really love me?*

'It is for you to birth the love, if you want it,' states Olympe.

I look up at her, confused.

'You can decide if it is something you want. Or not.' She speaks slowly and patiently, as if explaining to a backward child. 'If you do, then your task will be to bring Andrei to the realisation of what he feels for you.'

'How do I do that?' I ask. I've never heard of such a thing – surely people know if they love someone? Can it be something they don't realise until they are made to see it?

'There are ways.' I see a strangely hungry look in Olympe's eyes. 'Once, Andrei came to me and told me that he wished to submit himself to me completely. I knew then that, in a certain way, he loved me. His desire to prostrate himself before me and take whatever I wished to give him touched me. It moved me. It made me aware of what I might be able to feel for him, if I let myself. But . . .' She shrugs lightly. Beside her, her cat wakes up and blinks sleepily at me. 'I have never been in love and I did not want to begin at my age. And besides . . .' – now she smiles with an almost sly expression – 'I have many who offer me themselves like that. Too many for me to love them all.' She looks at me with that curious hungry look again and I wonder for a moment if she wants me to offer myself to her, as so many others have before now.

But that isn't the path I'm on.

I say slowly, 'You mean I should submit to Andrei? I've already done that. Last night, I gave myself to him completely.'

'Oh no. Not completely, my dear. Very far from completely. Believe me, you've hardly started.' She leans forward. 'I think perhaps I should teach you how to offer yourself to someone else without any boundaries at all.'

I stare at her, my mind racing with images. I see again the underground room that lies below us, with its equipment, the rack and the strange *prie-dieu*. Does she want me to offer myself to Andrei like that? Is that what she means? I don't understand. 'Madame, I would be honoured if you would teach me.'

She nods. 'I knew you would say nothing else. You adore Andrei, I can see that. You are soaked in his aura. You are already his creature.'

I want to protest and tell her that she is wrong, but her certainty is confusing. Can it be true? Do I adore him, that strange man with his ugly-handsome face, his unreadable expressions, the barely concealed animal toughness? He's ruthless. He's heartless. He's barely human.

Oh my God, I do love him.

The knowledge washes over me with the force of a tidal wave. I feel slapped in the face by it, and then lifted off my feet into a whirling vortex of emotion. Olympe is watching me, her eyes sparkling wickedly. She knows exactly what's happening inside me. I feel sure she wanted this.

She's making it happen. Are Andrei and I both under her spell? Can she manipulate us like marionettes for her amusement?

I realise that I don't care, as long as I get what I need. *Andrei.*

Olympe says, 'If you want the outcome you desire, you must do as I say.'

'But . . .' I swallow hard. I'm about to do what, right from the start, I promised myself I would not. I'm going to submit to this old woman and become her slave. 'Will it hurt?'

'My dear child.' She smiles, her red lips curving upwards to dagger points. 'I told you that you would have to birth this love. Did no one ever tell you that giving birth hurts?'

I leave Olympe's house in a daze, hardly able to understand what has happened. All I know is that I have walked out a different creature to the one who went in. For one thing, I now know that I've fallen in love with Andrei, the very thing I signed a contract promising that I wouldn't do.

Olympe has told me that I will be given further instructions by her at some point in the future. All I know is that I must wait and then obey. I feel like the little mermaid in the fairy tale, who agrees to lose her tongue and feel as though she is walking on needles for the rest of her life in order to win the man she loves. That makes Olympe a particularly nasty kind of sorceress. I don't know if she is that, but she is the most ambiguous person I've ever met in my life. I truly don't know if I worship her, or am terrified of her.

Perhaps both.

My phone rings and I jump, startled and already shaking

in case the next stage of my test is beginning immediately. To my relief, I see Summer's number.

'Where are you?' she demands. 'The day's nearly over! Come on, let's meet. Jimmy and I want to have some fun.'

I meet them in front of the Louvre where they are amusing themselves standing on the little stone pillars in the court-yard, striking poses and taking photographs of each other. They seem so young and joyful, so untouched by worries or cares. I feel about ten years older than both of them as they leap about, laughing. I smile, lifted a little by their high spirits, and try to join in.

After a while, we go inside. It's early evening and the museum will be closing soon. We just have time to look at one or two paintings before we have to leave.

'I want to see *The Raft of the* Medusa,' declares Jimmy, so we troop off through the galleries in search of it. It's in the nineteenth-century gallery and when we find it, we stand in front of the huge picture, staring.

Summer and Jimmy look with interest but I'm in a state of horror at the sight of this painting. Perhaps it's because of what's happened to me lately and my heightened emotional state, but the poor creatures on the raft, all that remain from the sinking of the *Medusa*, look tormented beyond endurance by what they've suffered. Their skins are green, their eyes wild, limbs twisted. Some, I suppose, are already dead and others close to it.

'What is this painting?' I say in a choked voice.

'It's based on one of those awful true stories,' Jimmy says. 'The ship was grounded and over a hundred people set off for the African coast on this raft they made. Apparently they went mad through starvation and dehydration, and began to eat each other. They killed the weak, threw others overboard, and some simply jumped in despair. When they were rescued, only fifteen men remained alive.'

'Well, I can see why you wanted to look at this, Jimmy!' remarks Summer. 'Very cheerful! Come on, let's go and see something beautiful.'

'It is beautiful,' Jimmy says. He's always loved art and knows a lot. 'And a seminal moment in French Romantic painting.'

'Not my idea of romance,' Summer says, and takes me by the arm. She seems to sense that this picture is wrong for me. 'Let's go. I don't like it one bit.'

I let her lead me away. As we walk down the gallery, she leans in to me and says, 'Are you okay, Flora? You don't look right at all.'

I gaze over at her and there must be something in my eyes, because her expression changes and she looks suddenly serious. She turns to Jimmy. 'Honey, will you go and get us a table at that place you want to try tonight? I'm worried it's going to be booked out.'

Jimmy regards us both and then understands that we need to be alone. 'Sure,' he says. 'I'll wander back through and look at my favourite Veronese on the way out. I'll catch up with you girls at the restaurant.'

'Great.' Summer waits until he's out of earshot and then pulls me closer to her, her arm linked through mine. 'Okay – so what's up, Flora? I'd have to be some kind of fool not to notice that something's not right with you.'

To my surprise, my eyes fill with tears. As soon as Summer notices, she looks horrified. 'What is it? Is something wrong?' She clutches at me. 'Oh, Flora, what is it? Is it the mysterious boyfriend you went to meet last night?'

'It's all right,' I say, my voice breaking. 'I'm just . . . I'm in love, that's all.'

'In love?' She looks relieved. 'Well, that's good, isn't it?' Then her expression grows worried. 'Or is it? Is he a jerk? Has he hurt you? Is he married? Oh my God, Flora . . . tell me right now, I can't stand this.'

Tears are rolling down my face but I'm laughing anyway. Her concern for me is so comforting, and her ideas of a nightmare scenario so far from the truth. 'He's not married. He might love me, I don't know. I don't think he does. It's just . . . it's been a great strain, that's all.'

'So . . . who is he? Do I know him?' She's curious again, now that the immediate edge has been taken off her worry for me.

'I don't think so.'

'Is he a student? How did you meet him? Come on, I've got a million questions. How long have you been seeing him?'

I hardly know where to start. 'Just a few weeks, I suppose. But it's been very intense.'

We stroll past priceless works of art, oblivious to their beauty.

'Weeks? So it's very early days.' She squeezes my arm. 'I'm happy for you, if you're happy – though I have to say that you don't look all that happy about it.'

'I am, I am.' I sigh. 'I'm just having a reaction, that's all. That picture . . .'

'What's his name? At least tell me that,' demands Summer. 'We can get down to all the other juicy details later.'

'Andrei.'

'Oh – he's Russian?'

I nod.

'And how old?'

'I don't know. Forty?'

'Forty!' she exclaims, and blinks at me. 'That's kind of old for you, isn't it?'

'Is it?' I've barely thought about the difference in our ages since the day we met. It doesn't seem to matter at all when we're together.

'Forty!' Summer seems shocked. 'But ... perhaps he's young at heart.' She obviously doesn't want to rain on my parade. 'So – what does he do?'

'He's a businessman,' I say vaguely. 'He works all over the world. Investments, or something. I don't really know.'

'Hold on.' A suspicion is growing in Summer's eyes. 'A forty-year-old Russian businessman called Andrei ... It's not ... Oh, Flora, it's not ...'

'Not who?' I say, my heart sinking. *Of course, I should have thought. She knows him too. We all do.*

My sister gazes at me almost furiously and hisses, 'Andrei Dubrovski! Say it's not him, Flora, please ...'

'What if it is?' I reply with a touch of defiance in my voice.

'He's dangerous! Dad talks about him sometimes, you must have heard him. He says Dubrovski is in all likelihood a total crook, no better than a gangster! He says he could be mixed up in very bad things and has made some powerful enemies. Oh, Flora, no – not him!'

'All right,' I shoot back. 'It's not him. If that's what you want to hear.' I'm getting angry. I don't want to know all this. The Andrei I know is not this cartoon businessman with baddie associates and a dangerous life. He's a man of flesh and blood, with a beating heart, and a hunger for me

175

that matches mine for him. No one knows him like I do right now.

Summer looks defeated. 'Oh Flora,' she says sadly. 'It is him. I can tell.' She holds my hand, her head drooping a little. 'If you love him, then you love him. But I can't help wishing it was someone else.'

'Don't tell anyone,' I say quickly. 'It's a secret. No one knows. You're the only one I've told. Please – don't breathe a word to Dad or Jane-Elizabeth.'

'Don't worry.' Summer's face is grave. 'Your secret is safe with me.'

Summer tries to rally from the news, but I can tell that it's affected her, even though she's her usual cheerful self all through dinner. There's a distance between us that I hate. I try not to imagine a scenario where I have to choose between her and Andrei.

It's hard to say goodbye to her the next day, but her relentless partying schedule is taking her on to a gathering of her crew in Monte Carlo. Jimmy is returning to LA.

'We'll see each other soon,' Summer says, hugging me. 'I'll come back as soon as I can. Or else we'll meet somewhere. Come to London maybe – I'm going to be there soon for Natasha's twenty-fifth.'

'Or maybe even at home,' I reply.

'Mmm. Maybe.' We exchange looks. Neither of us much wants to be at home these days.

'Will you please take care of yourself?' she asks quietly when she's kissed me goodbye. 'Don't rush into anything, that's all. Promise?'

'I promise,' I reply, wondering what exactly I'm promising. I know she cares and this is her way of telling me. I know she wishes I'd fallen in love with some poverty-stricken budding actor, someone uncomplicated, especially after Jimmy. 'I'm sorry,' I say.

'Don't be. I only want you to be happy, that's all.'

When Jimmy says goodbye, he adds, 'I'm really glad we're friends again, Flora. Really glad.'

'Me too.' I smile at him, meaning it.

'Will you come and see me in LA?'

'I'd love to.'

'Good. You take care. If you ever need me, I'm there for you.'

I look into his handsome face filled with affection. 'Oh Jimmy. If only you weren't gay,' I sigh, then add, 'I'm joking.'

He laughs. 'You had me worried there. Bye, honey, look after yourself.'

When they've gone, I walk around my apartment full of dejection at being alone again. I've still heard nothing from Andrei since our last night together, and there's no word from Olympe either.

But all I can do is wait.

CHAPTER FIFTEEN

I hear nothing from Andrei all the next day. All I can think to do to take my mind off it is to go to classes.

The tutor takes me aside afterwards and asks me where I've been. 'We've hardly seen you lately. This isn't like you, Flora.'

I'm shamefaced. 'I know. I'm sorry. There have been things happening . . . in my private life.'

'This academy is very prestigious. We expect complete dedication from our students. Anything less and we will have to consider your position here.' He looks confidingly at me. 'Besides, Flora, you have talent. I'm casting the show for the end of the year and I have you in mind for a big part. You know that the best agents in town come to our show. The leads almost always get representation. But I can only cast you if you're reliable.'

'I will be,' I promise, repentant at my recent bad behaviour and excited by the prospect of the end of term show. 'I'm sorry. I'd love to be in the show. Things will be better, I promise.'

No more skipping off to buy corsets and boots, I tell myself sternly. *I have to keep myself focused.* But I don't know how I'm going to reconcile my determination to commit to my career with my decision to submit to what Olympe chooses for me.

'Good,' says my tutor. 'I'm very glad to hear it.'

That evening, in the spirit of my renewed commitment, I eat a healthy supper and go to bed early after learning lines for the piece we're working on at the moment.

But in the morning, as I'm getting ready to leave, an email message arrives.

Miss X
Madame commands your presence at a ceremony. Be
at the Cafe Renoir on rue des Anges tonight at exactly
8 p.m. Request to be seated in the middle window.
Place your phone exactly in the centre of the table.
Wear a black dress, with sleeves, that reaches to your
knees and stiletto heels that are eight centimetres high.
Put your hair into a tight ponytail and wear mascara
and red lipstick. Madame prefers Guerlain. Ask at the
counter of Printemps for Madame's shade. Be prepared
to do exactly as you are told. Once inside the cere-
mony, phones and cameras are strictly forbidden.

There is no sign-off.

I stare at it. This will mean shopping. And I have to be at the Academie all day. I can feel the pull of both sides of my life. I need to show my dedication to my drama course, but how can I not show up for Olympe? The thought is actually terrifying. I know it would be the end of everything if I disobeyed.

So . . . I suppose I must obey.

I manage a compromise. At lunchtime, I rush out to Printemps and buy a dress, shoes and the shade of red lipstick that Olympe prefers. Sure enough, the assistant behind the Guerlain counter knows exactly what I want when I ask for Madame's shade, and shows no surprise at the request. It's the rich blood red I've seen on Olympe's own lips. I manage to get back to the academy and only miss half a singing lesson, which I don't mind so much. Singing is not what I most enjoy. After the day's study is ended, I go home to prepare for the evening, half afraid of what awaits and half excited.

Will Andrei be there? I really have no idea what Olympe intends for me.

I wonder if I can be truly submissive or if that will even be demanded of me. As far as I know, I'm going to learn how to bring Andrei to the knowledge that he loves me. And I'm mystified as to what that could be.

As I leave my apartment, dressed exactly as stipulated in the email, I feel like a knight setting out on a quest. Only if I pass the tasks set for me can I win the heart of my true love.

My true love? Andrei?

All I know is that I can't bear to imagine life without him. Isn't that the closest thing to true love there is?

I go to the cafe on rue des Anges as directed. When I ask for the middle window, there's no quibble. The waiter leads me there, to the table that's mysteriously empty in the busy cafe, despite its prime spot.

Olympe's influence must be extremely powerful. She can make everything happen exactly the way she wants.

I sit there and order a glass of red wine, to calm my nerves. Its ruby red colour makes me think of the lipstick I'm wearing, and of blood. I wonder what a cup of blood reminds me of, and then I remember. The Eucharist. Everything Olympe touches seems tinged with symbolism, even this drink of wine as I sit, dressed in my sombre, almost nun-like dress, ready to partake in the rites that Olympe will oversee like a high priestess.

It's 8 p.m. and I'm sitting where I'm supposed to be, the phone on the table in front of me. It pops into life, its screen glowing brightly in the dim cafe. I scoop it up and look at the message.

Finish your drink. Leave the cafe, turn right and go to the end of the road. Turn left and walk straight ahead. Take the third street on your left. Go to number 32 and ring the bell marked 'Cecile'.

I obey, draining my glass and leaving a note on the table to pay for it. Outside the night is dark and cold. It feels as though winter will never end as I walk through the darkness, my heels tripping on the pavement, following my instructions to the letter. No more than seven minutes later, I'm standing in front of the door and there is the bell marked as I was told it would be.

I stare at it, more than a little afraid. Then I reach and press it. There's no going back now. But then, there never was.

A beautiful older woman with a black velvet mask over her eyes, answers the door. I wonder if she is one of the tribe, the women permitted to wear silver masks at Olympe's gatherings. She has rich auburn hair and a milky white skin that I cannot help imagining Olympe would enjoy marking with whips. It would blush and welt most satisfactorily, the ivory staining with bright red in a pleasing contrast.

Am I really thinking this? Is this really me?

'Come in,' she says in a low sweet voice. 'You are expected.' She turns on her heels – exactly eight centimetres high, I notice – and walks away from me. At the end of the tiled hallway, a staircase with a wrought-iron banister curls away. My guide walks down and I follow her into the gloom below. Then we're in another, lower hallway and walking towards a door with red glass panels behind wrought-iron curls.

'Are you ready?' asks my guide in her musical voice. She hands me a black velvet eye mask. 'Put this on.'

I nod and slip the mask over my eyes.

She opens the door and leads me through an antechamber and then into a cavernous space lit by flickering candles and hung with velvet drapes. The scene has been carefully stage managed to create a dark red and black Gothic dream, with more than a hint of a church about it. Candles burn on many-stemmed black iron candelabra. Arrangements of trumpeting lilies, with all their virginal and religious symbolism, release a sweet perfume into the air. Around the room on little wooden chairs sit many observers wearing black, and masked in black velvet eye masks; there are both men and women. The soft strains of a string quartet fill the room but from where, I cannot tell.

'Come. This way.' My guide leads to me to one of the chairs. It's like something from a chapel with a slot behind for prayer books. 'Sit here. You are in a most privileged position. Madame must like you.' She gives me a strange look from behind her mask as I settle myself and then leaves me.

I look out over the room from my place and realise that in the middle, on a strip of red velvet carpet, is a long low stool and beside that a small chair with a polished wooden box next to it. Lights are arranged on the ceiling so that they point downwards on to the long stool, illuminating it with a golden glow. At the far end of the room, where I half expect to see an altar, is a pair of white columns set close together. More lights are directed on to these and I notice that hoops of iron are set into the columns at various intervals.

Oh my goodness – what's going to happen here?

I realise that my heart is racing and my nails are digging into the palms of my hands. I wonder if I'm about to observe my own fate.

She can't make me do anything I don't want to do, I tell myself. But I'm not altogether sure that's true.

The soft boom of a gong fills the room and the music ceases. Now there is an expectant silence and, as a small bell rings, a procession appears from some hidden doorway at the far end of the room. Four figures robed in black, their heads shrouded by hoods, are carrying a sort of stretcher between them, one that is covered in black velvet. On it lies the figure of a woman, and I can see why she cannot walk alone. She is wrapped in bands of pale chiffon, almost like a mummy, her legs bound together by the material, her arms tight at her sides. Her hair is pulled back and clipped out of the way. On her feet she wears extremely high spike sandals and round her neck a white leather studded collar. I can make out cuffs of the same material on her wrists and ankles.

I feel a movement beside me and realise that my auburn-haired guide from earlier is now sitting beside me. In a voice so low that it can scarcely be heard, she murmurs, 'The girl is offering herself to Madame.'

I'd guessed it was something like that.

Olympe wants to show me what submission looks like.

The figures bring the stretcher to the centre of the room

and place it on the stool. The woman lics there unmoving and we all watch her for a while. Her face is utterly impassive, almost like a funeral monument in the soft light trained on her from above. The chiffon around her body glimmers and is almost transparent. I can catch glimpses of her naked body beneath the material. Her nipples are so red I have the sudden idea that they've been coloured with Olympe's favourite lipstick.

At that moment Olympe appears from the hidden doorway and stands alone at the top of the room until all eyes are on her. Music strikes up again from somewhere but it's no longer the delicate string quartet. Now it's a haunting plainchant with a thudding beat beneath it. Olympe looks exactly the same as always, her hair pulled back, her lips bright red, but instead of her customary dark colours she now wears a white robe with long bell sleeves that hang almost to the floor.

The high priestess. I glance at the woman lying on the stool. *And her sacrificial victim.*

It is clear that Olympe, who is surely the architect of this ceremony, has a heightened sense of theatre and ritual.

She walks forward, gliding almost, and approaches the woman on the stretcher. She circles the supine figure, eyeing her carefully and then takes her place on the small chair next to her. One of the black-robed hooded figures comes forward and produces a pair of scissors so large they are almost shears, the blades shining in the light. Beginning at the woman's feet, the figure cuts quickly through the chiffon, slicing the material easily with the sharp blade, until the scissors reach the woman's neck. The chiffon falls away, revealing the woman's naked body in all its vulnerability.

I can't take my eyes off the strange sight, and I can't stop the way my pulse is racing and my breathing coming faster. It is not her nakedness that affects me. Rather, I'm fearful of what will happen to her. That skin looks so fragile, so easy to hurt. I'm also in awe of her courage. She must want this. It's hard to understand it. It has been drummed into me since childhood that I must avoid being hurt – no one must harm me at any cost. And here is someone willing, wanting, to experience what we are all supposed to fear most.

I'm afraid of what I will see, and what it will make me feel.

Olympe opens the polished box at her side and removes things from it. The box is on the other side of her and I can't see what she has in her hand, but she sets to work on the soft white flesh before her with the instruments she has taken out. Soon I can see black clamps on the white flesh, biting into it. They are put on and removed in some kind of order and pattern I don't understand. As Olympe goes about her work, the woman on the stretcher begins to moan and respond to the sensations on her skin. I see that Olympe is carefully attending to the most tender parts of the body in front of her: the red nipples, the soft belly, the delicate folds at the base of it.

We watch for what seems a very long time, as the whimpers and cries grow stronger. At one particularly agonised cry, I go to stand up.

I can't bear this any longer, I'm not going to watch it! It's awful, it's wrong!

But a hand on my arm restrains me. The auburn-haired woman beside me gives me a warning look and shakes her head. 'It's almost over,' she whispers.

At that moment, Olympe swiftly sets about removing all

the instruments she has attached to the body before her, and in another moment she has lifted up her victim and hugged her, whispering softly into her ear.

'After suffering . . . redemption,' whispers my guide. 'The blessings of love.'

I sit back in my seat, caught again by the spell of what is happening. The face of Olympe's victim is radiant; she's smiling even though her face is wet from the tears that the pain has brought forth.

'But . . .' says the woman beside me, 'she has more to endure before she has the final blessing.'

The figures come forward again. Olympe relinquishes her victim and they lift the woman to her feet and take her to the narrow columns at the far end of the room. They stand her with her back to us and, swiftly and efficiently, she is manacled with chains by the cuffs on her ankles and wrists to the hoops on the columns, so that she stands silhouetted before us, her legs and arms spread wide. Her entire back, bottom and thighs are bared to us and to Olympe, who walks forward with a white leather whip, its many slim strands knotted.

The small woman lifts her whip with a practised hand, and with a flick of her wrist, she brings the strands slicing through the air with a crack and they land right across the round buttocks, instantly bringing a rush of redness to the white skin.

The woman cries out, not so loud and with a kind of sigh, and her head droops a little. Her fists clench as she prepares for the next blow, which comes almost immediately, and another follows and another, laid on her in the kind of precise timing I would expect from Olympe. Some blows take her buttocks, others her hips and lower back, and others her thighs, and the woman's cries grow louder as her punishment continues. Olympe shows no mercy, but beats on and on. Around me the observers are sighing too, some making involuntary noises when the whip flicks down viciously on the naked skin, now criss-crossed with stripes, but whether of pity or relish I can't tell.

Beside me, the red-haired woman is breathing fast, her eyes fixed on the woman in chains.

'Madame knows,' she murmurs to me. 'Madame knows exactly how to make suffering beautiful.'

CHAPTER SIXTEEN

I barely know what is happening but I'm walking along a pavement in the dark night, my eye mask discarded on the way. What I've witnessed has left me dazed and in shock, unsure what I feel about anything. All I know is that I need Andrei with such an overwhelming force that I feel I won't be able to go on.

Pulling out my telephone with shaking hands, I send him a message.

Where are you? I must see you now.

I stop walking and lean against the solid stone of a building, feeling as though I can barely support myself. It is almost as though I've been at a crazy party and drunk so much that I no longer have any sense of how I'll get home or even where home is. All I know is that I long to be there.

The phone flashes back into life almost at once.

I'm available to you. Where are you?

I send back:

Where can we meet privately?

He responds:

Tell me where you are.

I look about and manage to see the street name, and the number of the building where I'm standing. I tap out the information and send it to him. Then I lean back against the cold stone, feeling safe again. *Andrei is on his way.*

The car draws up beside me fifteen minutes later. I'm cold now, but still in my strange state, where I'm both dazed and yet in a state of heightened emotion. The door opens and Andrei is inside, beckoning me in. I'm beside him in a second and the door closes. It is the first time I've seen him since I realised in Olympe's drawing room that I love him, and the sight of him makes my heart swell with pleasure. I know nothing except that at last I can feel the hardness of his body, absorb the strength of his maleness. I'm flooded with desire for him and turn my face to his, putting my hands on his cheeks so that I can take possession of his mouth. I begin to kiss him, my tongue probing at his lips and, after an instant, he responds, opening his mouth so that our tongues can meet and we can explore each other with intense hunger.

If Andrei is startled by the ferocity of my kiss then he doesn't show it, but instead answers my need with his own. As the car glides away, we kiss deeply and wildly, aware of nothing but the joy of our mouths meeting like this, and the mutual need to possess each other.

We kiss for long minutes as the driver takes us through Paris, our lust growing. I want to have him right now. I'm fired up beyond what I've ever experienced. I want to take him with the full force of my desire and give myself with complete abandon as well. I know that Andrei can match me, that his desire is equal to mine. Despite that, we don't touch each other but only kiss, the dance of our tongues stimulating a craziness in us that I know will soon be answered – but the anticipation is part of the fun.

At last, the car draws to a halt. We leave each other's mouths with reluctance, and I gather myself together enough to leave the car. We are in an underground car park.

'Where are we?' I ask, looking around.

'Somewhere I did not intend to bring you. But it doesn't seem to matter so much now.'

Andrei places his arm at my waist and guides me towards a lift. He keys in a code and a moment later we are in the silver box, gliding upwards. The lift opens directly into an apartment at the very top of a modern glass penthouse flat with a startling view of Paris laid out below, sparkling in the dark night with thousands of lights.

I step out, looking about me and taking in the luxury of the surroundings. This place is a perfectly designed modern home, everything in it quietly and discreetly very expensive. 'Do you live here?' I ask.

'It's one of my homes.'

'It's beautiful,' I say sincerely. It is – and yet, there is something a little soulless about it. There is not much I can learn about Andrei in this apartment, only about the taste of his interior designer. I feel sorry for him suddenly: the man with no family and no real home. I can't imagine him kicking back here, walking about in his socks and opening a beer while he watches a game on television.

He's over at a polished zinc bar and he turns to look at me. I forget the image of him as a regular guy, and see him as he is right now: elegant and darkly glamorous in his charcoal grey suit, his face craggy and his piercing eyes staring at me in that way that I can't decipher. 'Do you want a drink?' he asks.

I shake my head.

'Are you all right? What were you doing all on your own on that street at this hour?'

'I'd . . . been to a party. I came out, a little drunk. I felt suddenly that I needed you.' *It's almost true. Except that I've only had a glass of red wine tonight.*

'Oh.' Andrei looks a little amused. 'That kind of call for help. That's why you went so crazy in the car.'

I walk towards him, slipping my coat off my shoulders, my lust reigniting at the memory of what happened in the car. My body is on fire at once for him, my need stoked by what I witnessed earlier. As I move towards him, his face changes and his eyes darken.

I know what that means.

We face each other, staring into one another's eyes. Andrei's body seems to ripple with animal strength and I feel the crackle of the attraction between us. It's a powerful thing. It enslaves both of us when we let it.

He takes a step towards me and the next moment we are kissing wildly, not in the prolonged way we did in the car but with a ferocity that means we don't keep our mouths joined for long, we're both too eager to consume each other in other ways. I want to bite the skin on his neck, sink my teeth into his shoulder, lick and taste his flesh, and most of all I want the iron rod of his cock, in my hands, in my mouth and in my depths. We begin to wrestle with each other, struggling to get to each other's body, pulling and plucking at our clothes. He tugs at my dress, yanking the zip down and peeling it off my arms. Without waiting to examine, he's ripping at my bra, wanting it off. We want to be naked now. I push his jacket down and he frees his arms, then I pull at the buttons on his shirt, fiddling with them longer than I want, but then, a second would be too long. At last I can open the crisp cotton front and see his broad chest. I bury my face in it, smelling him, kissing him, letting my hands travel all over his skin. It doesn't last long. He wants me out of my dress completely, out of my knickers, out of everything so that we can make love.

The passion between us is growing more intense as we reveal ourselves to each other, our naked flesh pressing against one another, the heat of arousal burning between us. Everywhere we touch tingles and burns, and all we both desire is to feel our bodies united, as close as they can be.

Andrei is undressed now, his athlete's body firm and hard, his cock strong at his belly. I dip my head so that I can suck it, kissing it roughly, then drop down so I can take his balls in my mouth, licking them hard as I do. I want to feel every inch of him with my tongue, and give him my body in return. He pulls me up and we press our naked bodies together, my breasts squashed against him, his hands reaching down to caress my bottom and finger the groove between my legs. He pushes me firmly to the floor and we're lying there together, kissing, our hands roaming everywhere, feeling the delicious nakedness that promises so much pleasure. I find it exciting that the windows are uncovered and we can glimpse the great city below us while we make wild love without fear of being seen. We're exposed and yet private, and the thought makes me even hungrier to possess him.

Our mouths are desperate for one another; we are biting and licking, kissing and nibbling, wanting to suck each other's nipples, then graze skin with teeth, licking long strokes on each other. Our hands are everywhere, finding the secret places, digging into the flesh, stroking and sliding in wetness and against hot, hard flesh.

Andrei turns round so that he can apply his mouth to my entrance and I moan joyously as his tongue probes me, tickles my bud and then returns to my entrance, pressing inside me. When his tongue is busy on my clit, his fingers are deep inside me. I seize his cock and make him move so that he's over me. He presses down and I take one of his balls in my mouth while I rub his prick, moving the skin up and down as I lick the rough surface. Then he moves so that I can manoeuvre his cock right into my mouth and he lowers it deep into my throat so I can give him as much pleasure as possible. We work away on each other for long minutes, giving and receiving pleasure, half lost in the bliss we are getting as we kiss each other to heights of ecstasy.

My hips are moving and I'm about to come hard on his mouth while I've got his prick deep in my throat, when Andrei moves again. His cock pops out of my mouth and he turns round, moving me on to my hands and knees as he does. Within a moment, he's entered me hard from behind and is on his knees fucking me roughly. I throw my head back, groaning as the tip of his prick hits home deep inside me. He slaps my bottom as he rams it home, then reaches round in front and strums on my swollen bud that longs for his fingers to tickle as hard as they can.

'I'm riding you,' he says, his voice hoarse. 'I'm riding you hard.'

'Harder,' I beg, and he thrusts on, slapping my bottom and then rubbing my clit. I don't know how hard I can take this action, it's too delicious, too desperately exciting, to be naked up here above the city, with Andrei's hard cock thrusting into me, his fingers stimulating me unbearably, the palm of his hand slapping my arse whenever he wants to make me wriggle and push out my bottom to let him in a bit deeper.

I can't take it. I must come, I can't fight it now. I'm crying out with every deep thrust, taking him as he rides me.

'I'm going to come,' I cry out. My whole body is jerking with the ferocity of what I'm experiencing.

'Come,' he orders roughly and puts his hand over my mound, moving his whole palm over me hard, the heel of his hand rubbing down on my bud, and with that I begin to shriek and spasm convulsively as the orgasm takes me. I shake with the force of the pleasure for what seems like minutes and as it subsides, Andrei pulls out his prick. He turns me round and watches me panting with the force of my orgasm as I half sit, half lie, naked beneath him. Kneeling there, looking like a god, he takes his rearing prick in his hand and with several fast strokes he brings himself to a climax, bringing the head of it close to me as he does so that his spending spills all over my chest and breasts as it leaves him in hard pumps. I rub it into my body and take what is on my fingers and lick it down, relishing the hot, bitter-salt tang of it.

He sighs with pleasure as the last of it drips from his cock. I smile up at him, my legs still open to him.

'That was very nice,' I purr.

'Very,' he says, smiling back at me. 'A most pleasurable way to begin proceedings.'

I laugh. 'Your stamina is impressive. And . . .' I stroke his cock lightly. 'It's not the only thing.'

*　　　*　　　*

We go through to the bedroom and into Andrei's bathroom, and shower together. By the time we've exited the steamy cubicle we are aroused again, Andrei's cock standing proud and evidently eager for more.

We go to his bed and this time we make slow, infinitely tender and satisfying love. The wild ferocity has passed and now we take our time with sweet caresses, long kisses, gentle murmurings, until at last we come together in a delicious intense climax that's all the sweeter for the fierce agony of what went before.

When it's all over, I lie against his chest, running my fingers through the dark-blond hair there, savouring the musky scent of his skin. My fingertips run over a strangely raised patch of skin and I return to it a few times, tracing the pattern. There is a definite pattern to it, it's not simply random. After a moment, I prop myself up on my elbow and gaze at it more carefully in the low light from the bedside lamp.

'What's this?' I ask.

Andrei has been dozing beside me, almost asleep with the soporific effect of our recent exertions. His eyes open lazily. 'What?'

I touch the scars again. 'These.' Leaning forward, I peer at them, making them out beneath the dark curls. They are dark purple and they suddenly become clear as I stare. They are letters. A large O and then a small curling d and then an R. I know what they are but I wait for Andrei to say.

He hesitates and then says in a neutral voice, 'They are Olympe's initials, of course.'

I'd guessed but I'm still astonished. 'What are they doing on your chest?'

Andrei slides his dark blue gaze over to me. 'When they

were put there, I was clean-shaven. It was one of the conditions Olympe imposed on me. No body hair, at all.' He laughs a low throaty laugh. 'If you ladies think I don't understand the reality of waxing, you're quite mistaken. I was as smooth as a baby, all over.'

'But . . . her initials?' I trace them again with my fingers. 'How did she do this?'

'With a red-hot iron. It's a branding.'

'What?' I look up at him, horrified. He let her brand his skin, like a piece of livestock? 'She made you do that?'

'Oh no. I asked her to. I had the branding iron made up myself and sent it to her in a satin-lined box with a note begging her to give me this as proof that I was hers.'

I'm silent as I take this in. 'I don't understand,' I say at last. I think of the ceremony I witnessed this evening and the way the woman in chiffon gave herself utterly to whatever Olympe chose to do to her, the way she took the punishment of the whipping. By the end, she'd hung exhausted from her chains, her back and bottom a mass of red, blood just beginning to break through the skin. When Olympe had retired, handing her whip to one of the hooded figures and leaving the room, the acolytes had released the woman and begun a whole new ceremony of tending to her wounds and restoring her, an activity that became increasingly lascivious as the bowls of water they started with were replaced with lips and tongues. As it began to reach its climax, the people around me began moaning with their own heightened sensations and I became aware of movement everywhere. I got to my feet and, ignoring the hand of the auburn-haired woman on my arm, I stumbled out into the street and then called Andrei.

Why do they do it?

Then, I realise with a growing sense of appalled wonder that I am on the brink of doing the same myself. Olympe is working on me slowly to take me to the same place that Andrei has been, that the woman tonight went to.

Andrei says, 'It was some years ago now, a time in my life when Olympe gave me something I desperately needed. I'd achieved everything I set out to do. I was hugely powerful. No one dared disobey or gainsay me. A man cannot live with that for too long without becoming a monster. I craved a place where I could surrender everything and become a vassal myself. Olympe came into my life at that time and gave me that necessary release. Like a Caesar with a servant to remind him he is mortal, I needed Olympe to remind me that I was not infallible, a creature who could suffer and bleed like everyone else.' He stops and is silent for a moment as he remembers that time. I wrap my fingers around his and hold his hand. 'I was intoxicated by her power and by the sweetness of submission to her will. I would have done anything for her.' His dark gaze holds mine. 'I would have let her beat me to death if she'd wanted.'

I stare back, frightened. This is more than I can really understand, and certainly more than I ever want to experience.

'But of course, she didn't,' Andrei says. 'And in the end, we all know that our fantasies are contained within the greater reality that there will be no death in our games. The aim, after all, is ultimate sensation, not the end of sensation.'

I release a breath I didn't even know I was holding. 'But you still let her do that to you.'

'At the time it was the least I could do.' He grips my fingers in return and with the other hand he strokes my hair.

197

'But that is all a long time ago now. I don't have those compulsions or needs. I've been humbled in other ways.'

He means by Beth.

I lie back and wonder whether I should tell him about the ceremony I witnessed tonight, but I have a feeling it would anger him so I keep quiet. Instead I imagine a different ceremony, in which a branding iron is heated to sizzling white-orange and pressed into the flesh of the man beside me. The image makes me gasp with sorrow at his pain.

'Are you all right?' he asks, kissing my cheek softly.

I nod. Tiny hot tears are stinging my eyes. 'She hurt you.'

'Don't worry,' he says in a low voice. 'The pain was long ago and they say the marks will fade in time.'

But I can't help being afraid. *Does she still own you, Andrei? Is it Olympe, rather than Beth, that I should fear?*

CHAPTER SEVENTEEN

When I wake I have no idea where I am, and then I realise that I'm in bed with Andrei. His warm body is pressed against mine, heavy with sleep, his breath is hot on my cheek.

This is the first time we've ever slept together.

I lie there for a long time, relishing the closeness and the normality between us. We are like a regular couple, sharing their bed, waking up together. I revel in the way we're pressed together, my heart full of tenderness for him.

Olympe is right. I do love him. I know Summer and the whole world think he's bad news, but I can't do anything about that. I know he's damaged, and cold and all of that. But I can't help it.

I reach out a hand and stroke it through his soft dark-blond hair, noticing the shards of silver at the temples. He sighs in his sleep and turns a little closer to me, nuzzling in to my skin.

He probably hardly knows what he is missing in his life. He doesn't know what he needs.

The truth of what Olympe said to me suddenly bursts over me. That's why Andrei has to be led to knowledge of his own emotions. He has no idea of love. He's never really felt it. He is unconscious of what he craves. The way he hungers for sweet closeness in his sleep shows that.

But what about what he feels for Beth?

I'm surer than ever that his emotions for Beth are utterly bound up in the fact that he could never have her. The one thing in his life that wouldn't yield to him.

Beth and Olympe. The two women who've held Andrei in the palms of their hands.

But what does that mean for me? I've yielded to him, submitted. Does that mean I have to dominate him in order to make him love me? Is that the lesson that Olympe will teach me?

I lie there, kissing Andrei's bare shoulder and wondering what will happen next.

When Andrei wakes, there is an unusual awkwardness between us, perhaps because we're unaccustomed to going through the morning rituals with each other. We've never done such mundane things as shower, dress and breakfast together and Andrei seems a little uncomfortable with it.

But I love seeing him in his crisp white shirt, his hair damp from the shower, as he sits at the bar of his minuscule kitchen eating some cereal. He looks as fresh as a schoolboy ready for the first lesson of the day.

'My housekeeper will be here soon,' he says gruffly.

'I understand.' I've showered but I've had to wear the clothes I had on last night – my demure black dress and the high-heeled shoes. 'I must go home and change for class.'

Andrei gazes down at my outfit and then looks up at my face. For a moment I think I see the faintest look of suspicion on his face – he must have seen women at Olympe's ceremonies wearing this uniform before – but it's gone before I can be sure. After all, what's so unusual about a black dress and high heels? I'm not wearing the giveaway shade of lipstick now.

'I'll text François,' Andrei says, spooning more cereal into his mouth. He eats with a bear-like relish. 'He'll drive you home.'

'Thank you.' I smile at him. 'And will we meet again soon?'

He fixes me with a dark stare. 'I don't know,' he says slowly. I can tell he's thinking of our arrangement and how, slowly and perhaps even inevitably, it is being changed. The fact I'm here in his apartment is demonstration of that. The intensity of our lovemaking has gone beyond the mere comfort we agreed upon and become something else altogether. I can sense that, and I know Andrei can too.

I gather my coat. 'I will wait to hear from you,' I say.

Andrei continues to stare at me. Then he says stiffly, 'And . . . Jimmy. Is he still in Paris?'

'No,' I say. 'He's gone back to LA.' I return his gaze without blinking. 'He's become my friend.'

Andrei's expression does not change. After a moment, he says, 'I see.'

'I hope that won't change things between us.'

He looks away, returning to his breakfast. 'We'll have to wait and see,' he replies. Then he lifts up his phone. 'I'll text François now. He'll be waiting for you by the time you reach the car park.'

'Goodbye.' I smile at him.

He looks up briefly. 'Goodbye.'

As I walk to the lift, I think, *Olympe is right. It's not going to be easy for Andrei to realise what we have. I must do whatever she says.*

The next message from Olympe comes later that day, when I'm showering after a dance class. It says:

201

Miss X
Madame requests your presence this afternoon for tea
at 4 p.m. precisely.

With a sinking heart, I realise that I will have to cut my favourite class, my tutor's acting workshop. He's already said that I must attend if I'm to have a hope of getting the role he's marked out for me in the end-of-term production.

I try to imagine explaining to Olympe that I can't make her appointment and instantly I see a mental picture of her in her white robes lifting her whip.

I'll tell my tutor I'm sick. He might forgive me this time.

I arrive at Olympe's house ten minutes early. I've never been so careful to be on time for anyone before, but I still remember the vicious tug on my hair when I was late on that first occasion and I don't particularly want to experience it again.

At two minutes to four, I ring on the buzzer and at four o'clock precisely I'm being shown into the drawing room where Olympe sits on the sofa, her cat beside her. She's as neat as usual in a black jumper and skirt, a string of pearls falling almost to her waist.

A beautiful tea set is laid out on the table in front of her. A proper table, I'm relieved to see. Her black leather-clad servant comes in with a pot of tea and places it on the table before retiring without a word.

'How are you, my dear?' Olympe asks, pouring out the tea. The clear brown liquid steams as it rises in the delicate porcelain.

'Very well, thank you, Madame.'

'How did you find last night's ceremony?' Her grey eyes flick up to steal a glance at me before she returns to pouring the tea.

'It was . . . interesting.'

'Interesting?' The pencilled eyebrows go up again. 'I see. I hoped for a little more than that.'

'Of course, Madame,' I say hurriedly. 'It was very moving. I was most affected by it.'

'I should hope so. Not everybody is granted the privilege of witnessing such a thing.' She passes me the tea. There is no offer of milk, which is how I drink it, in the English way. I decide that the wisest course is to accept the tea as it is and thank her quietly. 'You are very lucky. My young acolyte naturally had to agree to your presence.'

'I see.'

'Nothing happens without consent, my dear, I'm sure you understand that.'

'Yes, Madame.'

'Good.' She gives me another of her penetrating looks. 'Now. I wonder if you truly understood the import of what you saw last night.'

'I think I did,' I say hesitantly. I don't want to sound arrogant. 'I know how far Andrei went to submit to you – I saw the brand on his chest.'

'Did you?' She smiles in that rather sly way of hers. 'Yes. That was his own idea but I liked it very much. It showed a grace of mind that appealed to me. And, of course, I approved of his desire to submit entirely to me.'

'Madame, do I understand that you think I should submit to Andrei in the way that he once submitted to you?'

Her eyes glitter almost dangerously. 'I believe that only

by showing the extent of your devotion will you awaken in him what lies dormant there.'

'I see.' I think about this for a moment. 'But how will I do what you suggest?'

'It is quite simple.' Olympe sips at her tea, still watching me over the rim of her cup. When she's swallowed the tea, she returns the cup to its saucer. 'I am willing to help you because I remain deeply fond of Andrei and I believe that you two are well suited. I'd go so far as to say that you are two halves of a whole. It is quite clear to me that you find your completion in the other. I also sense great potential in you, which is why I'm urging this course.'

I wait while she sips again at her tea, then she continues.

'I will arrange a private ceremony for you. Only members of my tribe will be permitted to be present, with Andrei too. You will oblate yourself before me for his pleasure, and I will, at the proper time, hand over the control of your submission to him. When he takes the instruments from me, he will understand the depth of your desire to be his. He will not fail to respond, my dear. It will be the beginning of the most beautiful journey of your life.'

I swallow hard, my heart beginning to pound at the thought of it. I'm afraid but there is also a strange excitement in the idea that I will be in the same position as that chiffon-wrapped woman of last night. At Olympe's words, I'm filled with a wild desire to give myself to Andrei to the ultimate extent. I know with utter certainty that I love him and I am suddenly sure that I'm prepared to go as far as necessary to convince him of the fact. Olympe is so sure that this will make him understand that he loves me, and I believe her. It makes perfect sense.

'How far must I go?' I ask.

She looks at me with that penetrating gaze. 'How far are you prepared to go?'

I pause for a moment on the brink and then I say firmly, 'As far as I need to.'

'Good. Good. You shall have your instructions. I will make the arrangement.' She glances at the teacup in front of me. 'Now, drink your tea, my dear, or I shall be forced to pour it over your hand. And you don't want that, do you?

My tutor accepts my excuse of a terrible migraine keeping me away from class, and he says I may be allowed another chance to audition for him. He chooses for me Ophelia's mad speech from *Hamlet,* and I begin to work on it whenever I can. The weekend passes very quietly. I stay in my apartment learning the words and recovering from everything that happened last week.

Even so, it's hard to relax. I move around the rooms, agitated and feeling as though I've drunk far too much coffee. My heart is continually racing and I find myself sighing and exclaiming at my thoughts, even when I'm hardly aware of what they are.

I've committed to something that terrifies me, but the idea that I'm also on a beautiful journey is seductive and exciting. My imagination is haunted by images of the naked figure strung between the pillars, and my sleep is disturbed by hot, passionate dreams in which my desires don't know any bounds. I want Andrei in every possible way, and I only wish there was a way to have his prick in my mouth and in my depths at the same time. I want him to possess me utterly at the same time as I make him slake my needs.

Over those two quiet days, as I come to terms with what I've agreed to, I begin to understand that my submission is also an act of dominance. By surrendering myself, I'll also be demanding something. Nothing is taken without something being given. I begin to see that now.

The only reminders of the outside world are the emails that are coming from Summer, bright, breezy and chatty and yet with an underlying current of anxiety in them. She wants to know how things are with Andrei. She wants me to stay in touch with her. I get the impression she's worried that I will vanish away with him, as Freya has with Miles Murray. I reply to her, hoping that my messages will allay her fears. Nothing will come between us, I reassure her. I might for the moment be taken up with Andrei and everything between us, but I will never leave her entirely.

But I cannot see into the future and what awaits me there. *I only hope that's true.*

On Monday a message arrives.

> *Miss X*
> *Go to the Guerlain counter at Printemps and ask for the package that Madame has left for you.*

As soon as classes are over, I head to the store. The same assistant is behind the counter and I wonder what has happened to her in the past that she is in on Olympe's secrets.

'I'm Miss X. I'm here for Madame's package,' I say.

The impassive assistant merely nods, and then takes a long narrow black package from beneath the counter. She hands it to me.

'Thank you.'

She nods again. I put it in my bag and leave.

In the privacy of my apartment, I open my bag and take out the package. I put it on the table and stare at it for a long time before I open it. When I do, the lid lifts easily, revealing a white satin-lined interior.

I let out a shuddering sigh.

Inside the box, cushioned by the satin, lies a long rod of black iron. I lift it out and see that at one end there is a circle and in the circle are two letters written backwards in dark iron. They are AD.

So that's what she wants me to do.

CHAPTER EIGHTEEN

Now that I've made my decision, I'm calmer and my fears – the dark, unnamed ones – begin to retreat. I know now what I need to be afraid of.

As I lie in the bath, looking down at my unmarked body, I wonder where she will put the brand. Will it be on my breast, the way Andrei took her initials on his chest? Or will it be on my arm, or my back? Or perhaps on the whiteness of my thigh or buttock?

When I'm feeling brave, I take out the iron from its white satin bed and look at it. It's heavy and cold and I imagine it white hot and smoking, ready to impress the mark on my flesh. The circle of iron is small and the letters are not large. She has obviously considered the fact that I cannot be marked with anything too large.

Then I put it away, full of trepidation and that dark excitement that lives permanently at the base of my stomach.

I go every day to my classes, and I'm a model student now. I do not go out at all. What is the point when this great event is waiting for me? I don't know if I could bear to be in a bar with my student friends, acting as though life is perfectly normal when I'm about to undertake this extraordinary trial.

I hear nothing from Andrei for the rest of the week, until Saturday dawns, bright and sunny, the first pretty day we've had all winter. The sky is a light blue, the sun is shining as hard as it can through the still cool air, and there is the faintest hint of spring approaching. I open my windows and look out at the fresh day with my spirits lifting.

At that moment, my phone chirrups and a message appears.

It's a beautiful day. Shall we spend it together?
A

My heart leaps with joy.

Yes, I reply at once. *Where shall we meet?*

The Tuileries Gardens. We'll start there.

I only understand how much I've missed him when I see him sitting on a bench in the place we've agreed, waiting for me. He's wearing a blue jacket over a pale shirt and buff-coloured twill trousers, smart but casual in that particularly European way. I hope I'm not too underdressed in jeans, a navy silk collared top and a white cotton jacket, teamed with gaucho-heeled brown ankle boots.

Andrei looks up as I approach, his face at once beaming with a smile I've rarely seen on his face – pure and uncomplicated. He stands up and holds out his arms.

'Flora! You look beautiful.' He embraces me and kisses my cheeks.

I laugh happily. I don't know if I've ever felt so sure that Andrei is happy to see me – not because we're going to satisfy each other, but simply because I'm me. It's a wonderful feeling.

'Thank you!' I do a twirl. 'As you can see, I'm all dressed up. What are we going to do today?'

'Today?' Andrei's blue eyes sparkle. 'I'm feeling very care-free and ready for some fun. Today – we enjoy ourselves!'

'That sounds great. What shall we do first?'

'First, we'll walk. Then we'll find somewhere for coffee. Then we'll visit a little curiosity shop I've been meaning to go to. Then I would like to see the Tomb of Napoleon, and in the military museum they have one of his hats and a coat, along with some of his travelling gear. I fancy taking a look at the belongings of a man who was unable to conquer Russia. After that – lunch. Then we're so close to the Eiffel Tower that I think we should go up it and be like proper tourists. Have you ever been up? No? Well, there we are then. You obviously should. Then we'll follow our noses back into town and find somewhere for tea. How does that sound?' He looks almost boyish with glee as he outlines our itinerary.

'It sounds marvellous,' I declare. 'Let's begin.'

We seem to be under a magic spell that day. Everything works out perfectly and neither of us puts a foot wrong. I feel at my most vivacious and amusing, and I make Andrei laugh all the time with my silly jokes. We walk without much caring where we go, except that we are heading west, and whenever somewhere catches our eye, we go inside to discover what treasures might lie within. We walk for miles – I've forgotten how enormous Paris is – until at last we stop for coffee and almond tart, not in a swanky place but in a down-to-earth working man's cafe, where the tables are bolted to the walls and the seats are coated in a shiny faux leather. All the time we chatter aimlessly, telling stories and musing on the impressions we have of the people around us. We find Andrei's curio shop and it's a funny old place, with its ancient proprietor sitting surrounded by glass cases full of his collection of oddments. Every now and then, among the rubbish, we find something to exclaim over – a pretty portrait miniature done in wax or a medal celebrating the victory at Austerlitz – and after an hour or so of browsing amongst the mounds of things, we each choose one thing to buy. Andrei selects an antique map of Paris from before the Third Republic, which he arranges to be sent to his penthouse apartment. I think hard before I choose an exquisite cameo brooch, with the head of Artemis in white upon a background of palest pink.

'It's beautiful,' Andrei says. 'It is just right for you.'

'Yes, I love it,' I say, holding it up, delighted.

'I would like to see you wear it against a white lace blouse,' he says solemnly. 'With your hair pulled back into a bun, like a demure little governess.' He presses his lips close to my ear. 'And only I would know what passion burns beneath your pure exterior.'

A delicious thrill runs through me. I cast a glance at the shop owner in case he has heard, but he seems oblivious to us as he examines his treasures through a magnifying glass behind his little counter.

'That sounds very tempting,' I breathe.

'So it should.' His eyes contain the look of desire in them and I draw in a sharp breath. 'Now. I think our appointment is with the dead.'

Half an hour later we are gazing down at Napoleon's tomb as it sits below us in the grand rotunda of the church of Les Invalides. It's a simple piece with a classical purity, and very impressive, a slightly squat box carved in a dark red stone and sitting on a plinth of green granite.

'He's in there?' I ask. 'I thought he died on an island in the middle of nowhere.'

'That's right. They brought him back here afterwards – well, what was left of him,' Andrei says. 'He died on St Helena, and I think it was some years later that he was interred here.'

We both stare at the tomb for a while.

'One of the greatest men who ever lived,' Andrei says quietly, 'even if he did try and take Moscow.'

After we've seen enough of the great man's tomb, we go into the military museum and spend a long time wandering among the glass cases full of uniforms and weapons, until at last I don't think I want to see another epaulette or red coat with hundreds of brass buttons all over it. Even Napoleon's coat – a rather tame dark green after all the jazzier uniforms – and his famous tricorn hat leave me feeling rather cold, while Andrei exclaims over them.

'I think perhaps ... lunch?' he asks, when he sees my lack of excitement.

'Lunch,' I say gratefully.

We find a boulevard cafe with views over Les Invalides and towards the Eiffel Tower, its famous iron structure soaring upwards against the blue sky.

'Shall we go up?' Andrei asks, after we've eaten our omelettes and salad.

I wrinkle my nose with a slight sense of disdain. 'Like a tourist?'

'Don't be so grand,' rebukes Andrei with a smile. 'What's wrong with being a tourist occasionally? Better than always being a world-weary sophisticate! Come on – I dare you to climb it!'

'The stairs?' I say disbelievingly.

'I dare you ...'

'You're on,' I say, confident that my dance classes and

the Pilates I regularly do will see me to the top without a problem.

An hour later, we stand on the top of the tower, buffeted by strong winds, both of us breathless and red in the face and agreeing that it was harder than we expected.

'A little more scary too,' I say, speaking loudly so my voice can be heard over the whipping wind. 'We're so high up! I'm sure I can feel the tower swaying.'

'You're not afraid, are you?' he asks, looking askance at me. 'Not you.'

'Of course I'm not! It's just . . .' I gaze out at the city spreading out before me in all directions, with the glint of gold on the gilded churches, the grand white buildings, the Seine curving away, and Sacré-Coeur with its Eastern-looking dome far away across the city. 'We're so high. Imagine if we fell . . .'

'I would never let anything happen to you,' Andrei says and the next moment he's taken me in his arms and is kissing me hard, his mouth warm and inviting as the cold wind beats around us.

Our romantic day includes a couple of hours browsing among the Impressionist masterpieces in the Musée d'Orsay, and rich hot chocolates topped with whipped cream in the cafe behind the clock face at the top. I can't believe how easy it is to be with Andrei. He's knowledgeable without being a show-off and I can tell that he has a broad expertise about art.

'I've always loved art,' he says. 'I'm a collector. I have some fine pieces. I've got a Millet and a Tissot – I saw you admiring those artists in the gallery downstairs. I'll show you them some day.'

213

'I'd love that,' I reply. I noticed some art on the walls of his penthouse apartment the other day, but it was modern abstract and I hadn't recognised the style. 'What else do you have?'

He shrugs. 'A Picasso or two. A Matisse. Some very fine Cézannes. A couple of Monets. Also, a tiny Renoir which I happen to love. Those are the best of my Impressionists, I suppose.'

I laugh. 'Yes – that does sound like a nice little collection,' I joke.

He smiles at me, aware suddenly of how ridiculous it sounds to mention so casually the masterpieces he owns. 'Like I said, I'll show you. I had a very fine Fragonard that Beth found for me—' He stops, catching himself up, and then says casually, 'but I don't have that any more. In fact, I haven't bought any art for a while, since my dealer very sadly died of cancer.'

'Oh. I'm sorry.' I try to pretend I didn't notice Beth's name or the way it made him stop short, a pained expression on his face.

It's the only sour note in our otherwise lovely day, and we try to put it behind us as quickly as we can.

Dinner is in a restaurant near Andrei's apartment, in a basement where he's clearly well known. The waiter brings a menu but he scarcely looks at it, ordering a wiener schnitzel with fries and creamed spinach. It sounds delicious so I order the same, and we eat ravenously with the accompaniment of a bottle of good strong red wine. I tell him all about my course at drama school, and the preparation I'm doing for my speech as Ophelia.

'But what do you intend to do when all this drama school

is over?' Andrei asks, spearing several fries at once on his fork.

'Well . . .' I blink at him. 'Become an actress, I suppose.'

'Really?' He looks bemused. 'That's what you want to do? Do you want to be famous?'

'No,' I say firmly. 'I want to act.'

He makes a dismissive face. 'People become actors to be famous.'

'Not all of them,' I counter. 'And certainly not me.'

He gazes at me with curiosity. 'You're not like the usual actress type then,' he remarks. 'They usually want to be adored.'

'Not me,' I say, and lean towards him with a conspiratorial smile. 'I want the opposite. I want to be anonymous!'

He laughs heartily. 'That's why you're Miss X, of course.'

'Of course,' I agree.

He looks at me oddly. 'One day, perhaps, you'll have to tell me your real name. Perhaps there's a reason why you don't want me to know it.' He gives me a playful glance. 'Are you really a princess or something?'

I blink and look away. 'No. I'm an average girl. But I'm also an actress, and I love to play a role. So for now, for you, I'm Miss X.' I shrug. 'That's all there is to it.'

'If you say so,' Andrei says. He doesn't seem that disturbed, I'm relieved to see. 'I'm happy with you as you are, Miss X or whoever.'

Those throwaway words fill me with joy.

That evening we go back to the penthouse, and make love like an ordinary couple. We go to his bed and, gently and tenderly, he kisses me all over until I'm begging him to enter me. The sex is not the crazy, passionate kind that usually sends us wild, but I find it beautiful as he gazes into my eyes while he moves deep inside me. We touch each other with a kind of tenderness we've rarely shared, caressing skin, adoring curves and muscles, sucking and kissing with slow intensity, until we shudder to a mutual climax so delicious, I'm surprised to find my face wet with tears afterwards.

'Are you all right?' he asks with concern when he sees my damp cheeks. 'Did I hurt you?'

'No . . . no . . . I'm not upset, I'm happy.' I can't explain to him how moving I found it to experience such natural sweetness in his arms.

Afterwards, we fall asleep together, Andrei drifting off first, his head pressed to my chest. As I look down at his dark-blond head against my breast, I wonder if soon he will be resting his cheek against his own initials.

CHAPTER NINETEEN

The awkwardness that was between us last time I stayed the night has completely gone. We breakfast together, chatting and laughing, as though it's something we do all the time. I head off to go to drama school, glad that this time I thought to put a change of underwear and a toothbrush in my handbag, just in case.

We say goodbye with a kiss and a promise to speak very soon, like a normal couple.

I'm making good time, so I take a scenic walk back to the Academie, enjoying a walk through the streets of Paris before the streets become really busy. As I wander into St Germain, I think back over yesterday and everything that happened.

Did we really kiss like that at the top of the Eiffel Tower, like a couple of lovestruck teenagers?

I laugh at the memory. Yesterday was so normal, capped off by the almost novel experience of delicious but undramatic sex, that I can't help wondering if my arrangement with Olympe is necessary.

We're practically like a couple now. We are in all but name. Perhaps Andrei is coming to the realisation that he loves me without the need for me to do anything drastic . . .

I hope suddenly and fervently that Olympe has not yet scheduled the ceremony. Just a few more days and perhaps I'll be able to tell her that we don't need any strange rituals and sacrifices.

I really hope so.

I walk along with a bounce in my step, enjoying the fragrance of early mornings that floats through the Paris streets. Everywhere seems to be perfumed with that particular aroma of croissants and coffee, and I realise that I would love to have a coffee myself. I choose a likely looking place – a bakery with a blue awning outside and the kind of queue that is short and yet somehow reassuring that the place is a worth a wait. A moment later, I'm at the end of the queue, thinking about my forthcoming audition and hoping that some of the trickier lines have lodged in my memory.

'Flora?' The voice breaks into my consciousness, dragging me back from the place in my imagination. 'What are you doing here?'

I blink, surprised. I know that voice. Who is talking to me? My vision lands on a familiar face, one I last saw a few weeks ago. On her wedding day.

'Beth?' I reply wonderingly.

She smiles. 'How lovely to see you. But what are you doing in this neck of the woods? I thought you lived in the Marais.' She looks fresh and pretty in a white A-line coat, dark cropped trousers and flat black lace-ups, and she's carrying a baguette and bag of croissants.

'Yes ... I do.' My face is growing hot, and I'm full of confusion. I ought to be happy to see Beth, she's been nothing but nice to me and I know that she helped Freya in her hour of need but I can't help a feeling of horror creeping over me at the sight of her. I try to keep my composure. 'I stayed with a friend last night. But what are you doing in Paris?'

Beth rolls her eyes and says, 'Dominic's work! Lucky for

him I'm so mobile and can do my job all over the world. He never stops flitting about. His latest deal has brought him back to Paris to talk to some billionaire about investment. He has a flat here, which is a relief.' She gives me a confiding look. 'I can't stand hotels. I like to feel at home.'

'I thought you were on honeymoon,' I say faintly.

Beth laughs. The queue edges forward and I step a little closer towards the bakery. 'Honeymoon! We had about three days of that before Dominic was itching to get back to work. But . . .' She smiles happily. 'Things are so lovely that I feel as if I'm on permanent honeymoon at the moment.'

'I'm glad to hear it,' I say sincerely. My immediate feeling of dread on seeing her is subsiding. She has no interest in Andrei, she's plainly as deeply in love with Dominic as ever.

'But how are you? And how is Freya?'

'I think she's fine,' I say slowly. 'I haven't heard anything from her lately but she warned me that might be the case.'

Beth nods. 'After everything that happened, she needed some of the quiet life to recover. I'm sure she's fine. She always said she would let us know the minute she needed anything.' She fixes me with a candid look. 'And you, Flora? You look a little . . . different.'

My wretched cheeks start to flush again and I'm sure she can read everything on my face. I have a strange desire to tell her everything. After all, she must know Andrei just about as well as anyone. Perhaps she could tell me more about his elusive character.

But she would see him completely differently to the way I see him. I don't want to hear more character assassinations of the kind that Summer was so quick to make. I owe Andrei the honour of taking him as I find him.

219

Beth is still regarding me steadily and I say with a slight stammer, 'I'm doing just fine. My course is great. I'm going to be a lead in the end-of-term show, I think.'

'That's good news. You must tell me when it is. If we're here, I'd love to see it.' The queue moves forward again, taking me into the interior of the shop itself. Beth says, 'I ought to get back to Dominic. He's like a bear until he's had his breakfast. Keep in touch, won't you, Flora? Maybe we can have lunch together and catch up properly. Goodbye.'

'Yes, that would be lovely. Goodbye.' We kiss each other's cheeks politely and I watch her go, walking off back to the straightforward happiness of her married life. I envy her and all she's got. But I'm also afraid.

What will Andrei do when he finds out Beth is here? I can't tell him. I just can't.

Everything we have suddenly looks in doubt.

After our romantic day, I hear nothing from Andrei again for twenty-four hours. The gaps between his messages are becoming more agonising, not less. As we grow closer, I expect more from him, more signs that he thinks of me when I'm not there and not simply when he desires sex. Waiting for another email is agony, but I can do nothing else. I don't want to badger him with messages if he doesn't want it. I'm sure that would be the worst thing I could do with Andrei, who needs to feel in control.

I find solace in going about my routine, attending all my classes and pouring my heightened emotions into my work. I sometimes think that if I didn't have the outlet of acting, I'd be locked up somewhere, or on a bucketful of pills.

Beating all the time at the back of my mind is the

knowledge that Beth is in Paris. Dominic's flat is in St Germain by the looks of it, not so far from Andrei's penthouse.

But what are the chances of him bumping into her? Surely they're tiny. Besides, Dominic has a flat here and they're obviously going to be here from time to time. I have to get used to that.

Nevertheless I can't help feeling fearful that Beth and Andrei might somehow meet.

If only things can be sorted between us, then I won't need to worry. Once I'm sure that Beth no longer has a hold over him.

I realise I have no idea if that's true or not. It's only Olympe who's told me that Andrei loves me; he's said nothing of the sort. I've still heard nothing from Olympe, but that is something of a relief. I don't yet have to commit to the step that I find such a fearful prospect. Even so, the sense that I'm entirely forgotten by the people who have such a huge influence over my life is not a pleasant one.

It's a relief when a message arrives from Andrei.

At last! I think with a wash of relief as I open it. Then, with a mental laugh, I remind myself that it's barely two days since I last saw him. I need to keep these things in proportion.

Can I see you this evening? I've missed you.

My heart leaps at the sweet simplicity. No false names or strange commands, just a straightforward message full of affection. Things are moving in the direction I've dreamed of. I type out a reply.

I've missed you too. Where shall we meet?

The answer comes back: the name of a restaurant and a time. No one could ever accuse Andrei of being too verbose.

I don't know the restaurant where Andrei wants to meet me. It's a dark, secret sort of place, with a gloomy, unprepossessing doorway that positively puts people off. It's the kind of place for a select clientele that knows that behind the anonymous dour frontage lies a luxurious, dimly lit restaurant with a maze of private rooms on the first floor. I'm led to one of them, a room with a small round table in the centre and a wide banquette lining the entire side of one wall.

Andrei greets me with a kiss, seeing my glance go to the broad velvet couch against the wall. 'Do you like it? This place used to be frequented by gentlemen to entertain actresses from the Comédie Française after the performance. And then they desired another kind of performance altogether . . .'

I laugh but I feel a little discomfited. I don't like the idea that Andrei has brought me somewhere where men paid for sex with courtesans. *Our relationship is not like that at all. Is it . . . ?*

I try to put that out of my mind, but as we sit down and order our food, I feel as though Andrei's mood has changed from the last time I saw him. Then he was carefree and affectionate. Now there is a distance between us again. His face is unsmiling and hard to read and those eyes have darkened to a hooded, steely blue.

We talk in a desultory way as the waiter brings our drinks and a basket of bread, and I can't shake the feeling that although Andrei is here with me, his spirit is somewhere else. I try to amuse him with the chatter he enjoyed on our day around Paris but it seems to wash over him.

We're not connecting. I can't seem to reach him.

A horrible desperation is growing in me, along with a misery that everything I've begun to believe about my relationship with Andrei could be wrong.

Nothing changes over dinner and I feel more helpless as we eat our food. At last I can't stand it any longer. My unhappiness is beginning to turn into anger.

'I don't know why you bothered to ask me here tonight,' I burst out, dropping my fork on to my plate with a clatter. 'You obviously don't want to see me.'

Andrei looks startled, frowning at my dropped cutlery. 'What?'

'You heard me. I could easily be at home studying something that really matters to me, not being ignored here.' I can tell my face is flushed with annoyance and my breathing is fast.

'What are you talking about?' he says shortly. 'I'm not ignoring you. What a ridiculous idea. We're having a perfectly pleasant dinner together. Or so I thought.' His icy blue eyes regard me impassively. 'What exactly is wrong?'

'You're being so distant. It's not like it was on our day around Paris, when we were so ... close.' I stop. I don't want to sound demanding, or worse, whining.

'Nothing has changed,' Andrei says but his voice is still cool. 'Why would it?'

I stare down at my plate, my appetite gone. 'I don't know.'

'There you are then. You're upset over nothing. Now, let's carry on and put this silliness behind us.'

The tone of his voice rankles me. I don't need to be

treated like a silly girl. I've given so much of myself to Andrei. He ought to respect that, and give my feelings some credence. He is being different with me, I can see that and feel it, and he can't simply brush it away as though my perceptions don't matter.

This agreement is about equality between us, no matter what power play we might choose to indulge in. I can't let him think he can order me around.

'Perhaps there is something that's made you so shut off,' I declare, filled with sudden recklessness. The apprehension that's been with me constantly since yesterday morning flickers into life and grows inside me, fed by my hurt at Andrei's treatment of me.

'Oh yes? What's that?' His voice is quiet and low, with a hint of menace.

I'm not afraid of you, Dubrovski!

'Beth is in Paris,' I say, and watch his reaction.

He slowly lifts another forkful of food to his mouth and eats it slowly, not looking at me the entire time. Then he says, 'I know.'

A wave of unpleasant feeling goes through me and my heart sinks. *So I was right.* 'You do?'

'Yes.'

'How? Have you seen her?'

He pauses and then says, 'I make it my business to know where Beth is.'

I gasp, a stab of pain hitting my belly. 'You have her followed?'

Andrei shrugs lightly. 'Not exactly. But I know where she and Dominic are at any given time. I knew when she arrived back in Paris last week.'

'Last week?' I stare at him, remembering our joyous day

together in Paris. So all along he was thinking about Beth and the fact that she was in the city. Maybe he only wanted to visit all those places in the hopes that we might bump into her.

'That's right.' His eyes have grown harder. 'I don't see why it's anything to do with you.'

I bite my lip, not sure how to respond to this. He's right. Our agreement was that we had no emotional involvement, but surely things have moved on since then. We've seen things, shared things, felt things . . . . I remember the tender affection of our nights together when his head lay on my breast, his arms around me. *Was that really all nothing at all? Have I just been a fool, thinking there is something in it, and that our relationship is changing and developing?*

'When I saw Jimmy, you went mad,' I say defiantly.

He flicks a steely gaze at me. 'I haven't seen Beth. If I do, I will tell you. That's the difference.'

I look away, not sure where this leaves us. I must seem like a jealous, hysterical woman, not the one he drew up our arrangement with. Have I put everything in jeopardy? *But he's still keeping tabs on Beth! He still loves her. It's all been completely pointless.*

We sit in uncomfortable silence for a moment or two, then Andrei puts down his cutlery and throws his napkin on his plate. The linen soaks up the dark sauce. I watch the stain creeping over the pure white. *He's spoiled it.*

Andrei gets to his feet. 'I've had enough of this. You're right, the evening isn't what I hoped. It's probably my fault. I apologise. I'm bad company. The best thing I can do is leave.'

I gasp and look at him pleadingly. 'No. Don't go – don't leave like this. I don't like this bad feeling between us.'

'No.' His voice is brusque. 'It's obvious that tonight is a washout. I'll go home and so should you.' His gaze flicks over to the broad banquette, as though he's thinking for a moment of what he intended should happen there this evening but now will not. 'I need to think.'

I get to my feet as well, twisting my napkin in my hands. 'I don't want you to go.'

He looks at me and for a moment I sense that he is torn. Then his resolve returns. 'No. I'll settle the bill on the way out. Stay as long as you want. Goodnight.' Without another glance, he marches out.

I watch him go in despair. This wasn't how it was supposed to end up. Have I ruined everything? Should I have kept my mouth shut? I sink back down into my seat, pour out another glass of red wine and take two big gulps.

The whole thing has been a waste of time. He doesn't love me and never will. He still loves Beth. I just have to accept it.

A feeling of utter bleakness possesses me. I thought tonight would end with the glorious feeling of Andrei's hard cock inside me, pushing me to the edge of pleasure. Instead I feel as though I've lost him for ever.

Then Olympe's words come back to me. She told me this would not be easy. She told me it would be painful. But in the end, I would have Andrei's love. I know I want that more than anything in the world.

I take another gulp of wine, feeling it burn my throat and my blood tingle with the hit of the alcohol.

I'll do it. I'll do whatever she thinks I have to do. I'll prove that I'm worthy of Andrei's love and push Beth out of his heart for ever.

CHAPTER TWENTY

My misery is alleviated a little the next day when I receive a message from Andrei.

> *My dear Miss X*
> *I apologise for my behaviour last night. I would like to see you again soon. I will be in touch to arrange something.*
> *A*

I feel better as I read and reread the email. As usual he gives so little away. I have no real idea how to read the message – is he building a bridge or preparing to tear it down completely?

All I can do is wait.

The next message I receive is not from Andrei, and I do not know who the sender is but as they know my secret email address, it must be via Olympe.

> *Miss X*
> *Please come to 356d rue de la Pompe at six o'clock this evening. You must begin your preparations.*
> *Josephine*

A flutter of fear moves through me. So I haven't been forgotten. Olympe intends to go ahead. I can't help feeling that although this ceremony is ostensibly to help me win Andrei, she relishes the idea of manipulating me towards submission. I wonder if she's seen me as a challenge, someone she wishes to test her power on.

Why should she help me if there's nothing in it for her? I suppose we all have our reasons for what we do.

I'm afraid at what is in store for me, but I know that I will be at the appointment with Josephine.

My palms are damp with sweat as I ring on the bell for apartment D at the given address. I have no idea what to expect and there is the possibility that I'll be made to experience some of what Olympe has in mind for me. I'm determined to be brave and endure whatever I have to.

Andrei is worth it.

A buzzer releases the door and I push it open. Inside an old wooden staircase leads upstairs and I climb in silence, my hand on the smooth wood of the balustrade. On the fourth floor the door is marked 'D' and I knock on it with a slight hesitancy. I'm on the brink of changing my mind and racing away down the stairs when the door flies open and there stands the woman I remember from the rite I attended, unmistakable even without her mask. She is tall with milky white skin and rich red hair worn up. She is wearing a low-cut dress and round her neck is a black velvet ribbon.

'Flora. You came.' She smiles at me. Her mouth is like a china doll's, small and rosebud-ish, with little white teeth. 'I'm glad.' She steps back to allow me inside. 'Please, come in.'

I follow her in. The apartment is comfortable and well furnished, not in the opulent style of Olympe's townhouse but in a more everyday way.

'Are you Josephine?' I ask.

'That's right.' She gives me a warm look over her shoulder as she leads the way to a small sitting room. 'Olympe has asked me to prepare you for your ceremony.' She laughs. 'You're so lucky. I'd give anything to experience my first ceremony again. I've never been so transported, before or since. It was life-changing for me.' She gestures for me to sit down on one of the chairs.

'Was it frightening?' I ask, sitting down where she suggests. Josephine seems much more normal and approachable than Olympe. *But how normal can she really be?*

'Of course! There's not much point if it isn't! I was terrified out of my skin. But Olympe has a beautiful way of reminding you of the skin you are in.' She smiles at me again, her eyes friendly but with a slight glassiness that makes me think again of a china doll. 'You will never feel so intensely human, or so close to the divine.'

'When is my ceremony to be?' I ask.

'Very soon. You won't know until close to the time. Olympe understands how to play upon our hopes, fears and desires in such a way that she gives us the perfect experience.'

'When was yours?'

Josephine looks dreamy for a moment. 'Ten years ago now. I can hardly believe it, the time has gone so fast. It was quite amazing. Now – can I get you some tea? Then we will talk about what must done.'

I refuse the tea but accept a glass of water. Josephine sits down opposite me and looks at me intently before asking me a series of questions: my dress size, my underwear and shoe size. And my blood type.

'Don't be worried, it's never been needed. Well . . .' She

laughs. 'Only once. And all was well. But we must take precautions.'

I look at her nervously.

She moves quickly on. 'Now – your hair. It's very beautiful. But Olympe likes to see necks. You will be called on the morning of the ceremony and you must devote the rest of that day to your preparations. You will be required to be completely clean and hairless. Please see to it that all removal is done first thing so that your skin is smooth by the end of the day. The hair on your head must be worn up, as I mentioned. You will also need to undergo an enema. Your skin must be soft but all lotions should be well absorbed by the hour of the ceremony. You are, naturally, forbidden to touch yourself in a sexual way on the day. Tempting though it may be.' She smiles at me. 'When you arrive, you will be given specific instructions but you must be without make-up – all adornment, including the rouging of your nipples and private parts, will be done by acolytes on the day. All clothes will be provided, as will any immediate care that is needed afterwards. There are trained first-aiders in attendance at every ceremony. They are rarely needed but occasionally minor dressings are necessary.'

My throat is dry and I try to swallow. My stomach flutters with nervousness. I cannot really imagine this will happen to me. *But it will. I've decided. Olympe has decided. There is no going back now.*

'Is that all?' I ask, my voice coming out hoarsely.

'Yes, just about.' Josephine sits back in her chair, still smiling happily at me as though she's just been telling me about a lovely outing I'll be enjoying, rather than being viciously beaten before an audience. 'Any questions?'

'What happens afterwards?'

'Ah . . .' she says softly. 'Afterwards . . . you must understand that Olympe will do no more to you than inflict the necessary pain. She doesn't charge for this service, even though her expertise is quite simply priceless. You will be in the hands of a true artist. Once she has left, you are obliged to do nothing that you do not want to do. But many celebrants wish to . . .' Her eyes grow darker, even glassier than before '. . . douse the flames that Olympe has conjured within them. There will be many on hand who will be happy to help in that regard.' She is looking at me with a hungry expression and I notice her eyes roving over me. 'You may find that you will require a great deal of help to regain your equilibrium. And we in Olympe's honoured band, we are happy to help one another wherever necessary.'

I stare back at her, saying nothing. I understand her implication but don't know exactly how I should tell her that her services will not be required. My entire focus is Andrei. I don't intend to join in the orgy that I suspect follows the ceremonies. Then I speak. 'How do you know Olympe? What can you tell me about her?'

Josephine's blue eyes glitter a little. 'I met Olympe at a party. I already knew who she was, of course, because she is famous in Paris's demi-monde. I knew that she had married very young to a man who had unusual tastes. He soon realised that he had no desire to have normal intercourse with his wife, but instead required her to submit to his passion for inflicting pain. From then on her relationship with him was chaste and it was understood that there would be no children, but it was rich in many other lessons. Her reward for submitting – besides his undying love and material security for life – was that she could take as many lovers as she wished. She took many, men and women, but she is adamant that she has never been in love. Instead, she is the loved one. Worshipped. Adored. The magnetism of her personality ensures it, her extraordinary self-control demands it.'

I frown, puzzled. 'But when did she stop being her husband's submissive?'

'He died, and after that, she realised that she could never be anyone else's creature. She discovered that her great pleasure was to become the dominant one. It was her purpose, her mission. It has changed many lives.'

'Does she still have lovers?' I ask, fascinated by this glimpse into Olympe's life.

Josephine shakes her head. 'No. She hasn't had lovers for years. Not in a conventional sense. Once she became a dominant, she ceased it almost completely.'

Does that mean before Andrei? I can't imagine him sleeping with Olympe. *But maybe that's because I don't want to.* I gaze over at Josephine. She's watching me intently and I feel uncomfortable under her stare. I ask her quickly, 'So what did you do? When you met her?'

'I introduced myself and I knew within two minutes that she was the most fascinating person I had ever met. I went home and wrote a letter to her, in which I explained that I intended to devote myself to her and do anything she wished. It took a while before she replied – it was agony, I can tell you, to wait – but then she invited me to her house for tea. We discussed what I would do for her, how I would prove my devotion.'

'What did you do?'

Josephine smiles enigmatically. 'I left my husband and family, I moved here to Paris from my home in Italy and I moved in with Madame. Before she would offer me anything, she had to be sure of my motives so there was a long probationary period while she tested my resolve. It was gruelling but beautiful. I learned new things about myself and about endurance. I felt the burden of love and desire. I experienced the pain of delicious release and utter submission. Then I became the leader of the little tribe, and moved out into my own place.' She leans forward, her expression almost transfigured. 'You too, could learn the same thing if you wish. I know Madame would accept you. She wants you. When she speaks of you, I've seen a look in her eyes that has been there only a few times before. You could become her creature, just as I have. You would not regret it.'

For a moment, her voice is hypnotic, tempting. I consider for an instant whether I should do as she says and submit entirely to Olympe's will. I would learn things in that underground chamber of hers that would bring tears coursing down my face, but perhaps I'd also know a strange and otherworldly bliss. Then I shake my head. 'No.'

I don't want to submit to Olympe, no matter how much she wants me to. I only want Andrei.

'Very well.' Josephine pulls herself together with another of her luxurious sighs. 'Now . . . are you ready to sign?'

'Sign?'

'Oh yes.' She gives me a candid stare. 'We don't go to all this trouble without being sure that you will play your part. This would all be for nothing if you decide on the day that you will pull out, or become possessed by unexpected cowardice when the hour strikes. Olympe would not allow herself to be humiliated in that way. We, the tribe, would not allow it.' Josephine opens a folder lying on the coffee table before us. 'Here.' She extracts a printed contract and passes it to me to read.

It's printed in an archaic script on yellow parchment-style paper, and worded in an old-fashioned way, but it is clear enough that I'm undertaking to be at the appointed time and place, and to allow unspecified actions to be performed on my body, acknowledging that they may lead to pain and mild injury. While I'm assured that I will not be seriously hurt and there is no risk of death, I must still indemnify Olympe and her tribe against whatever may happen to me. I may not sue. I must take what is coming to me, and accept it. If I fail to attend or withdraw from the ceremony or refuse any ministrations, I will be bound to pay a sum that draws a small gasp from me.

It is a truly huge amount of money.

'Don't worry, we've never had to ask for the money,' Josephine says cosily, as though that is a comfort for me. She can guess what I've just read. 'Now – will you sign?' She holds a fat Mont Blanc fountain pen.

I take it. There is my name beneath a dotted line. *Flora Hammond.*

I look up quickly to see Josephine's eyes fixed on me. She knows at once what is in my mind.

'Oh, yes, we know who you are,' she says. 'Plenty of our friends like to protect their anonymity, but of course we make it our business to find out identities. We must protect ourselves as well. You might be a journalist or a black-mailer, with a desire to expose Madame to the cruel and uncomprehending gaze of the world.'

I blink at her, trying to absorb what she has said. So all along, they've known my name. 'Does ... does Andrei know?' I ask.

She shrugs. 'I have no idea. We never tell anyone what we know. But if Andrei Dubrovski is as astute as he seems, I don't think it will have taken him long to find out your name.' She laughs her tinkling little laugh. 'And of course, you have less reason than most to fear pulling out of your ceremony, with all the money you have at your disposal!' Then her eyes glitter darkly again. 'But you won't pull out. I can read in your face that you mean to do it. And believe me – you won't regret it.'

I go home full of apprehension.

I've signed now. There's no going back.

I spend the evening on my own as I have done so often lately. In my inbox are dozens of messages from friends, and invitations to events, parties and gatherings are piling up. But I have no desire to go anywhere or see anyone. My life has narrowed down to my classes at drama school, and the other, darker drama playing out in my private life with its own cast of characters – the Russian tycoon, the aged dominatrix, the tribe of upper-class citizens who spend much of their free time indulging in the practice of pain and pleasure. Only Summer's emails can lift me out of that circle just for a while and remind me of another life that I also belong to, and that one day soon I'll have to return to my family.

I feel as though I will be quite a different person when they see me again. *Will they notice? Will Dad even care? He's only obsessed with Freya right now. I've heard nothing from him for weeks. Even Jane-Elizabeth hasn't contacted me. I suppose she thinks I'm safely sorted out at drama school.*

I look at the unread messages in my email inbox and on

a whim, I delete a dozen or more without reading them. It feels strangely powerful.

Then I get up and go to my bedroom and take out the long black box. It's been calling to me ever since I returned home, with a subtle but insistent voice. Now I can no longer resist it.

I open it and look at the cold bar of black iron. Turning it in its satin bed, I see again the reversed initials, AD, and stare at them. Soon they'll belong to me for ever.

The woman who goes home will be marked as someone else's possession.

The dreamy look on Josephine's face comes back into my mind.

But will I belong to Andrei ... or Olympe?

CHAPTER TWENTY-ONE

Two days go by. No summons comes. I'm living in a constant state of heightened expectation. I have no idea how I'll be told of the time and place of my ceremony, and as a result I'm a bag of nerves every morning, jumping out of my skin when anybody behind me coughs or passes me too close. When a lorry suddenly begins beeping as it reverses, I almost have a heart attack. By the time ten o'clock comes, I begin to calm down, thinking that the hour for the summons is now past. I'll need to be told early if I'm to prepare in the way I've been told. I have a clinic on my speed dial so that I can call as fast as possible and book the necessary treatments.

The only upside to my nervousness is that I'm finding it easy to play Ophelia in her mad scene, as she veers from happiness to tears and back again. That kind of emotional state is all too familiar to me at the moment.

Then, at last, I hear from Andrei.

My silence is because of work. I would like to see you. Can you meet me for lunch tomorrow? It's going to be sunny. Let's eat outside.

It's a Saturday tomorrow and for some reason I feel sure that I won't be summoned on a Saturday, even though it would be best for me if I was. I have a feeling that Olympe will test me by making the day as difficult as possible. Sunday is surely not likely. So I have two clear days to enjoy myself.

I type back.

That sounds lovely. Tell me where and when, and I'll be there.

When I've sent off the message, I sit and look at the screen for a while, wondering what Andrei would think if he knew what I am planning. But the element of surprise is all – I know that Andrei must be overcome by the sacrifice I'm prepared to make for him, startled, moved – and in that moment, know the truth. If he were forewarned, he would only see the dark side of it, not the beauty and power of the submission. Olympe has made that perfectly clear to me.

I feel almost carefree as I head off to meet Andrei. The decisions have all been taken, I've signed away my right to choose or change my mind. At some point, I'll have to undergo the thing I fear but after that, life will be delightful again. I'm determined to enjoy my last two days of freedom in the meantime.

Last time Andrei and I met, it was a disaster. I don't want that again. We should feel joy in each other – that's what this is all about, after all.

He's waiting for me at an outside cafe table on one of the beautiful Parisian streets on the Left Bank. It's on one side of a square dominated by a huge white stone church and bordered by plane trees, and the pretty bistro tables outside it are perfect for watching the chic residents of this expensive area as they walk their little dogs, or go shopping at the pricy boutiques. Andrei is sitting there, his eyes obscured by Ray-Bans, the light breeze ruffling his hair. There's almost a sense of spring about the bright sunshine and blue skies, and the tiny green buds on the plane trees, but nevertheless, I'm glad of my shearling coat.

Andrei stands up as I approach. 'How delicious you look,' he says with a smile, and kisses my cheeks.

'Thank you.' I'm also in sunglasses, and beneath my coat I'm wearing a simple but extremely expensive white shirt, and a pair of elegant navy trousers with flat ballet slippers. 'So do you.'

He smiles again and I'm pleased to see that he seems to be in a good mood. I hope we can put the memory of our last encounter behind us. 'It's hard to be depressed on a day like this, in Paris as the spring arrives, lunching with a beautiful woman.'

I feel myself melting a little inside. He's right. It's very romantic. 'And not so very far from your apartment,' I say in a low voice.

'Ah.' He laughs conspiratorially. 'It's been too long, hasn't it? Are you feeling the hunger? I know I am.'

I think of our last delicious bout of lovemaking and its tender fulfilment. Today I feel the stirring of something else inside me. I want something a little spicier, a little more interesting. Suddenly, all I can think of is my need to have Andrei. Perhaps it's the way I can see the outline of his muscled shoulders under his wool jacket, or the bulge of his thighs, or the way his huge hands rest lightly on the table, but the overall effect is the fizz of lust tingling over me.

'Shall we go now?' I ask quietly.

Andrei laughs again. 'We share the same desire,' he replies. 'Let's have our lunch and enjoy the delicious anticipation. We have all afternoon, don't we?'

'But I'm not sure if I can wait,' I whisper.

'Perhaps we won't have to wait too long,' he says, a promise inside his voice.

Lunch becomes a decidedly erotic affair, every bite we take a foreshadowing of what we'll later do with our mouths. I find it delightfully exciting as Andrei eats a dish of oysters, savouring the briny tang as he sucks them out of their shells and swallows them. I can hardly keep my hands from wandering to him, I want to touch him all the time, feel the hardness of his flesh under my hands. The thought of his solid, powerful body between my thighs sends shivers of desire down my back.

We don't linger over our lunch, and without ordering coffee, Andrei signals for the bill. We leave the cafe and take a walk together to the nearby park.

'Aren't we going to your apartment?' I ask him.

'Soon,' he says, sliding a hooded glance over at me. 'But let's get some air first.'

The park is busy as people enjoy the sunshine, and I wonder what Andrei has in mind for us. We walk on until we come to a boating lake, and I'm surprised when he goes to the attendant and pays for the hire of a boat. It doesn't seem like his kind of thing but perhaps that simply shows how little I really know him.

I sit in the little craft and Andrei takes the oars, handling them expertly. He pulls out until we are in the middle of the lake. There's no one else about. Most of the families stay close to the shore and few others have

ventured out so far. It's peaceful on the water. I dip my
fingers in and let them trail there, losing myself in the
rhythm of the oars and the squeak of the rowlocks as they
move.

'Open your coat,' he says suddenly. 'Let me see you.'

I glance up at him, startled. It's sunny but there is a
definite chill out here on the lake.

'Do as I say,' he says with a smile. I can't see his eyes
behind the sunglasses but I sense that they are steely.

I open my coat to reveal my white shirt.

'Unbutton your shirt.' His face is impassive as he
goes on rowing, putting his back into every stroke of the
oars.

I do as instructed. My fingers are cold from the water
and it takes a while for me to open the buttons up. I pull
back the shirt and show him my white lace bra underneath,
my breasts rising from it in soft mounds. He gazes at me
without expression.

'Now undo your bra.'

I obey, reaching around to unclasp it, flinching a little
under my own cold hands. The white lace falls away and
my breasts are exposed, the nipples hard as bullets in the
cold air, the flesh covered in goose bumps.

'Very nice,' Andrei says. 'Rub them please.'

Still I say nothing, but begin to run my hands over my
breasts, caressing the skin and pinching at my nipples so
that they stand even harder. Andrei watches. I think I can
see a bulge at his crotch and that makes me tingle in
response, my sex throbbing a little and the rush of arousal
making it swell. I lick my fingers and then run them over
my nipples to wet them.

241

'Very nice,' Andrei remarks. 'Keep playing with them with one hand. With the other, undo your trousers.'

I pinch my left nipple and cup my breast, massaging it as I slide the other hand downward and undo the button at my waistband. The zip slides down easily, giving a glimpse of my white knickers underneath.

'Push the panties down,' orders Andrei.

I obey, raising myself a little so that I can wriggle the trousers and knickers down far enough to expose me. I sit there, waiting for my next instruction. Andrei rows on, watching me silently, his mouth hard. I'm sure that there is a massive hardness at his crotch but his movements make it hard to see.

After a while he says in his hoarse voice, 'Touch yourself.'

I move my fingers down to my clitoris and start to rub it gently with my index finger.

'Lick your finger,' he commands.

I suck my finger deep into my mouth and then return it to my clit, rubbing it lightly and rapidly so that it swells under my touch, protruding out and showing its eagerness to be caressed. I lower my finger down into the folds below and slide it in the juices there. It comes up glistening and I rub again at my clitoris. I moan lightly and lick my lips, opening my legs a little wider and working a little faster at myself.

'Let me taste you,' orders Andrei.

I dip my fingers back to my entrance and pick up the juice there, then I lean forward and press my fingers into his mouth. He sucks them in hard and I can feel his tongue licking them clean.

'Again.'

I repeat the process until he has licked me clean three

times. We're both excited now but Andrei's face is still impassive as he pulls on the oars.

'Make yourself come,' he orders.

A shiver of excitement goes through me. I never would have dreamed that I'd be able to do something like this but now I don't hesitate. I put my fingers back on my bud and start to rub it. It loves the pressure of my fingers, sending delicious sensations shooting out from my centre, making my heart pound and my eyes half-close. I love the idea of Andrei watching me, and what it's doing to him to see me pleasuring myself like this. I rub harder, the little bud growing ever more sensitive under my fingers. I can feel it wanting to flower into an orgasm. I dart my fingers into my hole and press them inside, moving them in and out of the soft wetness of my tunnel, then return to my clit, rubbing it hard with short round motions.

'Are you coming?' Andrei's voice is thick with lust. 'I want you to.'

'I'm coming,' I sigh and then moan as my clit explodes with the pent-up lust and I shake with my beautiful, electric orgasm. As it subsides and my spasm finishes, Andrei stops rowing.

'Suck me,' he orders.

I don't hesitate but kneel down in the boat, half naked as I am, and work quickly to release his cock. As soon as it's free, I take it into my mouth and suck him hard while working the flesh in my hands. It's hot and smooth, and throbs under my hand. It doesn't take long before he's moaning, his hands on the back of my head, pressing me down on his rod. His hips move and I suck harder, licking the top of his cock, running my tongue around its rim, rubbing harder at the shaft. In a moment, he swells under my hand and then, with a choked sound from Andrei, his prick pours forth a gush of hot white thickness and I swallow it down, savouring every drop. When at last his orgasm is over, I sit back.

Andrei puts his cock away and buttons up. Then he picks up the oars.

'You'd better make yourself decent,' he says gruffly but with a hint of lightness in his tone. 'I'm taking us back to shore.'

I say nothing as I do up my clothes. The outing was much more enjoyable than I could have hoped.

Breathless and a little dishevelled, we return the way we came and now we're heading in the direction of Andrei's apartment. I can hardly wait to get there but Andrei is in a more languorous mood.

'Let's stop here,' he says, indicating another cafe bar with chairs out on the pavement. This is not as fancy as the place where we had our lunch. Burly working men are at the bar and a football game is being broadcast from televisions mounted near the ceiling. 'I want a drink. I feel like something strong. We can drink it in the last of the afternoon sunshine.'

'All right.' I smile at him. 'Let's do that.'

I take a seat at one of the tables and Andrei goes into the bar to order drinks. It's crowded inside and I have the feeling that he half wants to watch whatever is happening on the screens. I've never seen Andrei show any interest in football, but for all I know he's mad on it.

Something else to learn about him.

I sit at my table outside and watch the world go by. The afternoon is certainly cooling and it will be dark before too long. Families are hurrying home from the park, and there is a general air that the day is almost over and it's time to think about getting inside.

I notice a figure walking along the pavement towards me, a woman in heels that are not really suited to walking, though her fur coat is no doubt keeping her warm. She has long caramel-coloured hair that falls in thickly blow-dried tresses over her shoulders, but her face is half concealed behind huge sunglasses. She's smoking a cigarette as she goes, moving in the kind of hip-swivelling way that draws the eyes of men as she passes.

As she goes, I feel a strange flicker of recognition. I know that tanned skin and the provocative sashay, but . . .

Just as she reaches me, the realisation floods my mind but not before she has stopped, dipped her sunglasses and said in a surprised tone, 'My, my! It's Flora! Fancy seeing you here.'

I feel a cold chill of dislike sweep over me. 'Estelle,' I reply coolly. 'This is a surprise.'

'Isn't it?' She takes off her glasses altogether so I can see her big doe-like eyes framed with kohl and huge black lashes. I get the feeling that this meeting is not so much of a surprise to her as she is pretending. *But how on earth would she know where I am?* 'What are you up to?'

'I'm having a drink with a friend,' I say in as brief a tone as I can manage without sounding too rude. Behind me, a cheer comes up as someone scores a goal for the favoured side. I pointedly ask her nothing about what she's doing here, but my mind is racing. What is Estelle doing in Paris? Is my father here too? He doesn't let her out of his sight for very long as a rule. But I don't want to ask any questions that might give her an excuse to linger.

It's a waste of time. She sways over on her heels and drops down into the chair beside me. 'How charming. So how are things? How is drama school? Are you still having lots of fun?' she says in the acidic way that makes it sound as if I'm just amusing myself with acting and nothing serious will ever come of it.

'Yes.' I can't stem my curiosity any longer and besides, the last thing I want to do is discuss myself with my father's girlfriend, the woman none of us can stand. Freya's warnings ring through my head. If Freya is right, Estelle is the one who betrayed everything about Freya's affair to the press and almost got her into serious trouble. 'So – what are you doing in Paris, Estelle?'

She smiles at me. 'Oh, a lightning trip to see my dermatologist. Dear Doctor Schwartz, I couldn't live without him.'

'I thought you were looking a little frozen.'

'Luckily I don't need to gurn for a living,' she throws back with faux sweetness. 'And anyway, I'm so happy that I don't need to frown. All I have to do is smile.' She leans forward and whispers, 'And open my mouth nice and wide.'

I recoil. She's disgusting. I don't want to think about what she gets up to in order to keep my father entranced.

'What are you really doing here?' I ask, my voice as frozen as Estelle's face.

'I told you. Seeing my doctor. And doing a little sightseeing. I've heard that there are some lovely views in the park. The boating lake is particularly pleasant – as long as you can get some privacy.'

I go still. Estelle watches my face change with evident pleasure. I curse the way I show everything in my expressions. Now my cheeks are aflame with embarrassment and anger.

'I can see we both know what I'm talking about,' Estelle murmurs.

'What do you want?' I say stiffly. 'What the hell are you after?'

'My dear Flora, please.' She looks hurt, her big Bambi eyes wounded. 'There's no need to talk like that. I'm fascinated by the man you're so ... kind to. He's so *interesting*. And with such a varied portfolio of businesses that make him so terribly rich. But you know ...' She wrinkles her nose and frowns. 'I'm not altogether sure that your father would approve of Mr Dubrovski. If he ever saw a photograph of you and him together, perhaps ... boating ...'

'Why are you doing this?' I hiss through clenched teeth. 'What on earth do you hope to gain?'

Estelle's expression hardens. 'I know that you girls hate me and you'd do anything to get rid of me. Well, you need to know that I'm not going anywhere and I intend to do all in my power to make sure that I stay exactly where I am. I've already dealt with Freya. Your father is on the brink of disinheriting her. He's furious about her little vanishing act and the way she's obsessed with her two-bit bodyguard. He's going to be even angrier when he finds out who you're fucking.'

'You're unbelievable,' I say, shaking my head. Anger swirls inside me and I feel as though I could lean across the table and slap her smug face. What right does she have to try to destroy my family?

She leans towards me again, her arms folded. 'Well, you know what? You hate me because you think I'm not good enough to be in your precious family. You have so much and yet you resent sharing one penny with me, even though I make your father happier than he's ever been. That's why I intend to show all three of you – and that stupid cow Jane-Elizabeth – exactly who is the boss around here.'

'I don't hate you because you're not good enough,' I say icily. 'You're much better than the bubblehead you pretend to be. I hate you because you don't love my father. You only want to use him. If he ever stopped being rich, you'd be gone.'

She shrugs. 'I love him enough. I can put up with him and give him all he needs from me as long as I get security in return. And I'm here to stay, so you have to live with that.' Her eyes flick up to someone approaching from behind me, and she murmurs, 'Unless, of course, I get a better offer . . .'

Andrei is there, putting down two Campari sodas on our table and looking curiously at Estelle.

She smiles at him, batting her eyelashes and cocking her head winsomely so that her thick hair falls over her shoulders. 'Well, well, and who is *this* incredibly handsome man, Flora?'

'This is Andrei,' I say in a mechanical voice. 'Andrei, this is Estelle. My father's girlfriend.'

'It's a pleasure to meet you, Andrei,' Estelle purrs. She gives him the most flirtatious look I've ever seen, practically licking her lips as she moves her bosom suggestively. 'I hope we see some more of you – now that you're Flora's friend.' She stands up, wiggling her hips. 'I have to go now. Flora, I do hope I can see you soon, I've got some pretty pictures of the park to show you. Goodbye, Andrei, it was charming to meet you. I do hope you'll visit us before too long. You'll always be welcome at the Hammond house. Bye!'

She slips on her sunglasses and trips away on her high heels, her rounded bottom swaying as she goes.

CHAPTER TWENTY-TWO

I'm speechless. In one breath, Estelle has let me know that she has pictures of me and Andrei on the lake, virtually offered herself to him and given away the secret of my identity.

I feel as though the blood has drained from my face and my lips are dry as I turn to look at Andrei. He's sat down and is sipping his Campari.

'She seems quite a character,' he says drily.

A ripple of hope goes through me. Perhaps he hasn't noticed that she used my surname. 'Yes,' I say in a croaky voice. 'She's just . . . sweet.'

He laughs and raises an eyebrow at me. 'I don't think you really mean that, Flora.'

I laugh too, relaxing a little. I know that I'm in a fix, with Estelle having photographs of me that will enrage my father and cause all sorts of bother, but I'm also sure that her little blackmail tricks aren't going to work either. Freya wouldn't take it, and neither will I.

But, says a little voice in my head, *maybe that's what she wants. Maybe she wants us all to just get lost and leave her in charge, the queen of the castle, with all of Dad's money at her disposal.* I feel so sad at the thought. If only Dad knew that we'd always love him, money or not, while Estelle wouldn't be seen for dust if he lost his cash.

'Now,' Andrei says, draining his drink. 'Shall we go home? I feel like a little . . . recreation.'

I push Estelle out of my mind. I'm not going to let her ruin my afternoon with Andrei. *I'll deal with her later – perhaps I'll even find Beth and ask her to get a message to Freya.* Then I push the thought of Beth out of my mind too. I have to concentrate just on Andrei and me now. That's all that matters at this moment.

Andrei gets up and offers me his arm. 'Let's go home,' he says and gives me a hot look. 'I don't think I can wait much longer.'

At the apartment, we are hardly through the door before we are kissing wildly. My coat drops to the floor and by the time we reach the bedroom, I'm only in my underwear.

'You were glorious today,' he murmurs as he undresses, not taking his eyes off me. 'The way you obeyed me. I wasn't sure if you would. But you were very exciting.'

'I know when to obey,' I say playfully. 'But my obedience is always because I want it.'

'Very true.' Andrei smiles. 'That is what makes it so beautiful, simple and clever. Your submission is also your dominance and so is mine.'

'Would you ever obey me?' I ask, lying back on the bed. I start to run my hands over my body invitingly.

'Of course. If I wanted to.'

We smile at each other.

'Luckily we both have the same wants,' I say lightly.

'Absolutely. So, my little obedient mistress, let's see how much you want to obey me now.' He stands there and takes his cock in his hand. I sigh with pleasure at the sight. I don't know how I would ever grow tired of its magnificence, the girth, the way it feels when it fills me up, when it swells and jerks with its orgasm.

'I'm ready to do whatever you command,' I say.

'Good. Lie down and stretch out your arms. I want to tie you to the bed.'

I do as he asks, noticing the little hoops on the sides of the bedhead. A moment later he has used a stretch of leather to tie my wrists so that I can't move my arms.

'Delicious,' he says, looking down at me happily and lazily stroking his cock. He climbs on to the bed and straddles me so that my view is of his wonderful stiff prick and his balls on my breasts. He rubs his cock over my breasts a little and then brings it to my mouth. I lick it lightly, the tip of my tongue playing over its smooth warm head. When I've kissed and licked it enough for his liking, Andrei moves down my body, trailing the hot shaft across my breasts and then over my belly. I open my thighs for him and he drops down to kiss and lick me, pushing aside my white panties so he can tickle my bud with his tongue and probe inside me. I can't move my arms at all but my hips wriggle with the delicious feelings he is stimulating in me, with the added sensation of my knickers cutting into me and pressing down on my clit. After a while, he pushes his prick in under the knickers, and enters me, his length sliding home and stretching me delightfully around his girth as he goes in.

I sigh with pleasure, pushing my hips up to meet him, wanting to take him in and feel the pressure of him on me.

He lies down heavily on top of me and runs his hands over my pinioned arms. He evidently likes the sight of me tethered and helpless, yearning for him and unable to touch him. He begins to move slowly in and out. The feeling is incredible. Without the use of my arms, I find the focus of pleasure in my body is greater, my sex more alive to him, my bud more desperate for the touch that sends lascivious thrills racing through me.

He pumps harder and harder, his breath coming in pants. He holds on to my arm and feels my taut muscles, his other arm supporting him as he fucks on. He goes on for a very long time and I can't get enough of it. The day darkens outside and still he fucks me, building a slow orgasm of great intensity for us both. It's not until I've come in a screaming agony of pleasure that he releases his own orgasm, spending hard inside me before we collapse together in a hot, sweaty and satisfied mass.

Afterwards, when I'm untethered, we lie in each other's arms until at last we rouse ourselves. It's dark outside, Paris coming to life in a carpet of lights beneath us. Andrei showers and then prepares us a simple supper – bread and pâté with a bottle of cold Chablis – while I take my shower and dress in a pair of his silk pyjamas.

'They suit you,' he says admiringly as I pad into the kitchen. I do a twirl. They're sky-blue silk edged in dark blue cord.

'Thanks!' I say. 'I rather like them. Can I keep them?'

'Hmm, we'll see. They're my favourites.' He carries a wooden board loaded with bread, butter and pâté to the table. 'Come on, let's eat something. I'm starving.'

'I suppose that's what sex does,' I reply, coming over.

'It's a very healthy activity,' Andrei says, sitting down. 'Some wine?'

'Yes please.' He offers me a glass and I sit down, sipping the cold, flintily dry liquid. 'Delicious.'

'Not as delicious as you,' he says, his eyes glinting.

We smile at each other. I'm happy again. Let Estelle do

her worst. We have a bond that she will not be able to break.

Or does she even want to? I bet she's counting on me choosing Andrei, just as Freya chose Miles.

'What are you thinking?' he asks, regarding me carefully as he butters his bread. 'Your face is like the sun with a cloud passing over it. You've darkened.'

'I'm just thinking about that woman – Estelle. She's not my friend. It makes life difficult.'

'I sensed that. She obviously hoped to make some kind of trouble for you.' He stares at me. 'Can she do that?'

'If she wants to, I suppose,' I say carefully. 'But I don't intend to let her.'

'Good.' Andrei nods. 'I get the sense she likes to play dirty. So don't let her win, will you? I'm sure your father's good sense will win out in the end.'

There's a pause as I absorb this, and then my stomach flips over and I clutch the table. 'What?' I say in a strained voice. 'What did you say?'

'I said your father will see sense in the end.'

'But . . .' I can hardly get the words out. 'You don't know who my father is.'

Andrei goes very still, his knife freezing in the act of buttering his bread. Then he moves again, more deliberately. 'Of course I don't,' he says, 'but I'm sure he's a man of good sense.'

I stare at him, apprehension growing inside me. 'You know who he is, don't you? You know!'

Andrei's expression cools and when he looks up at me again, his face has hardened. 'All right then. Yes. I do know.'

'How long?' I demand, my voice rising in anger. 'How long have you known?'

'Not that long. Only recently in fact,' he says. He pauses, then sighs and says, 'Flora, I had to know who you are. I have my reasons. Besides, you could have been an assassin. Or a crazy woman. Or both. A man in my position can't afford to start sleeping with a stranger who won't tell him anything about herself.'

'So you found out behind my back.' I'm furious now. I feel like an idiot. He's been calling me Miss X and all the time it was just a stupid game. He was patronising me, indulging me, making me believe I was a woman of mystery and all along, he knew . . . 'Why didn't you tell me?'

'You wanted it to remain a secret and that was fine with me,' he snaps back. 'But you can't be so childish, Flora. You must understand why I had to know.'

'I've done everything you wanted!' I shout. 'I've played your games, done what you asked. Gone with you to Olympe, given myself to you in every way.'

'Yes, and I've enjoyed every minute—'

'But it's been meaningless if you were just toying with me!'

Andrei puts down his bread, his expression exasperated. 'I haven't been toying with you, Flora, that's ridiculous . . . We both entered into this arrangement knowing it was a pose.'

'I didn't! I thought it was real.'

He makes an expression of annoyance. 'Yes, of course it was real, I didn't mean that. What we've done and shared doesn't become any less real because I know who you are.'

'But it does if you never told me, can't you see?'

'You knew who I was, why shouldn't I have the same privilege?'

'Because you pretended it didn't matter, but all along it did.'

He looks baffled. 'I don't understand, Flora, I really don't.'

I bite my lip. I can't explain the frustration I feel, the sense of hurt pride and foolishness that is turning into anger and recrimination. 'It was part of my side of the arrangement,' I protest. 'You've broken it!'

He goes very still and when he speaks again, his voice is colder. 'Perhaps we should think again about this arrangement.'

I stare, frozen, and then say in a low voice, 'What do you mean?'

'I've been thinking about this . . . charade we've been playing. I think it should come to an end.'

I pull in a sharp breath. I haven't seen this coming. All day and then tonight – we've been in such harmony, enjoyed each other so much. Did he, all the time, intend to finish it? 'But . . . why?'

'Why?' His blue eyes are frosty. 'It's messing with our minds, that's why. We don't know who we are. You're Miss X and you go crazy when you find out I know who you are. I'm your lover and I've never even been in your bed, or seen your apartment.'

'I didn't know you wanted to,' I say, suddenly sad.

'You're the one obsessed with me knowing nothing about you.'

'Because I don't want to be Flora Hammond all the time.'

He tuts in annoyance. 'You can be who you want with me – don't you know that by now? Do you think I care who your father is, or where you get your allowance from? I see rich kids and poor kids all the time, and you know what? None of it matters to me.' He takes a furious bite of his bread.

I watch him for a moment. I can't help admiring him even now. He's so utterly sure of himself. A man with complete confidence who looks out on the world knowing he is strong enough to cope with anything.

'Things have changed,' he says. 'They'll never be what they were.'

'What's changed them?' I ask, misery soaking my voice.

'We have.' He glances at me. 'We can't help it, I guess.'

'So you want to end it?' I feel like my heart is breaking.

He fixes me with those blue eyes, so hard to read. 'I think we need a break. I think we need some time to think. You're angry with me and I'm worried about you. And . . .'

'And?' I supply, a sense of dull horror growing inside me. It's almost with a sense of the inevitable that I hear him say:

'And there's Beth.' He looks away. 'I'm sorry, Flora. But that's the way it is.'

In a numbed state I go to the bedroom and get dressed. Without another word, I collect my things together and ride the lift down to the ground floor, too stunned to do anything but move on automatic pilot. I feel as though I've been punched but haven't yet felt the pain, only the dazed feeling of being half-conscious. But in the taxi that I hail to take me home, I have enough of my wits about me to send a message to Josephine.

Dear Josephine
I don't mean to be presumptuous but I need your help.
I would like to have my ceremony soon, if Madame
wishes it. As soon as it can be arranged.
Flora

CHAPTER TWENTY-THREE

The summons finally comes. When it does, I feel sick and yet excited at the same time. I knew that it would arrive and perhaps my entreaty to Josephine made it all the more rapid. I'm not sure what I expected but it was not a courier arriving at my apartment with an envelope sealed with wax inscribed with the initials OdR, just as I saw them on Andrei's chest. Inside is a beautifully calligraphic letter directing me to the address where I witnessed the last ceremony. I have to be there at 8 p.m. exactly tonight.

I quickly call the clinic I have on speed dial and arrange an appointment first thing. I have to pay double to secure the slot, but that doesn't matter. The main thing is to fulfil the requirements explained by Josephine.

In the clinic, as every hair on my body is removed, I wonder if this is the first instalment of the pain I'm supposed to endure. The wax goes on as soft and dripping as warm honey, and is as vicious as a razor blade when it's pulled off. I'm surprised at how long and how intricate an operation it is to wax off all hair. I thought I was well trimmed in all areas but now I know that is not the case – there is much, much more to be lost. After the depilation, I experience the entirely new sensation of an enema, which is strange at first, and then not unpleasant as I get used to it and become accustomed to the embarrassment of being cleansed like this in front of a latex-gloved clinician. When it's finished, I feel much lighter, cleaner, and strangely refreshed. I sense that I'm almost ready for the final purification awaiting me tonight. Before then, I go home and soak in a long bath, looking down at my plucked body with interest. What will it be like for me tonight? Can I really endure what I saw there so recently?

I will endure it. I have to. It's the only way to win Andrei back, I'm certain of it.

I make sure to smooth the body lotion into my skin well beforehand so that I won't be greasy or slippery when the time comes. I begin to slip into an odd, half-hypnotised state, moving with full knowledge of what I'm doing and going about my preparations with perfect precision, and yet I'm only half there. My mind seems to be detaching from my body, as if to prepare myself for the mental struggle of what lies ahead. I remember something that Josephine said as I left her apartment that day. 'Remember, Flora, your mind controls your body absolutely. The battle will be with your mind not with your flesh. Exert yourself over your body and take the transfiguration that comes from suffering.' She gave me one of those smiles of hers. 'There's a reason why there were so many martyrs, you know. They longed to experience it themselves.'

I wonder if it will come to me, this state of miraculous elation Josephine described. I hope it will, but I can't be sure. What if it doesn't work for me and I only know agony and not the thrill I've been promised?

Don't think about that. It will happen. Olympe is a mistress of her art, Josephine promised me that. Besides, what am I really afraid of? Pain will pass.

The hands of the clock seem to be flying through the

259

hours. At six o'clock I eat a very light supper, all I can manage with my stomach in knots. By seven, I'm dressed in my simple black dress and I'm ready to go. I take a taxi, as though afraid that my purified, cleansed state will be sullied by the streets. I also don't want to be followed. Estelle's little revelation about the photographs of Andrei and me has made me suspicious that someone in her pay is on my trail.

I direct the driver to a wrong address, get out, double back and take another taxi, hoping that this will give anyone pursuing me the slip. Then I stand in front of the door, ready to ring the bell. My hands are shaking violently as I lift them to press the buzzer marked Cecile. A voice comes through the intercom.

'Yes?'

My lines are clear. They were written in the letter. 'I have transgressed. I require absolution.'

'Come in, my child. Here, you will be made clean.'

The buzzer sounds loudly and I hear the catch release. Pressing the door open, I step into the hall.

This is it. I'm here. It's going to begin.

My heart is pounding, and I feel faint and dizzy from a tight pressured feeling inside my heart. I know I mustn't panic, I must stay calm, but the fright that's growing inside me is very hard to damp down.

A woman in a black robe, the hood down, appears from the stairs. She beckons me without a word and I follow her into the depths, across the lower hall and through a door. We're in a preparation room, laid out ready for me.

'Do you have the box?' asks the woman. She is in her forties with fair hair pulled back tightly in the same style as Olympe.

I nod, unable to speak, and produce the long slim box that contains the iron branding tool.

'Good.' She smiles. 'The brazier is being prepared upstairs. It's always more interesting when we have that to deal with too. Now, shall we begin?'

At some secret signal, three more women appear and all four begin work on me. I'm told to undress and when I'm completely naked, they inspect me all over. At first, I'm shaking hard, and my trembling body seems to please them rather than not, but as they treat me with gentleness, the first shock of fear subsides, and I calm down. After they've examined me, perhaps ensuring I've followed all the instructions, I seem to pass muster. The first woman leads me to a chair, the kind you see in a hairdressing salon, that can be raised and lowered, placed before a mirror. I'm asked to sit. I'm not offered a towel or a robe, and they start to make up my face and do my hair. It's all very subtle, in shades of brown, taupe and peach, but effective. There's an undoubted air of glamour about me as they finish.

When that is done, the first woman looks at my body again with the same appraising eye, and then she produces a lipstick. It is Madame's shade, of course. She twists it out and then applies it to my nipples, making them a dark blood red. She moves towards my sex with it and I hold up my hand to stop her.

'No. I don't want that.'

She looks shocked that I've spoken to her, and then doubtful. 'Madame likes it.'

'No,' I say firmly. I don't want to be painted there, like a toy.

After a moment, she puts the lipstick away. Then she gestures behind me.

'Stand over there,' she orders, and I turn to see a table covered in pieces of chiffon.

I go over to the table, and the other three women join the first to start wrapping me up in the pale gossamer-light fabric. It is a very strange feeling to have the tightness of it wound around me while my flesh remains visible beneath, particularly the red stain of my nipples. I can see now why the lipstick is applied. When I'm bound in several layers of chiffon, effectively preventing me from walking, I'm adorned in strings of pearls – one as a belt, another strung between my shoulders, another entwined in my hair, more round my back – and then I realise that I look almost exactly like the woman I saw worked upon last time, but without the white leather collar and manacles. I'm her now. The sacrificial victim.

'You look very beautiful,' says one of the women admiringly. She strokes the chiffon across my arms, and looks at me almost lovingly. 'You are going to be a marvellous novice, I can tell that.'

'You'll receive a superb absolution,' coos another.

'We are looking forward to it.' One of the others, a small dark-eyed woman, smiles with anticipation. 'It's not often we get to see . . . what you're going to suffer.'

I feel a shudder down my spine and my skin tingles with vulnerability. I know what they're talking about and the idea makes me feel simultaneously sick and faint. They have taken the long box and it has vanished. I can't help imagining the cold iron already being placed in the brazier, warming up on the hot orange coals, its blackness turning into the white-orange of searing heat.

Can I stand it? There's still time to escape if I need to!

I turn and catch a glimpse of my reflection in the mirror

across the room. I look otherworldly in my costume, but also like the subject of a romantic Gothic painting.

I'm not going anywhere. I've come this far. There's no turning back.

I don't know how I sense that people have arrived and are filling the upstairs room, but I do. It must be like preparing to go on stage, making up in the dressing room and knowing that the audience is filing into the auditorium, full of expectation of the performance that awaits. I remember going to the opera with Andrei and the pleasant sense of anticipation that filled me as the theatre grew busy and the orchestra began to tune up. Somewhere, offstage, the actress playing Carmen was kohling her eyes, rouging her cheeks, painting strong lines over her eyebrows and colouring in her lips, while perhaps she felt that fear of failure, scared that she might disappoint everybody.

Or else she bubbled with confidence, knowing that all she had to do was sway across the stage and let that rich voice soar through the auditorium and she would possess everyone.

I realise, suddenly, that the audition for my tutor means nothing at all. It's the most basic of play-acting, a self-aggrandisement, a clamour for attention. This is the greatest role I'll ever play, in front of an audience that expects the ultimate performance. I'll be simultaneously abasing myself and raising myself far above anything they would ever expect of themselves. I'll be like a gladiator in Ancient Rome, prepared to give a show that might end in the most extreme suffering but will be beyond most people's capabilities, with a kind of magnificent confidence in taking the greatest risks possible as the people watch.

One of the women appears at my side. She's hooded now. I don't know which one she is. She holds a goblet that looks like gold but must be some kind of silver gilt. 'Drink this,' she urges quietly, and loosens my chiffon bonds so that I can take it.

The liquid is a dark ruby red and I suspect it is wine spiked with something that will calm me without reducing my sensations. I sip it. It slides down my throat with a sweetness that's followed by a fiery burn. At once, I feel exhilarated and more at one with every sensation my body can feel. The glass is taken away and my bonds are refastened. I can't move but my skin prickles to the touch of the chiffon that enfolds me.

The figures stand around me now, the lights in the underground room are dim, music is floating through the air.

I'm ready.

They have a stretcher for me, a silk-wrapped platform with four poles for them to carry me. They manoeuvre me into place, lying me down on it with gentleness and tenderness. I am euphoric, every nerve end tingling.

I'm ready. I can take it. I will show him what I'll do for him.

A bell rings somewhere far away.

'It's time,' mutters one of the hooded figures. They take their places at the four corners of my bier. They lift me up and I feel as though I'm floating upwards towards heaven. I close my eyes and feel the tightness of my soft bonds. Every inch of my skin feels more alive than I've ever known it.

No matter what happens from here, I've felt this, and it's extraordinary. I think I'm beginning to understand.

CHAPTER TWENTY-FOUR

The air is filled with sweet music but the boom of a gong disrupts it. I'm in a lift, ascending smoothly to a level above the underground room. I imagine myself as I was so recently, coming into the chamber unaware of what lay in wait. How could I have foreseen this?

The lift comes to a halt with a small bump. Doors are opened and then my stretcher is carried out into a dim antechamber lit by candles. I hear the low murmur of voices beneath the floating music and close my eyes. Terror is growing somewhere inside me, but there's something that's keeping it at bay, that same detachment I felt earlier as I prepared for tonight – *it's happening and not happening, that's the only way to describe it.*

I hear a gong sound loudly, close at hand, and jump inside my cocoon of chiffon. I remember Olympe say that birthing Andrei's love will hurt. But the surest thing I feel is that I am about to be born myself, through pain into a new world.

The stretcher is hoisted up. Red, black and orange flicker before my eyelids. We're moving forward. The music stops and is replaced by the eerily beautiful sound of plainchant.

It is time.

A door opens – I can't see it but I sense it – and we emerge through it into the chamber I remember from before. I know that a diminutive figure in white robes waits for me, beside the low stool and the box of instruments.

Make me brave.
Who am I talking to?
Let me endure.
Is this a prayer?
Enable me to stand my fate.
Oh God. We must be close. She must be there. She is there. I'm here. It's beginning.

I'm staring at the ceiling. It's panelled and carved, and intricately interesting but at the same time as I stare unblinking at it, I'm aware that one of the hooded figures has come forward with the glinting scissors and is slicing through the chiffon. I feel it fall away, first from my heels and ankles and then up my legs, releasing my tightly bound limbs. As it reaches the apex of my thighs, I pull in a tiny, sharp breath, but the blades chop relentlessly on, and a moment later, I feel I'm exposed in my most intimate parts to the eyes of the people I know are watching around the room. That feeling lasts only a second, then my belly is naked and then my lower chest, and then, with another long bite of the blades in the chiffon, my breasts are exposed. The ropes of pearls fall upon my naked skin, then they are gently removed.

I lie, utterly naked, beneath the glow of the lights, for everyone to see.

Olympe is there. I would sense her powerful personality even if I did not see her small, pointed face over mine.

'You are the perfect sacrifice,' she breathes in a voice that only I can hear. 'He will be compelled by you.'

Compelled? He's supposed to experience a blinding revelation that he loves me!

A flicker of fear goes through me.

What if she's wrong?

It's too late for that now.

Olympe's hands run over the skin on my arms and shoulders, then up from my lower belly to below my breasts. Her touch is surprisingly gentle, her skin soft and pampered. She strokes at first, lulling me into a sense of safety, then her little nails begin to scratch and dig into my skin.

I gasp at the first touch. It hurts with nasty little pinches but it's bearable. She pinches where I had no idea I was so tender – on the soft underside of my arm, at the side of my breasts, on my stomach and on my thighs – and the pressure and sharpness of the pinches grow. I can't help tiny sounds emerging from my throat as the talon-like nails dig into me. It hurts – and the anticipation of the pain is almost as bad as the pain itself. *But I have to stand it. This is just the beginning.*

She strokes me again and seems pleased. Then she reaches into the polished wooden box at her side and takes out a white leather collar, which she slips under my neck and then pulls tight – not tight enough to prevent me breathing but so I can feel the restriction. She buckles it in place. Then she takes something else from the chest, but I can't see what it is until her hands hover over my nipples and then she attaches a biting clip to my right nipple. I gasp with the pain as the little thing clamps down on my tender nipple, and sends a burning shimmer all over me. She attaches the other, and the burning feeling doubles. I moan. It's taking all my strength not to reach up and rip them off but I have to endure. What is surprising is the way the pain is making my body react, the way I can feel my sex throb and grow wet. I'm horrified. I don't want to show arousal to this old woman as she inflicts pain on me.

And I'm not aroused. I'm not.

I close my eyes. My heart has sped up and I'm breathing fast. I wonder if Andrei is in the audience. I can feel the spectators shifting, craning to get a better look. Has he recognised me yet? Is he here at all? Would it be in character for Olympe to put me through this and then reveal that Andrei was never here to witness it?

More clamps. She attaches one to the soft flesh on my stomach, and then a line of them along the thigh that is closest to her. Tears come into my eyes as the agony of the tiny teeth biting into my flesh grows. I'm sure I must be bleeding. In my mind's eye, I see trickles of blood going down my body where the clamps are attached. When I think I can't bear it any longer, I feel something else and open my eyes.

Olympe is holding a flat leather paddle and she is stroking it up and down my skin. It's soft and smooth but I gasp with anticipation of what the flat black surface will do to me when she strikes me with it. I know it will sting with viciousness. Olympe starts to flick it lightly on my skin. It doesn't hurt much – certainly not compared to the bite of the clamps that are making my nipples burn and sing – but it makes a loud noise. She flicks me over my belly and then puts two sharp blows across my nipples where they are already being violently squeezed by the clips. I can't help crying out and this seems to stimulate Olympe on. She flicks me harder with the paddle, striking me on the belly and thighs. It's hurting now, a burning sting with each blow. Then she pulls back the leather and flicks it hard over my sex. It strikes my clitoris, which is full and red at the apex of my slit, and I cry out again. My body starts to shake and I clench my fists hard with the desire to defend myself and stop her doing that again. My clit is burning with pain and yet it is sending out electric currents all over me that send a warm honey trickling through me at the same time. I hate it and yet ... something hot and pleasurable is running through my veins.

Olympe seems to sense my struggle with my urge to fight her off. She puts down the paddle and beckons two of her acolytes forward. Each one lifts one of my arms over my head. Olympe produces a long stiff bar of leather with a cuff at each end and she quickly fastens the manacles round my wrists. I'm bound to it, my arms held out above my head and unable to move. She regards me for a while, no doubt enjoying the spectacle, and then I see that she has something else in her hand – a long wooden handled needle.

I gasp with real fear. *What's she going to do with it?*

I soon know. She presses the wicked sharp point right on the tenderest point of my right nipple. It sends a bolt of severe pain racing through me and I cry out again, almost with a scream. She does the same to my left and then, with a smile that only I can see, she presses the point towards my slit. For one awful moment I think she is going to insert the needle inside me, but she drags the point up me and then pushes it against the bud of my clitoris, making me cry out again and my limbs shake. Tears of agony roll down my cheeks.

I don't know if this enrages her or pleases her, for she drops the needle and returns to the paddle. With a hard slap over my mound, she sends coruscating pain soaring through my clit. I scream and there's a kind of sigh from the audience. Then she beckons to the acolytes and they turn me over on the black velvet so that I'm lying on my belly. I've left the shreds of chiffon behind and I'm now completely naked, my bare bottom exposed. With another nod from Olympe, the acolytes spread my legs and fasten my ankles into a pair of cuffs attached to the same kind of stiff rod as my arms. Now I'm in an X shape, held out firmly and unable to change position. I cannot see Olympe now and can only make out dim shapes in the shadows around me.

She picks up the paddle and begins to beat my buttocks, softly at first and then harder, hitting with a regular stroke. At first it barely hurts. The sensation of the paddle bouncing off my buttocks is almost a welcome relief after the tormenting attentions of the needle and the burning bites of the clamps, which are pressed even harder on me now that I'm on my stomach. I feel the blows come with an almost comforting rhythm and the room is full of the sound of the leather slapping loudly over my skin. My buttocks tingle and then begin to burn. I can feel the blood rushing to the surface of my bottom, more with every smack. The pain begins to bite but it's a pain that is growing gradually, bringing with it the strangest sensation of satisfaction, though why it should be, I have no idea.

Nevertheless, the pain begins to grow and I start to wonder how long I can stand it, as my bottom feels more and more raw. I have no idea what it must look like, but the burning flesh must surely be scarlet. I wonder if she will go on until she breaks the skin, and I see my own skin dripping with blood so vividly I'm almost certain that it is bleeding already.

I'm gasping with every blow and then moaning, and then, as it hits me again, I'm shouting, twisting my head, shaking my bottom, trying to move my legs and arms against the restraint. I can hear answering moans from the audience as they watch me being punished.

Where is Andrei? Does he know I'm doing this for him?

Then suddenly the beating stops and I'm left for several minutes to recover. I'm still twisting and jerking under my restraints for a few moments, breathless, groaning, and then gradually, as I realise that the blows have ceased, I become still and begin to get my breath back. One of the acolytes darts forward and sponges my bottom lightly with a cool fluid, and then rubs in a mint-scented lotion that makes my skin sting and tingle again. My ankles are uncuffed so that I can close my legs. It hurts my poor bottom as I move my thighs together.

I'm lifted into a kneeling position, now blinking against the contrast of light and dark after so long looking down. I can't make out anything beyond Olympe.

'Now,' she declares loudly. 'A special moment for a special novice, who is about to dedicate herself to a new master.'

I look at her, dazed by what I've endured so far. She leans forward and swiftly removes the clamps from my skin. My nipples enjoy the blissful release from the pain.

If only it didn't bring this strange pleasure with it, I could understand.

Then, something unexpected. Olympe brings out a gag, which she puts round my head, filling my mouth with a thick leather bit. Then, just as I'm adjusting to the thick wodge in my mouth, she produces a leather hood, with netting at the eyes, nose and mouth, and in a deft movement she puts it over my head. For a moment I struggle, but there is not much I can do with my arms still raised high and held stiffly outwards. I'm panicked by the sensation of the hood encasing my head and the restriction of my breathing. Olympe slaps me hard twice and the blows do, strangely, calm me down. I begin to become accustomed to the hood and my breathing starts to become more regular. But I'm still struggling to understand what she has done. And then it hits me.

I can't be recognised. It's impossible to see me. I can't speak.

All sense of arousal drains from my body. I'm afraid now. I've been hidden, made anonymous, all trace of my identity gone. I'm just a body now, a body at the mercy of Olympe.

But there's nothing I can do.

A cold sweat breaks out all over me and I start to shake. Then there are hands at my wrists. The cuffs are undone, the stiff rod of leather taken away. My arms fall to my sides, aching but with the relief of release. Nevertheless, the hood and gag still fill me with panic. I'm shaking all over.

Hands lift me to my feet. I'm naked now, possibly smeared in blood, but that seems of little account. I'm led a few steps forward and hands move my limbs gently apart. I sense that I must be by the columns I saw the previous woman chained to and sure enough I feel myself fastened again at the wrists and ankles, this time with cold iron.

A smoky incense fills the air and I'm aware of warmth nearby.

The brazier! I can't help a whimper escaping the gag. *Oh God. What have I done? Where is Andrei?*

Olympe's voice sounds loud and clear. 'This novice wishes to become the servant and possession of a master, and win his approval. She will submit to him here before us as proof of her devotion to him. She will allow him to make the mark of possession upon her.'

A murmur from the audience. I think they like the idea.
'Bring in this slave's master!'

I hear a door open behind me and then footsteps. A wave
of relief rushes through me, helping me forget the pain I'm
already in. I want to drop down and hang from my manacles, turn my face up and cry, but I don't. I stay strong,
wondering what he can see: a naked woman with her back
to him, her bottom stained red with her beating, a hood
over her head, her hands and ankles chained, waiting for
his ministrations.

Does he know it's me? What has she told him?

Olympe speaks again, in her clear, authoritative voice.
'Sir, here is a most willing victim who has particularly
requested that you inflict the blows she longs to suffer. Will
you do so?'

There's a pause, agonising in its length, though in reality
it can only be a few seconds.

'Yes.' It's Andrei's voice and I thrill to hear it. He's so
close to me. I long for him so much that if he wanted to
ravish me here, in front of all these people, I wouldn't mind.
In fact, I long for it.

'She has asked that you lay it on, with no mercy.'
Olympe seems to relish her words. 'I have selected the
whip for you.'

I sense Andrei approach me. He's standing behind me
and I guess he's taking in the sight. How can he recognise
me, with my body already changed with a beating and my
head covered by the hood? *Can he? Will he?*

'Lash her,' orders Olympe.

A moment later, I hear the whistle of leather strips and
then the blow across my already tender buttocks.

I shout and my head falls back. The shout is muffled by

273

my gag and the leather hood. *I can't be heard.* Inside the hood, I start to pant.

Slap! It hits me again, feeling as though it is flaying the skin off me. I cry out loudly, and then another stroke comes, beating down relentlessly on my raw bottom. The only thing that can comfort me as the fiery strips of leather hit my poor skin is that it is Andrei who is inflicting this pain. I tell myself that every blow I endure will bring us more closely together.

But does he know it's me? Has she told him? Oh God, I can't stand it!

Hot tears are burning my eyes and running down my cheeks. I'm breathless and gasping round my gag and under the hood, my voice small and ineffectual. I scream and shout inside my hood but I'm sure that nothing much can be heard beyond.

The tenth and eleventh strokes hit me. I begin to wonder if I will faint under the agony.

'Another lash,' cries Olympe, her voice resonant with happiness.

I wait for the next, certain that I will not be able to stand it. I'm sure I'll pass out, and drop down, and all this will have been for nothing.

But it doesn't come. Then I hear Andrei's voice. 'It seems to me that the slave has reached her limits.'

'Oh no, she wants more. As much as you can give. As hard as you can,' urges Olympe.

What does she want from me? How much I can give? Already I've endured much more than I ever supposed I could . . .

'No.' Andrei's voice is firm and cold. 'Only if she asks me herself.'

There's a pause. It seems that Olympe doesn't want me to be unmasked quite yet.

'Very well,' she says. 'Then we shall complete the ceremony. You must mark this slave.'

Icy terror floods through me.

'The fire is hot, the iron is ready,' she goes on. 'You must choose where on her body she is to take the mark.'

I don't know what is going on behind me. I can only pant in racing horror, powerless to stop this and yet now wondering if Olympe was right in what she predicted. I cannot sense that Andrei is fully involved.

He doesn't even know it's me. I'm sure of it.

After a moment, he says, 'She is determined to take this mark?'

'She is! It is the point of this experience for her.'

Another pause and something like a sigh from Andrei. 'Very well.'

Now I'm aware of the heat that is coming from the brazier. It makes me almost unconscious with fear. *I shouldn't do this. I don't believe it's what Andrei will want. I think I've been fooled by Olympe. But how can I stop it?* Even if I could speak and make myself heard, I don't know if I would have the strength.

I hear him walk to the brazier and remove something from the coals, releasing a waft of scented smoke as he does so. Then a bar of heat approaches me. I'm sweating and moaning. *No, no, no . . . Andrei, it's me!*

I twist against my manacles but it's no good. There's nothing I can do to escape. Hands touch me, holding me still.

'Don't fight it,' whispers a voice close to my head. Olympe.

But I want to fight it. I'm in horrified anticipation of the searing sizzle of my flesh burning.

I sense Andrei's nearness and the heat comes closer and closer. I can feel it eating into my skin already. I moan and throw back my head again but someone seizes me. The white-hot heat is very close to me now, already burning me before it's touched me.

There's nothing I can do. It's too late. I bite down hard on the gag, waiting for the agony to commence.

It doesn't come.

'What is this?' Andrei's voice is rapping out, hard and cold. 'What the hell is the meaning of this?' The heat is abruptly removed from my skin and I hear it dropped back into the brazier. 'Those are my initials, Olympe!'

'And she is your slave,' coos Olympe. 'Naturally. It is what she wants.'

'What? I'm not in the market for a slave, you know that! Why have you allowed this?'

'I haven't,' retorts Olympe, her voice as powerful and strong as Andrei's. 'You have. You might not know it but it's what you want. And so does she. Get the brand and do it!'

'No.' Andrei's voice is as stubborn as I've ever heard it. 'I refuse. And who is it who wishes to be my slave?'

'That cannot be revealed until you mark her,' returns Olympe, almost with a jeer in her voice.

I moan, overcome with everything I've experienced. I sense a change in Andrei – an alertness. Suddenly I can hear him coming swiftly towards me, shouting at the acolytes, 'Let her down for Christ's sake, let her down!'

They wait an instant and then obey. My chains are undone and I fall to my knees. My eyes are closed to blessed darkness. I feel Andrei beside me, undoing the leather hood and lifting it off.

'Flora! Oh God, no, no . . . I had no idea . . . oh no . . .'
He discards the hood and unbuckles the gag, pulling it free
so that my mouth is at last clear of it. I look up at him and
his expression is more agonised than I've ever seen. 'What
have they done to you, my beautiful girl?'

I can't speak, but only stare mutely up at him, hoping
that all my love and gratitude to him is in my eyes.

He turns in a fury to Olympe. 'What the hell have you
done to her?' he yells.

'Nothing she didn't want!' replies Olympe icily. 'Ask her.'

'I will. Believe me. Once she's recovered from whatever
you've done to her.' Scorn enters his voice. 'I didn't expect
this of you, Olympe. You know the difference between a
true submissive and an impressionable girl, don't you?
What were you thinking?'

'I do,' answer Olympe. Her own voice is full of anger.
'But do you, Andrei? Do you ever see what is in front of
your face? She was doing all this for you, not for me.'

Andrei seems startled and says nothing for a second, then
he turns from Olympe and begins to lift me up, tenderly.
'Give me your robe,' he orders one of the acolytes and a
moment later, I'm being wrapped in black cotton, my aching
nakedness covered at last. Andrei lifts me up and carries
me with complete ease.

'Come on,' he whispers in my ear. 'We're getting out of
here right now.'

CHAPTER TWENTY-FIVE

I hardly know what happens next. I'm vaguely aware of Andrei carrying me upstairs and into a waiting car. He holds me gently, careful to avoid where my pain might be, and murmurs softly to me as the car glides through Paris. We stop, and he carries me again. The next thing I know, I'm on the bed in his penthouse apartment, so very tired I can hardly think.

Andrei runs me a tepid bath and lowers me carefully into it. I yelp as the water stings my lacerated behind and then sigh as it begins to soothe and comfort me. Andrei tends to me, washing me gently with a sponge, talking to me as though I am a frightened child who needs calming. When I'm clean and feeling better, my head clearing, he dries me with infinite gentleness, wraps me in a bathrobe and leads me back to the bed. He makes me take painkillers for my inflammation and drink a hot cup of tea.

'Flora, my darling, what were you thinking of?' he asks, sitting on the bed beside me and holding my hand. 'What were you doing there?'

'It was for you,' I say in a small voice. 'I wanted to show you that . . . that I love you. Olympe persuaded me that it was the best way.'

Andrei smiles ruefully. 'To let me beat you up and brand you with my initials?' He shakes his head. 'Olympe has been at this game a little too long. Perhaps she has begun to lose her grip on things.'

I say hesitantly, 'Her friend Josephine . . . there was some-thing she said that made me wonder. She hinted that Olympe wanted me to become her submissive. She more or less asked me if I would. But I said no.'

Andrei nods. 'That does not surprise me. Olympe is many incredible things but she is also an arch manipulator and she hates to be thwarted. I suspect that if she knew who you are, she was excited by the prospect of making you one of her submissives, and no doubt, in time, one of the tribe.'

'I never would have wanted that,' I declare. 'I only wanted you. And Olympe told me that this was the way I would show you my love. She was very convincing. I believed her completely.'

'She probably meant it, in her way.' Andrei looks at me tenderly. 'I'm in awe at what you were willing to do for me, she was right about that. But when I think how I whipped you . . .' He blanches and looks quite ill. 'I feel terrible.'

'You didn't guess it was me?'

He shakes his head. 'Not at all. I imagined you were a practised submissive. Many of them are, you know. In fact, I've always admired Olympe's ability to judge perfectly what a novice should endure, and when to allow an old hand to play the ingenue. She misjudged badly here.'

'She did things to me . . .' My voice trails away and then I find the strength to go on. 'She did things I hadn't seen, I didn't expect.'

'She let something in her get carried away. We had an intense relationship at one point. Perhaps she still feels some ownership and let herself punish you beyond what you could stand.' He rubs my hand gently. 'This is my fault, Flora. I got you into this position. Olympe never likes to lose a submissive. When I left her, I believe she never quite got over it. Perhaps that, along with her desire to own you herself, made her lose some of her legendary control. I'm to blame.'

'It isn't your fault. I made it happen. I didn't have to go through with it.'

He stares at me, those blue eyes soft as a summer sea again. 'Why did you?'

'Because you wanted to break off the arrangement,' I say wretchedly. 'I couldn't bear to lose you. I realised that I love you and I wanted to show you just how much, so that you would stop loving Beth.'

'Oh Flora.' He shakes his head slowly. 'I haven't stopped loving Beth.'

'I know.' My eyes fill with tears. My emotions feel raw, so close to the surface, as though they've been as battered as my flesh. My heart sinks with sadness. 'I know.'

'I haven't stopped loving her because I never did love her. I see that now. I thought I loved her, because I wanted her so badly and she refused to be mine.' He holds my hand tighter. 'But the kindest thing she ever did for me was to refuse me. I didn't understand then. Even when I tried to force her to do what I wanted, she held firm and wished me love in my life.'

I stare back, trying to take this in. 'You ... don't love Beth?' The idea seems ridiculous. The fact of his love for Beth has dominated my life for what feels like a very long time.

'No.' He laughs. 'I don't.'

'But then ... why did you want to break off our relationship?' I'm bewildered. It doesn't make sense.

'I didn't want to break off our relationship. Where did you get that idea? I wanted to review that arrangement. The contract we agreed before all this started properly. I wanted to end it. I had the idea we should tear up that blasted bit of paper and burn it.'

I blink with astonishment. 'So . . .'

'So I wanted us to be together, properly. I was tired of the games, fun though they were to start with. I realised we didn't need them. We had moved beyond them to see the people we really are.'

A spring of happiness is bubbling inside me. Darkness is turning, wonderfully and unexpectedly, to sunshine. 'You wanted us to be a couple!'

'Yes. I know there'll be trouble with your family – no decent family would want me in it, let's be honest – but I'm prepared to face it if you are.'

A thought strikes me. 'Estelle . . . she knows. She has pictures of us.'

'Not any longer,' Andrei says coolly. 'François was keeping watch and he saw your idiot bodyguard Alphonse taking some photographs with a long lens camera, and made it his business to find out exactly what he thought he was doing. My men are sorting out the situation right now.' He laughs. 'I think it was when I saw you with her that I realised I love you. I saw you from the cafe when you thought you were alone with her. My little tigress facing her enemy.' He kisses me tenderly, his lips divine on my mouth. I feel hungry at once for more. 'I was so utterly on your side. Don't be worried about her. She won't hurt you.'

I gaze at him, wishing that were true. But Andrei doesn't know the whole story. 'My father won't be overjoyed, she's right about that, pictures or not.'

'I know.' Andrei nods. 'I shall just have to convince him

of my honourable intentions and the fact that, despite my reputation, I'm not actually a monster or a criminal.'

'You're not?' I say hopefully.

'No!' He laughs with a loud guffaw. 'I'm not. Don't believe everything you hear.'

I lie back on the pillows. The pain in my body doesn't seem half as bad now. The bath has done its soothing work. I'm relaxed and now that what Andrei has said has sunk in, I'm feeling elated. 'You love me!' I say happily. 'And I love you!'

'I suppose that's right, yes.' He gazes at me, smiling one of those broad happy smiles that transform him into a handsome man. 'And even though I'm not a monster or a criminal, I have to admit that I can be a handful. Do you think you can cope?'

I lean forward to kiss him. 'I've had some practice. And besides, you're exactly the kind of handful I like best.'

Andrei returns my kiss and then pulls away, looking at me with a kind of wonder again. 'I can't believe what you were prepared to go through for me. You were going to let me brand you with my initials . . .'

'Like you did for Olympe,' I reply simply. 'To show your love.'

'Hmm. Well. Olympe and I are very different creatures,' he says. 'I'm glad we didn't mark your lovely skin.'

'We did a little, if what I can feel is anything to go by.'

'Yes, a little. But it will heal.' He leans in towards me and mutters, 'I will be the only one to do such things to you in future, eh?'

My body tingles despite the aching in my limbs.

'But we will make sure you are better first.' He raises an eyebrow at me. 'Still, I'm looking forward to giving you a proof of my love.'

'Now ... now,' I beg, taking his hands in mine and kissing them.

'No. You're very tired and you've been through a lot tonight. But ...' He kisses me and says, 'I cannot promise that tomorrow I'll be able to restrain myself.'

'But I want to,' I plead.

'Tomorrow. Now you should sleep. I want you to forget the nightmare. We will cut our ties with Olympe and rely only on ourselves for pleasure.'

I sigh happily. 'You know what? That sounds good to me.' I lie back on the pillows again and yawn. Andrei tucks the covers around me. I want to talk to him more about when he realised he loved me and what he really thought of our arrangement but I don't think I will make much sense.

In fact, I'm asleep before he turns out the light.

EPILOGUE

The auditorium is full of cheering, and this time it's for me – and the rest of the cast of the end-of-term show. We're taking our bows, relieved and euphoric now that it's over. My tutor was as good as his word and gave me a leading part. I think I pulled it off – at least, it felt right and the cheers and whoops from the audience seem sincere.

As I take my bow, a bunch of flowers lands at my feet – a beautiful bouquet of roses. I know which of the people in the front row threw that. I look to him with a beaming smile to see him on his feet, clapping and glowing with pride.

Andrei. I'm so happy he's here.

It's crowned the evening that he was here to see it.

Afterwards we toast the success of the show at a smart restaurant.

'You were marvellous, darling,' Andrei says. 'I knew you were talented, of course, but even so . . .'

'Thank you.' I squeeze his hand with gratitude at his compliments. 'My tutor tells me that some very important agents were in the audience and at least two of them asked for my mobile number. So here's hoping . . .' I hold up my glass and Andrei clinks it with his.

'Hmm.' He frowns slightly and says, 'Not that you

will need them. You don't seriously intend to act, do you?'

'If I can,' I say, my smile fading. 'You don't mind, do you?'

Andrei considers and then looks up with a smile. 'I suppose not. There's plenty of time to decide that anyway. We should think only of now and what we have.'

'Good,' I say, relieved. 'I wouldn't want anything like that to come between us.'

'Perhaps it's good you'll have plenty to occupy yourself,' Andrei says, sipping his champagne. 'I need to go on urgent business. I'm not sure how long I'll be gone.'

'What is it?' I ask, even though I hardly know what he does.

His face hardens just a little. 'A private matter. Let's just say that I have the opportunity to get my own back on a previous employee of mine. One who treated me with unforgivable impudence.' His mouth twitches in a strange smile. 'But I'm going to take a particular pleasure in my revenge.'

I stare at him, wondering why this remark causes a flicker of anxiety in my stomach. 'Oh. That doesn't sound good.'

'Don't worry about it,' he replies, firmly closing the subject.

We put it behind us and enjoy the rest of our evening, the triumph of the show still filling me with pleasure.

It's only when we are in the car on the way back to Andrei's penthouse apartment that everything changes. A text comes to my phone. To my astonishment, it's from Beth.

Flora, I've got to see you. Freya has sent me a message that I must give you in person. She needs your help. And so do I. I'll tell you more when I see you. Can you come to the apartment as soon as possible? Tell no one. Not even A.

I gape at the message.

She knows. She knows I'm with Andrei! But how?

And more importantly, what can be wrong with Freya? I'm filled with the impulse to get to Beth right now and find out, but I restrain myself. Something tells me that no matter what Andrei has told me about his feelings for Beth, it's still dangerous territory.

The words about his ex-employee float into my mind.

Can it be Beth? Is that who he means?

'Who's your message from?' asks Andrei, who has been absorbed in his own phone.

I say nothing for a moment. I hate this. Do I have to lie to him? *But what else can I do?*

'Summer,' I say. 'She wants to talk to me.'

'Your sister. I can't wait to meet her,' Andrei remarks. 'Flora and Summer, the season twins. It's a beautiful notion.'

I rest my head against the window, watching the city go by. Sadness fills my heart. I've not told him the truth. I'm going to see Beth without letting him know.

Why does life get in the way and complicate things?

Andrei leans over and kisses me. 'You're my beautiful spring girl,' he says. 'And when we get home, I'm going to show you how much you invigorate me.'

I kiss him back and smile.

Oh, Andrei. If only it could be you and me, alone, making love for ever. But it can't . . . I have a feeling reality is going to intrude sooner than we'd want.

'You're my passion,' he murmurs into my ear. 'Do you know that?'

'You're mine too,' I reply, and lose myself in the dark pleasure of his kiss. Reality can wait till tomorrow at least.

ACKNOWLEDGEMENTS

Thank you to everyone who has helped me on this book, in particular Francesca, Sharan, Justine, Naomi, Lizzi and all of the marvellous team at Hodder. Also to Lizzy and Harriet, and to my family and friends for their support.

**Have you read the first novel in Sadie Matthews's
exhilarating, intoxicating *Seasons* trilogy . . .**

SEASON OF DESIRE

Freya Hammond is used to people fulfilling her every whim.
Wealthy and spoiled, she lives a butterfly existence of fashion
and parties and is accustomed to getting her own way.
Which is why the new bodyguard is riling her. Miles Murray
is ex-SAS and obeys her instructions with barely repressed
scorn. She can sense that he doesn't think much of her.

The Hammonds have been staying at their luxurious retreat
high in the Alps. Now Miles is driving Freya to the airport
but the rapidly worsening weather and a near-miss with
a dangerously driven jeep cause him to lose control, and
send the car plummeting off the side of the mountain.

When Freya comes to, she is lying on the freezing ground, Miles
beside her. The car is a mangled mess far below them. Now
Freya needs Miles to save her life. Using all his survival skills,
Miles manages to locate an old shepherd's hut and get them
both there despite Freya's twisted ankle. Rescue will surely
come before too long . . . but until then Freya is no longer in
control. The tension between them is soon at fever pitch as
she tries to dominate a man who no longer obeys her orders.

And when rescue does come, how will they
return to their old life of mistress and bodyguard
after what has happened between them?

Out now in paperback and ebook.

HODDER

Have you read the *After Dark* series by Sadie Matthews? Deeply intense and romantic, provocative and sensual, it will take you to a place where love and sex are liberated from their limits.

Read on for a taste of the first book in the series ...

FIRE AFTER DARK

It started with a spark ...

Everything changed when I met Dominic. My heart had just been broken, split into jagged fragments that can jigsaw together to make me look enough like a normal, happy person.

Dominic has shown me a kind of abandonment I've never known before. He takes me down a path of pure pleasure, but of pain, too – his love offers me both lightness and dark. And where he leads me, I have no choice but to follow.

Out now in ebook, paperback and audio.

HODDER

CHAPTER ONE

The city takes my breath away as it stretches beyond the
taxi windows, rolling past like giant scenery being unfurled
by an invisible stagehand. Inside the cab, I'm cool, quiet
and untouchable. Just an observer. But out there, in the hot
stickiness of a July afternoon, London is moving hard and
fast: traffic surges along the lanes and people throng the
streets, herds of them crossing roads whenever the lights
change. Bodies are everywhere, of every type, age, size and
race. Millions of lives are unfolding on this one day in this
one place. The scale of it all is overwhelming.

What have I done?

As we skirt a huge green space colonised by hundreds of
sunbathers, I wonder if this is Hyde Park. My father told
me that Hyde Park is bigger than Monaco. Imagine that.
Monaco might be small, but even so. The thought makes
me shiver and I realise I'm frightened. That's odd because
I don't consider myself a cowardly person.

Anyone would be nervous, I tell myself firmly. But it's no
surprise my confidence has been shot after everything that's
happened lately. The familiar sick feeling churns in my
stomach and I damp it down.

*Not today. I've got too much else to think about. Besides,
I've done enough thinking and crying. That's the whole
reason I'm here.*

'Nearly there, love,' says a voice suddenly, and I realise

it's the taxi driver, his voice distorted by the intercom. I see him watching me in the rear-view mirror. 'I know a good short cut from here,' he says, 'no need to worry about all this traffic.'

'Thanks,' I say, though I expected nothing less from a London cabbie; after all, they're famous for their knowledge of the city's streets, which is why I decided to splurge on one instead of wrestling with the Underground system. My luggage isn't enormous but I didn't relish the idea of heaving it on and off trains and up escalators in the heat. I wonder if the driver is assessing me, trying to guess what on earth I'm doing going to such a prestigious address when I look so young and ordinary; just a girl in a flowery dress, red cardigan and flip-flops, with sunglasses perched in hair that's tied in a messy ponytail, strands escaping everywhere.

'First time in London, is it?' he asks, smiling at me via the mirror.

'Yes, that's right,' I say. That isn't strictly true. I came as a girl at Christmas once with my parents and I remember a noisy blur of enormous shops, brightly lit windows, and a Santa whose nylon trousers crackled as I sat on his knee, and whose polyester white beard scratched me softly on the cheek. But I don't feel like getting into a big discussion with the driver, and anyway the city is as good as foreign to me. It's my first time alone here, after all.

'On your own, are you?' he asks and I feel a little uncomfortable, even though he's only being friendly.

'No, I'm staying with my aunt,' I reply, lying again.

He nods, satisfied. We're pulling away from the park now, darting with practised agility between buses and cars, swooping past cyclists, taking corners quickly and flying through amber traffic lights. Then we're off the busy main roads and in narrow streets lined by high brick-and-stone mansions with tall windows, glossy front doors, shining black iron railings, and window boxes spilling with bright blooms. I can sense money everywhere, not just in the expensive cars parked at the roadsides, but in the perfectly kept buildings, the clean pavements, the half-glimpsed maids closing curtains against the sunshine.

'She's doing all right, your aunt,' jokes the driver as we turn into a small street, and then again into one even smaller. 'It costs a penny or two to live around here.'

I laugh but don't reply, not knowing what to say. On one side of the street is a mews converted into minute but no doubt eye-wateringly pricy houses, and on the other a large mansion of flats, filling up most of the block and going up six storeys at least. I can tell from its Art Deco look that it was built in the 1930s; the outside is grey, dominated by a large glass-and-walnut door. The driver pulls up in front of it and says, 'Here we are then. Randolph Gardens.'

I look out at all the stone and asphalt. 'Where are the gardens?' I say wonderingly. The only greenery visible is the hanging baskets of red and purple geraniums on either side of the front door.

'There would have been some here years ago, I expect,' he replies. 'See the mews? That was stables at one time. I bet there were a couple of big houses round here once. They'll have been demolished or bombed in the war, maybe.' He glances at his meter. 'Twelve pounds seventy, please, love.'

I fumble for my purse and hand over fifteen pounds, saying, 'Keep the change,' and hoping I've tipped the right amount. The driver doesn't faint with surprise, so I guess it must be all right. He waits while I get myself and my luggage out of the cab and on to the pavement and shut the door behind me. Then he does an expert three-point turn in the tight little street and roars off back into the action.

I look up. So here I am. My new home. For a while, at least.

The white-haired porter inside looks up at me enquiringly as I puff through the door and up to his desk with my large bag.

'I'm here to stay in Celia Reilly's flat,' I explain, resisting the urge to wipe away the perspiration on my forehead. 'She said the key would be here for me.'

'Name?' he says gruffly.

'Beth. I mean, Elizabeth. Elizabeth Villiers.'

'Let me see . . .' He snuffles into his moustache as he looks through a file on his desk. 'Ah, yes. Here we are. Miss E. Villiers. To occupy 514 in Miss Reilly's absence.' He fixes me with a beady but not unfriendly gaze. 'Flat-sitting, are you?'

'Yes. Well. Cat-sitting, really.' I smile at him but he doesn't return it.

'Oh yes. She does have a cat. Can't think why a creature like that would want to live its life inside but there we are. Here are the keys.' He pushes an envelope across the desk towards me. 'If you could just sign the book for me.'

I sign obediently and he tells me a few of the building regulations as he directs me towards the lift. He offers to take my luggage up for me later but I say I'll do it myself. At least that way I'll have everything I need. A moment later I'm inside the small elevator, contemplating my heated, red-faced reflection as the lift ascends slowly to the fifth floor. I don't look anywhere near as polished as the surroundings, but my heart-shaped face and round blue eyes will never be like the high-cheek-boned, elegant features I most admire. And my fly-away dark-blonde shoulder-length hair will never be the naturally thick, lustrous tresses I've always craved. My hair takes work and usually I can't be bothered, just pulling it back into a messy ponytail.

'Not exactly a Mayfair lady,' I say out loud. As I stare at myself, I can see the effect of everything that has happened lately. I'm thinner around the face, and there's a sadness in my eyes that never seems to go away. I look a bit smaller, somehow, as though I've bowed a little under the weight of my misery. 'Be strong,' I whisper to myself, trying to find my old spark in my dull gaze. That's why I've come, after all. Not because I'm trying to escape – although that must be part of it – but because I want to rediscover the old me, the one who had spirit and courage and a curiosity in the world.

Unless that Beth has been completely destroyed.

I don't want to think like that but it's hard not to.

Number 514 is halfway down a quiet, carpeted hallway. The keys fit smoothly into the lock and a moment later I'm stepping inside the flat. My first impression is surprise as a small chirrup greets me, followed by a high squeaky miaow, soft warm fur brushing over my legs, and a body snaking between my calves, nearly tripping me up.

'Hello, hello!' I exclaim, looking down into a small black whiskered face with a halo of dark fur, squashed up like a cushion that's been sat on. 'You must be De Havilland.'

He miaows again, showing me sharp white teeth and a little pink tongue.

I try to look about while the cat purrs frantically, rubbing himself hard against my legs, evidently pleased to see me. I'm inside a hall and I can see already that Celia has stayed true to the building's 1930s aesthetic. The floor is tiled black and white, with a white cashmere rug in the middle. A jet-black console table sits beneath a large Art Deco mirror flanked by geometric chrome lights. On the console is a huge white silver-rimmed china bowl with vases on either side. Everything is elegant and quietly beautiful.

I haven't expected anything else. My father has been irritatingly vague about his godmother's flat, which he saw on the few occasions he visited London, but he's always given me the impression that it is as glamorous as Celia herself. She started as a model in her teens and was very successful, making a lot of money, but later she gave it up and became a fashion journalist. She married once and divorced, and then again and was widowed. She never had children, which is perhaps why she's managed to stay so young and vibrant, and she's been a lackadaisical god-mother to my father, swooping in and out of his life as it took her fancy. Sometimes he heard nothing from her for years, then she'd appear out of the blue loaded with gifts, always elegant and dressed in the height of fashion, smoth-ering him with kisses and trying to make up for her neglect. I remember meeting her on a few occasions, when I was a shy, knock-kneed girl in shorts and a T-shirt, hair all over the place, who could never imagine being as polished and sophisticated as this woman in front of me, with her cropped silver hair, amazing clothes and splendid jewellery.

What am I saying? Even now, I can't imagine being like her. Not for a moment.

And yet, here I am, in her apartment which is all mine for five weeks.

The phone call came without warning. I hadn't paid

attention until my father got off the phone, looking bemused and said to me, 'Do you fancy a spell in London, Beth? Celia's going away, she needs someone to look after her cat and she thought you might appreciate the chance to stay in her flat.'

'Her flat?' I'd echoed, looking up from my book. 'Me?'

'Yes. It's somewhere rather posh, I think. Mayfair, Belgravia, somewhere like that. I've not been there for years.' He shot a look at my mother, with his eyebrows raised. 'Celia's off on a retreat in the woods of Montana for five weeks. Apparently she needs to be spiritually renewed. As you do.'

'Well, it keeps her young,' my mother replied, wiping down the kitchen table. 'It's not every seventy-two-year-old who could even think of it.' She stood up and stared at the scrubbed wood a little wistfully. 'I think it sounds rather nice, I'd love to do something like that.'

She had a look on her face as if contemplating other paths she might have taken, other lives she might have lived. My father obviously wanted to say something jeering but stopped when he saw her expression. I was pleased about that: she'd given up her career when she married him, and devoted herself to looking after me and my brothers. She was entitled to her dreams, I guess.

My father turned to me. 'So, what do you think, Beth? Are you interested?'

Mum looked at me and I saw it in her eyes at once. She wanted me to go. She knew it was the best thing possible under the circumstances. 'You should do it,' she said quietly. 'It'll be a new leaf for you after what's happened.'

I almost shuddered. I couldn't bear it to be spoken of.

My face flushed with mortification. 'Don't,' I whispered as tears filled my eyes. The wound was still so open and raw.

My parents exchanged looks and then my father said gruffly, 'Perhaps your mother's right. You could do with getting out and about.'

I'd hardly been out of the house for over a month. I couldn't bear the idea of seeing them together. Adam and Hannah. The thought of it made my stomach swoop sickeningly towards my feet, and my head buzz as though I was going to faint.

'Maybe,' I said in a small voice. 'I'll think about it.'

We didn't decide that evening. I was finding it hard enough just to get up in the morning, let alone take a big decision like that. My confidence in myself was so shot, I wasn't sure that I could make the right choice about what to have for lunch let alone whether I should accept Celia's offer. After all, I'd chosen Adam, and trusted him and look how that had turned out. The next day my mother called Celia and talked through some of the practical aspects, and that evening I called her myself. Just listening to her strong voice, full of enthusiasm and confidence, made me feel better.

'You'll be doing me a favour, Beth,' she said firmly, 'but I think you'll enjoy yourself too. It's time you got out of that dead-end place and saw something of the world.'

Celia was an independent woman, living her life on her own terms and if she believed I could do it, then surely I could. So I said yes. Even though, as the time to leave home came closer, I wilted and began to wonder if I could pull out somehow, I knew I had to do it. If I could pack my bags and go alone to one of the biggest cities in the world, then maybe there was hope for me. I loved the little

Norfolk town where I'd grown up, but if all I could do was huddle at home, unable to face the world because of what Adam had done, then I ought to give up and sign out right now. And what did I have to keep me there? There was my part-time job in a local cafe that I'd been doing since I was fifteen, only stopping when I went off to university and then picking it up again when I got back, still wondering what I was going to do with my life. My parents? Hardly. They didn't want me living in my old room and moping about. They dreamed of more for me than that.

The truth was that I'd come back because of Adam. My university friends were off travelling before they started exciting new jobs or moved to other countries. I'd listened to all the adventures waiting for them, knowing that my future was waiting for me back home. Adam was the centre of my world, the only man I'd ever loved, and there had been no question of doing anything but being with him. Adam worked, as he had since school, for his father's building company that he expected one day to own himself, and he was happy enough to contemplate living for the rest of his life in the same place he'd grown up. I didn't know if that was for me, but I did know that I loved Adam and I could put my own desires to travel and explore on hold for a while so that we could be together.

Except that now I didn't have any choice.

De Havilland yowls at my ankles and gives one a gentle nip to remind me that he's there.

'Sorry, puss,' I say apologetically, and put my bag down. 'Are you hungry?'

The cat stays twined around my legs as I try and find the

kitchen, opening the door to a coat cupboard and another to a loo before discovering a small galley kitchen, with the cat's bowls neatly placed under the window at the far end. They're licked completely clean and De Havilland is obviously eager for his next meal. On the small white dining table at the other end, just big enough for two, I see some packets of cat biscuits and a sheaf of paper. On top is a note written in large scrawling handwriting.

Darling, hello!
You made it. Good. Here is De Havilland's food. Feed him twice a day, just fill the little bowl with his biscuits as if you were putting out cocktail snacks, lucky De H. He'll need nice clean water to go with it. All other instructions in the useful little pack below, but really, darling, there are no rules. Enjoy yourself.
See you in five weeks,
C xx

Beneath are typed pages with all the necessary information about the cat's litter tray, the workings of the appliances, where to find the boiler and the first aid kit, and who to talk to if I have any problems. The porter downstairs looks like my first port of call. My porter of call. Hey, if I'm making jokes, even weak ones, then maybe this trip is working already.

De Havilland is miaowing in a constant rolling squeak, his little pink tongue quivering as he stares up at me with his dark yellow eyes.

'Dinner coming up,' I say.

When De Havilland is happily crunching away, his water bowl refreshed, I look around the rest of the flat, admiring the black-and-white bathroom with its chrome and Bakelite fittings, and taking in the gorgeous bedroom: the silver four-poster bed with a snowy cover piled high with white cushions, and the ornate chinoiserie wallpaper where brightly plumaged parrots observe each other through blossomed cherry tree branches. A vast silver gilt mirror hangs over the fireplace and an antique mirrored dressing table stands by the window, next to a purple velvet button-back armchair.

'It's beautiful,' I say out loud. Maybe here I'll absorb some of Celia's chic and acquire some style myself.

As I walk through the hallway into the sitting room I realise that it's better than I dreamed it could be. I imagined a smart place that reflected the life of a well-off, independent woman but this is something else, like no home I've ever seen before. The sitting room is a large room decorated in cool calm colours of pale green and stone, with accents of black, white and silver. The era of the thirties is wonderfully evoked in the shapes of the furniture: the low armchairs with large curving arms, the long sofa piled with white cushions, the clean line of a swooping chrome reading lamp and the sharp edges of a modern coffee table in jet-black lacquer. The far wall is dominated by a vast built-in white bookcase filled with volumes and ornaments including wonderful pieces of jade and Chinese sculpture. The long wall that faces the window is painted in that serene pale green broken up by panels of silver lacquer etched with delicate willows, the shiny surfaces acting almost like mirrors. Between the panels are wall lights with shades of frosted white glass and on the parquet floor is a huge antique zebra-skin rug.

I'm enchanted at this delightful evocation of an age of elegance. I love everything I see, from the crystal vases made to hold the thick dark stems and ivory trumpets of lilies to the matching Chinese ginger pots on either side of the shining chrome fireplace, above which is a huge and important-looking piece of modern art that, on closer inspection, I see is a Patrick Heron: great slashes of colour – scarlet, burnt orange, umber and vermillion – creating wonderful hectic drama in that oasis of cool grassy green and white.

I stare around, open-mouthed. I had no idea people actually created rooms like this to live in, full of beautiful things and immaculately kept. It's not like home, which is comforting and lovely but always full of mess and piles of things we've discarded.

My eye is drawn to the window that stretches across the length of the room. There are old-style venetian blinds that normally look old-fashioned, but are just right here. Apart from that, the windows are bare, which surprises me as they look directly out towards another block of flats. I go over and look out. Yes, hardly any distance away is another identical mansion block.

How strange. They're so close! Why have they built them like this?

I peer out, trying to get my bearings. Then I begin to understand. The building has been constructed in a U shape around a large garden. Is this the garden of Randolph Gardens? I can see it below me and to the left, a large green square full of bright flower beds, bordered by plants and trees in the full flush of summer. There are gravel paths, a tennis court, benches and a fountain as well as a plain stretch of grass where a few people are sitting, enjoying the last of the day's heat. The building stretches around three sides of the garden so that most of the inhabitants get a garden view. But the U shape has a small narrow corridor that connects the garden sides of the U to the one that fronts the road, and the single column of flats on each side of it face directly into each other. There are seven altogether and Celia's is on the fifth floor, looking straight into its opposite number, closer than they would be if they were divided by a street.

Was the flat cheaper because of this? I think idly, looking over at the window opposite. No wonder there are all these pale colours and the reflecting silver panels: the flat definitely has its light quota reduced by being close to the others. *But then, it's all about location, right? It's still Mayfair.*

The last of the sunshine has vanished from this side of the building and the room has sunk into a warm darkness. I go towards one of the lamps to turn it on, and my eye is caught by a glowing golden square through the window. It's the flat opposite, where the lights are on and the interior is brightly illuminated like the screen in a small cinema or the stage in the theatre. I can see across quite clearly, and I stop short, drawing in my breath. There is a man in the room that is exactly across from this one. That's not so strange, maybe, but the fact that he is naked to the waist, wearing only a pair of dark trousers, grabs my attention. I realise I'm standing stock-still as I notice that he is talking on a telephone while he walks languidly about his sitting room, unwittingly displaying an impressive torso. Although I can't make out his features all that clearly, I can see that he is good looking too, with thick black hair and a classically symmetrical face with strong dark brows. I can see that he has broad shoulders, muscled arms, a well-defined chest and abs, and that he is tanned as though just back from somewhere hot.

I stare, feeling awkward. Does this man know I can see into his apartment like this while he walks about half naked? But I guess that as mine is in shadow, he has no way of knowing there's anyone home to observe him. That makes me relax a little and just enjoy the sight. He's so well built and so beautifully put together that he's almost unreal. It's like watching an actor on the television as he moves around in the glowing box opposite, a delicious vision that I can enjoy from a distance. I laugh suddenly. Celia really does have it all – this must be very life-enhancing, having a view like this.

I watch for a while longer as the man across the way chats into his phone, and wanders about. Then he turns and disappears out of the room.

Maybe he's gone to put some clothes on, I think, and feel vaguely disappointed. Now he's gone, I turn on the lamp and the room is flooded with soft apricot light. It looks beautiful all over again, the electric light bringing out new effects, dappling the silver lacquer panels and giving the jade ornaments a rosy hue. De Havilland comes padding in and jumps on to the sofa, looking up at me hopefully. I go over and sit down and he climbs onto my lap, purring loudly like a little engine as he circles a few times and then settles down. I stroke his soft fur, burying my fingers in it and finding comfort in his warmth.

I realise I'm still picturing the man across the way. He was startlingly attractive and moved with such unconscious grace and utter ease in himself. He was alone, but seemed anything but lonely. Perhaps he was talking to his girlfriend on the phone. Or perhaps it was someone else, and his girlfriend is waiting for him in the bedroom and he's gone through there now to take off the rest of his clothes, lie beside her and drop his mouth to hers. She'll be opening her embrace to him, pulling that perfect torso close, wrapping her arms across the smooth back . . .

Stop it. You're making it all worse.

My head droops down. Adam comes sharply into my mind and I can see him just as he used to be, smiling broadly at me. It was his smile that always got me, the reason why I'd fallen in love with him in the first place. It was lopsided and made dimples appear in his cheeks, and his blue eyes sparkle with fun. We'd fallen in love the summer I was sixteen, during the long lazy days with no school and only ourselves to please. I'd go and meet him in the grounds of the ruined abbey and we'd spend long hours together, mooching about, talking and then kissing. We hadn't been able to get enough of one another. Adam had been a skinny teenager, just a lad, while I was still getting used to having men look at my chest when I walked by them on the street. A year later, when we'd slept together, it had been the first time for both of us – an awkward, fumbling experience that had been beautiful because we'd loved each other, even though we were both utterly clueless about how to do it right. We'd got better, though, and I couldn't imagine ever doing it with anyone else. How could it be so sweet and loving except with Adam? I loved it when he kissed me and held me in his arms and told me he loved me best of all. I'd never even looked at another man.

Don't do this to yourself, Beth! Don't remember. Don't let him keep on hurting you.

I don't want the image but it pierces my mind anyway. I see it, just the way I did on that awful night. I was babysitting next door and had expected to be there until well after midnight, but the neighbours came back early because the wife had developed a bad headache. I was free, it was only ten o'clock and they'd paid me for a full night anyway.

I'll surprise Adam, I decided gleefully. He lived in his

brother Jimmy's house, paying cheap rent for the spare room. Jimmy was away so Adam planned to have a few mates round, drink some beers and watch a movie. He'd seemed disappointed when I said I couldn't join him, so he'd be delighted when I turned up unexpectedly.

The memory is so vivid it's like I'm living it all over again, walking through the darkened house, surprised that no one is there, wondering where the boys have got to. The television is off, no one is lounging on the sofa, cracking open cans of beer or making smart remarks at the screen. My surprise is going to fall flat, I realise. Maybe Adam is feeling ill and has gone straight to bed. I walk along the hallway towards his bedroom door; it's so familiar, it might as well be my own house.

I'm turning the handle of the door, saying, 'Adam?' in a quiet voice, in case he's sleeping already. I'll go in anyway, and if he's asleep, I'll just look at his face, the one I love so much, and wonder what he's dreaming about, maybe press a kiss on his cheek, curl up beside him . . .

I push the door open. A lamp is on, the one he likes to drape in a red scarf when we're making love so that we're lit by shadows – in fact, it's glowing darkly scarlet right now, so perhaps he's not asleep. I blink in the semi-darkness; the duvet is humped and moving. What's he doing there?

'Adam?' I say again, but more loudly. The movement stops, and then the shape beneath the duvet changes, the cover folds back and I see . . .

I gasp with pain at the memory, screwing my eyes shut as though this will block out the pictures in my head. It's like an old movie I can't stop playing, but this time I firmly press the mental off switch, and lift De Havilland off my lap onto the sofa next to me. Recalling it still has the capacity to floor me, to leave me a sodden mess. The whole reason for coming here is to move on, and I've got to start right now.

My stomach rumbles and I realise I'm hungry. I go through to the kitchen to look for something to eat. Celia's fridge is almost bare and I make a note that grocery shopping will be a priority for tomorrow. Searching the cupboards, I find some crackers and a tin of sardines, which will do for now. In fact, I'm so hungry that it tastes delicious. As I'm washing up my plate, I'm overtaken suddenly by an enormous yawn. I look at my watch: it's still early, not even nine yet, but I'm exhausted. It's been a long day. The fact that I woke this morning in my old room at home seems almost unbelievable.

I decide I'll turn in. Besides, I want to try that amazing-looking bed. How can a girl not feel better in a silver four-poster? It's got to be impossible. I go back through to the sitting room to turn out the lights. My hand is on the switch when I notice that the man is back in his sitting room. Now the dark trousers he was wearing have been replaced by a towel tucked around his hips, and his hair is wet and slicked back. He's standing right in the middle of the room near the window and he is looking directly into my flat. In fact, he is staring straight at me, a frown creasing his forehead, and I am staring right back. Our eyes are locked, though we are too far apart to read the nuances in one another's gaze.

Then, in a movement that is almost involuntary, my thumb presses down on the switch and the lamp obediently flashes off, plunging the room into darkness. He cannot see me any more, I realise, although his sitting room is still brightly lit for me, even more vivid than before now I'm watching from the dark. The man steps forward to the window, leans on the sill and looks out intently, trying to see what he can spy. I'm frozen, almost not breathing. I don't know why it seems so important that he doesn't see me, but I can't resist the impulse to remain hidden. He stares a few moments more, still frowning, and I look back, not moving but still able to admire the shape of his upper body and the way the well-shaped biceps swell as he leans forward on them.

He gives up staring and turns back into the room. I seize my chance and slip out of the sitting room and into the hall, closing the door behind me. Now there are no windows, I cannot be seen. I release a long sigh.

'What was all that about?' I say out loud, and the sound of my voice comforts me. I laugh. 'Okay, that's enough of that. The guy is going to think I'm some kind of nutter if he sees me skulking about in the dark, playing statues whenever I think he can see me. Bed.'

I remember De Havilland just in time, and open the sitting-room door again so that he can escape if he needs to. He has a closed litter box in the kitchen that he needs access to, so I make sure the kitchen door is also open. Going to turn out the hall light, I hesitate for a moment, and then leave it on.

I know, it's childish to believe that light drives the monsters away and keeps the burglars and killers at bay, but I'm alone in a strange place in a big city and I think that tonight, I will leave it on.

In fact, even ensconced in the downy comfort of Celia's bed and so sleepy I can hardly keep my eyes open, I can't quite bring myself to turn out the bedside lamp. In the end, I sleep all night in its gentle glow, but I'm so tired that I don't even notice.

Find your next delicious read at

THE
Book
BAKERY

The place to come for cherry-picked monthly reading recommendations, competitions, reading group guides, author interviews and more.

Visit our website to see which great books we're recommending this month.
www.TheBookBakery.co.uk

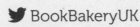 BookBakeryUK
TheBookBakeryUK